TIM PARR

BELOW THE STRANDLINE

Waggabolly ™

First published by Waggabolly 2020

Author website: timparr.uk

First edition

ISBN: 978-1-8382051-1-9

This book was professionally typeset on Reedsy.
Find out more at reedsy.com

For my family and those friends who know me best

Contents

IV PART FOUR

Preface

BELOW THE STRANDLINE

"Strandline"

Definition: The mark along a shore formed by water-borne debris that is beached on a falling tide.

Praise for 'Below The Strandline'

'Parr is adept at portraying his fictional world's most unpleasant elements' - *Kirkus Reviews*;

'An impressive debut that leaves the reader wanting more. Perfect for murder-mystery fans ... I could not put it down once I started it. I was forced to finish the book in a single day. It is wonderfully crafted.' - *Reedsy Review;*

'How Tim wrote so exactly about young lads growing up in that particular era is uncanny – it was so accurate. I was in London in the period when this book was set, and it's so feasible you wonder if he has some inside knowledge.' - *Goodreads Review;*

'I would have read this in one sitting had time allowed. The author has clearly done his research to produce a story with details true to their era.' - *Amazon Review;*

'The short punchy chapters reminded me of Dan Brown. The moral ambiguity reminded me of Line of Duty.' - *Author's Website;*

'An enjoyable page-turning read. Set in the 1970's, this thriller captures the atmosphere of low-life London really well. There are some good plot twists as well as some funny moments - the book was a nice way to spend a lockdown weekend!' - *Goodreads Review;*

'Congratulations and well done. I think you have set us up for a sequel!' - *Author's Website;*

'A rough novel that's as engrossing as it is bleak … there are worse things than leaving readers wanting more, and they'll find it hard to leave Parr's grim story behind.' - *Kirkus Reviews.*

timparr.uk/reviews

Prologue

The clink of milk bottles could be heard outside as the milkman went about his early morning rounds. Curtains had already been pulled in houses up and down the street. People readied themselves for the day ahead, sipping tea and scraping toast. Number forty-two was identical to all the other terraced dwellings in the street except that its blinds and drapes remained tightly closed while the house slept on. In a tiny bedroom, a small boy with a mop of black hair lay wide awake in the damp cot that he had outgrown, looking at the shapes of the rabbits on the mobile that bounced in the draughts from the poorly fitting crittall windows. As the morning sunlight pierced the tatty curtains and threw shapes on the wall of the bedroom, the boy became restless and strained to listen.

After a long while, he heard noises in the room next door, sounds of someone getting up. He climbed out of the damp cot awkwardly, hampered by the low-strung terry cloth nappy that had not been changed for two days. He dropped silently to the floor and approached his mother's bedroom, watching shyly through the hinged gap in the door. He waited, out of sight and quiet as a mouse. Her latest overnight companion had just risen and was coughing up morning phlegm. The boy spied through the narrow gap and watched as the man lit a cigarette, buttoned up his shirt, found his shoes and opened the bedroom door to leave. The man smelled the pong before he laid eyes on the boy.

"You've got to change your kid, for pity's sake," remarked the man to the slumbering woman. "He's stunk the place out!" The woman did not rouse.

Heavy feet thudded down the stairs and the front door shut behind, rattling the letterbox flap. The child wandered into his mother's room, chewing his thumb and hugging Bear. He stood right next to her bed and snuffled loudly at her. She slept on. He whimpered like a puppy and she still slept on. The crying started in earnest, first in low notes, gradually climbing up the scales. It was persistent in rhythm and rose in pitch until it caught her attention. She stirred and opened a bleary blood-shot eye but rolled over, away from the ruddy-faced child. Weighed down by her latest hangover, she sank back into her slumber. Jerry was indignant. He screwed up his face and bawled his lungs out until his chest hurt, feeling with every intake the injustice of being little and helpless. The crying became uncontrollable and emotional release that oddly soothed him. It took his mind off his discomfort, hunger and boredom. At last, she could take no more and seeing the toddler with his arms outstretched to her and drenched in tears, she finally came to her senses. She lifted the rank child, and Bear, into the bed until she was ready to face the day.

Neighbours observed the comings and goings at number forty-two, tutting and talking in hushed tones over their garden fences. They shook their heads at the shame of it as they watched Jerry's mother emerge from the corner shop at the end of the street in headscarf, sunglasses and bright red lipstick, her basket laden with bottles but little to eat. It was obvious that she had left the child at home again on its own. Word got round.

"She had another man over last night," one would say.

"That poor child!" exclaimed another.

"What a racket next door, did you hear?"

"Playing that music again. It went on until after midnight, so inconsiderate!"

"And that's not the worst of it. My Henry had a glass to the wall and did he blush!"

One day there was a knock on the door. The distraught mother wept as her sobbing toddler, her only child, was wrenched away from her. She understood the reasons. She accepted that she was a hopeless mother and that she was unable to care for herself, let alone for the young life.

"It's for his own good," reassured the kindly doctor, looking around him with dismay at the filthy room, the empty bottles stacked by the bin. "Rest assured he will go to a good family! Come on, I'll help you to pack a bag for him."

When they were ready to leave, the doctor turned to the boy, knelt to his level and looked compassionately into his eyes.

"It's alright, Jeremy," he said. "You go with the nice man here, just until your mother gets better." The tall visitor in the black coat and wire framed glasses had not spoken and smiled coldly.

That night, Jerry's fragile mother took an overdose as a cry for help. But help never came.

Little Jerry's bottom lip trembled as he looked up at the sinister building, squinting at words that he could not decipher that were carved above an enormous doorway. He hugged

Bear closely, whispering to him softly, "Don't be scared," and stroked his brow as his mother did to him when she was sober.

The boy was afraid and tried to pull away but the grip around his wrist only tightened. The tall man in the black coat and round glasses held the child firmly and forcibly led him up the steps, pressing a large bell that rang somewhere deep within. Bolts slid and the door was opened by a stern-looking woman in the uniform of a nun. She had been expecting them. She looked down at the child.

"What's this one's name?" she asked in clipped tones.

The bespectacled man replied and passed her the envelope that the doctor had written. She nodded, took the small bag that the man handed to her, the bag that Jerry's mother and the kind doctor had packed for him that morning.

"I'll be back for him, in a week or two," he said.

The woman held his gaze, snorted in distaste, then closed the door on the man. She took the bewildered Jerry inside the cold, dimly lit hallway.

"Come on, Jeremy," she said. "You'll be safe here. At least for now. Let's find you something to eat."

* * *

1975

Crystal waters bubbled up in a freshwater spring in a green and lush meadow in rural England. The stream coursed through the landscape, widening as it flowed. It was home to freshwater trout and dazzling blue kingfishers. Cows lazily chewed the succulent grass along the banks. Boaters rowed and punted, fishermen cast their lines.

The upper river ran eastwards and meandered under ancient stone bridges, through villages and towns. Over its journey of two hundred miles from its conception to the sea, the river gathered pace as the tributaries along its route merged to fill and energise the maturing River Thames that was taking on a bolder personality, now fast and swollen. Beyond Teddington Lock, the waters were tidal and turbulent, churning the mud into brackish brown. The river flowed swiftly, funnelled by the high embankment walls that served as flood defences to protect the city. It raced on, battling or running with the tides that surged past London's landmarks. It rushed under Tower Bridge, past the docklands to the east of the city and out to the silty Thames Estuary before finally discharging into the North Sea.

Along its tidal reaches, beyond London's bridges that spanned the waterway, little beaches were exposed at low tide. On one of these mudflats, oystercatchers, dunlin, ringed plover and a solitary avocet picked at the waterline as it sparkled in the morning sunlight. Opportunist gulls hung around shiftily, looking for easy pickings and fighting over washed up food waste, their speckled young boisterously demanding to be fed. Two adult gulls danced a circular dance at full stretch, stamping three-toed prints in the mud as each bird possessively gripped the river food in their beaks, seeking to rip from the other the sinewy oyster that stretched as they tugged.

The stronger gull prised the oyster away, swiftly gulped it down and flew up to a high vantage point on a channel marker above the mudflat. It raised its head, puffed its breast and raucously proclaimed its success to the seagull world.

A few yards along the beach, a man's body lay partly submerged just below the strandline. It was swollen and bashed from the undercurrents. The head rocked gently from side to side in the wavelets. A barge laden low in the water passed on the far side of the river, its engine drumming steadily. The wash from the boat reached the mudflat. The body lifted and sank back, briefly turning full face to the sky as the head lolled on the wave. One misty eye stared out unseeingly. The other displayed a raw empty socket, drilled out by the bird for its gristly meal.

The body was also missing its hands.

I

PART ONE

1

Over The Back

The doorbell chimed and he ran downstairs. His mother had already opened it to find a skinny boy with fair hair and freckled face looking up at her expectantly with a big grin and supporting a battered bicycle that was clearly too big for him.

"Hello Mrs Castle, can Robbie come out to play?"

"Robert?" his mother called over her shoulder, adding in a sing-song way, "It's Peter."

"Yes, I know!" he said irritably, eyes rolling in mock disbelief as he squeezed between her and the doorframe. The two boys exchanged grunted greetings.

"Over the Back?" Pete asked.

"Let's go," said Robbie. "Bring your bike round to the side gate and I'll meet you at the kitchen door."

Pete did the early morning paper-round six days a week and being a Saturday morning he had already covered five miles on his delivery round before Robbie had even stirred, home for breakfast then back out on his bike across town on the off-chance that Robbie was allowed to play.

They had met on their first day in the boys' grammar school. Pete and Robbie had been placed in the same form group. The class all had to sit in alphabetical order of surname, an uninspired seating plan that made it simpler for the form master to take the morning register. The two boys had found themselves sitting at desks next to each other and quickly hit it off.

A boy of similarly skinny build sat immediately behind them in the class. He saw the funny side of life and often shared his bag of penny chews from the school tuck shop at mid-morning break time. Soon Robbie, Pete and Andy had become inseparable and were usually found at break times in a huddle with a pack of cards, marbles, sniggering over a Beano comic or kicking a tennis ball around the quad.

The school was not without its share of bullying. They were quick learners and avoided the people and places where trouble often brewed. They were particularly alert to the combative fourth and fifth formers who were twice their size and whose sport was picking on any first years in the dinner queue that they took exception to. A bad haircut, sticky-out ears or a crooked tie were all valid reasons for inflicting sly punches, dead-legs and Chinese burns while passing the time in the heaving lunch queues until the dining hall doors were opened.

They got together out of school whenever they could, as a threesome or in pairs if one was grounded or had to do something for their parents. Robbie's home was a popular choice and not just because it had a rented black and white television, which neither Pete nor Andy's parents had yet. They seemed to have everything - a telephone, a radiogram for playing vinyl records and a larder that was always well stocked with biscuits. But what was special about the house was its garden, backing as it did on to a private estate. The estate land was officially out of bounds. There was a wide overgrown no-man's land between the back of their garden and the estate boundary fence. Robbie's dad had occasional bonfires with the garden waste they threw over, building a stile in the chain link fence to climb over more easily.

The stile at the end of Robbie's garden was their gateway to a hidden world and that soon became their private playground of choice. It accessed expansive woods, marshes, a lake frequented by prehistoric-looking herons and Canada geese, a narrow river that could be jumped with care and beyond that a pine-forested shooting estate. The estate held occasional organised shoots. The beaters could be heard entering the far away woods to flush out the cultivated stock of pheasants, shouts and barking carrying on the wind, guns cracking. This fuelled their imaginary play.

Early expeditions in wellie boots were just short forays from Robbie's garden, taking them over the stile, across a wide grassy path, negotiating a rusted barbed wire fencing with No Trespassers signs and slipping down the steep bank at the perimeter of the woods. The three lads climbed nearby trees, taking in glimpses of the silver lake and the woods. They discovered a raised island of mud with a small clump of decaying trees that stood proud in an otherwise flat marshy area. This they claimed as their own and named it Pong Island. They built stick shelters, dug bear traps, imagined the gathering invading armies of Germans or the Red Indians ready to take their scalps. They scratched into the earth secret symbols that only they could encode and tried to speak in pig latin learnt in playgrounds, moving the beginning of words to the end and adding 'ay'. Want to have a fight? became "Ant-way to ave-hay an ight-fray", which was an open invitation to be tackled to the ground and pushed in the mud.

They were absorbed in a make-believe world but when teatime came and went, the distant bellowing from Robbie's mother calling them in would pop the magic bubble in an instant. They reluctantly left the secrets of Over the Back for another day, dragging their tired legs back over the chain-link fence to drop into the garden, stomping up the lawn in water-filled wellies and mud-encrusted jeans to demolish sandwich spread and crab paste sandwiches. If they were in luck Robbie's mum would bring them a plate of bourbon biscuits and custard creams. If they were not, then they politely accepted a solid slice of Mrs Castle's latest sponge cake disaster.

As they got to know each other, they recognised each other's natural skill. Robbie was the natural navigator, good with numbers and could always plot the best route back. Andy could draw a bit and had access to his grandad's camera. Pete had a good head for heights and could always be relied upon. Robbie mapped out the territory. Andy was their wildlife photographer and sketched out a club logo. Pete picked a good tree and a built treehouse at their first base camp just inside the fence.

A year on and the eleven-year-olds turned twelve, and as the seasons continued to fly by, before long they were crashing head long into their teenage years. They continued to meet up at weekends and would usually plan a trip Over the Back, but when they visited the woods, they now ventured much further. They heaved a fallen tree branch to span across a more accessible section of the river, opening the pine plantation to them for the first time. In rucksacks they carried pen knives for whittling sticks to sharp points, string for stringing taut bows, matches for lighting fires, beer pilfered from their dads and occasionally a tatty girlie magazine that was doing the rounds at school that somebody had traded with an elder brother and had to be returned within a day or two, or else on pain of death.

They experimented after dark with smoking dry twigs they had gathered to mimic cigarettes, lighting the tips and blowing out the flaming ends so that they glowed like charcoal. Some were so vile when they inhaled that they triggered fits of coughing and spitting but others that had a natural filter-like core were more palatable. They attempted to track deer and photograph them. With great anticipation, they waited a week for the film to be developed at the high street chemists but when Andy excitedly brought the unopened packet in to school to show them having shared the cost between them, they watched with growing disappointment as picture after picture was either over-exposed, under-exposed, or just an inky blackness with an advise label stuck on by the photo lab.

They were more successful at building a strong waterproof hide deep in the woods, covering a robust frame of branches with canvas sheets, laying a tartan picnic rug inside and disguising it all with twigs and leaves. The three of them each picked a tree nearest the hide and carved his initials deeply into the bark of that tree, the wounds weeping sap as they firmly cut and recut the lines. The markings would help them to find their forest camp again in the rows and rows of many lookalike trees and marked their territory. When it was finished, they whelped with triumph and danced around the hide, their voices echoing through the woods, causing startled

7

wings to rustle up to the sky.

Their playing now included target practice, throwing small stones at tin cans balanced on a low branch or shooting arrows at a hand-drawn target they pinned to a tree. In mock battles they threw homemade spears, tossed pine-cone grenades at each other and in the reed beds on the edge of the marshes where the mud was deeper they waded through stinking water and ripped off ripe bulrush heads, chucking them at each other. A direct hit produced a satisfying explosion of seed heads all over their victim, resulting in gales of laughter. These times were fun and rich and cherished.

And then came Jerry.

2

The New Boy

Jerry had joined from a different school after the Easter holiday which marked the beginning of the summer term. The story was that he was a bright child but had been expelled from another school for reasons undisclosed but enough for his previous foster parents to give him up. After some difficulty he had been relocated to a new foster family within their school area.

School can be cruel and he was initially marked out as a misfit, ignored and left to wander by himself at break times around the edges of the playground. Their school still had an old bomb shelter from the Second World War, now a boarded-up relic from times gone by, and he would disappear round the back, returning at the end playtime smelling of cigarette smoke. He was slight in build but taller than his peers and looked older, as though he might have been moved down to retake the academic year. He was distinguished by jet black cropped hair, sticky-out ears and unfortunate purple scars, more like burns than birthmarks, that ran up one side of his neck, over his left jaw line and tapered up to the corner of his mouth. He was obviously self-conscious about it and remained tight-lipped when challenged about it, as other boys often did in their direct, no-filter way. But what he lacked in brawn and looks, he made up for with a cunning, calculating mind that always seemed to be cranking behind sharp, glinting eyes. People who met him and gained his trust were struck by a charisma that either appealed or repelled. Had people taken the time to get to know him better, they would have discovered that Jerry got off on taking risks, the more extreme the better, regardless of the consequences to himself or those around him. He was disruptive and destructive. And because of the first letter of his surname, he was seated at a spare desk next to Andy, just behind Pete and Robbie.

Jerry was routinely getting into trouble in and out of class and was usually among those in detention after school. He would be hauled by one of his protruding ears, or more painfully a pinch of his hair near the scalp, to stand at the front of the lesson to be verbally belittled by a physics or Latin master and humiliated in front of the other pupils. This upset him deeply and he found himself digging his fingernails into the palms of his hands to keep his emotions under control. A crisis point came one Thursday morning in a Geography lesson held in one of the terrapin huts before lunch. Exasperated beyond reasonable limits, the popular geography teacher Mr Penrose had shown himself incapable of tackling Jerry's gnawing petulant behaviour or ignoring the clever slanging quips spoken in under tones directed at him and just not quite audible to him. Empty threats undermined his authority and Mr Penrose told Jerry to wait behind after the lunch-time bell had been rung and the hut had emptied.

The rest of the class were dismissed for lunch, apart from

Jerry who was instructed to remain sitting at his desk while Penrose wiped away the hand-drawn map of the six states of Australia from the blackboard. He had been chewing paper balls and as Penrose turned back to him, brushing his hands of the chalk dust that whirled in the rays of sunlight like spotlights on a theatre stage, the master was hit in the face by soggy projectiles flipped from the flexed twelve-inch ruler. He pulled a drawer open and stormed over to Jerry, grabbing him hard with a ferocity that he did not know he was capable of. Penrose pushed the boy across the nearest desk and vented his rage and frustrations on Jerry with a wood-soled slipper that the pupils knew as Horace, kept as a punishment, like a nuclear deterrent but until then rarely used in anger. Jerry's chair was ominously empty when the register was taken on Friday morning.

Jerry felt bitter and vengeful. He would never have told his foster-parents of the incident and would have had no support from them if he had, so he took matters into his own hands. He would watch and bide his time. He was no ordinary boy.

Occasionally Jerry would be seen on the bench outside the deputy headmaster's office which was at the end of a highly polished wood-floored corridor in the east wing of the old block. Boys waiting their reprimand had to sit in silence outside the door, a loudly ticking wall clock building the tension. Shouted words heard through the closed door were enough to shake most of them to the core and were a precursor to the threat of the cane from the diminutive bespectacled Scot. For Jerry, rather than altering course, these disciplinary episodes had only encouraged his delinquent behaviour.

A couple of weeks before the end of the summer term, the ultimate action had to be taken. He was sent to the headmaster's office who would decide on a course of action. The headmaster had the whitest hair mismatched by the darkest eyebrows. He would rarely be seen outside of morning assemblies or parent events but occasionally crossed the quad in his flowing gown resembling a sinister crow. The headmaster had reviewed his file and did not like to see failure as it reflected on him. He would give Jerry one opportunity to fall in line. He would see how he responded to a lashing delivered with great reluctance, accuracy and force by the be-robed headmaster himself. Either this would knock the devil out of him, or his school would acknowledge failure and expel him before the term was out. Jerry was called into the inner sanctum, where the crow was waiting for him, a long knobbly bamboo cane placed within reach. He was told to stand, to remove his hands from pockets and the magazine from down the back of his trousers, before verbal and corporal punishment were delivered.

And to the surprise of many in the staff room, Jerry took the headmaster's punishment tearfully but without comment or whimper. He sat his exams and was expected to pass them. In the last few weeks of school term, it was noticed how he had become uncharacteristically docile in class, almost attentive and cooperative. Those who did not know him well only saw a boy who had withdrawn into himself, but behind those eyes the cogs were turning fast.

Before long, the last hymns had been sung at the final assembly of the summer term, the bell had been rung and school holidays had begun.

3

The Holidays

The summer holidays stretched ahead. One hot July day, the three boys had again patrolled their territory Over the Back. They had collected spent shotgun cartridges found in the wide woodland paths that criss-crossed the plantation, finished the picnic lunch of pork pies and lump of cheese in bread with radishes from Pete's dad's allotment, all washed down with a can of beer. They spent the time crouching quietly in the undergrowth, passing the binoculars between them and watching in wonder a family of deer grazing little more than fifty yards ahead of them out in the open. Andy had brought along his grandad's cine camera and had captured a minute of film with the herd dead centre in the view-finder only to realise later when it had been developed and they ran it through the projector that he had been holding it at the wrong tilt. Insects buzzed lazily and from the distant lake came cackles of geese and fowl. Out of the peace, there came a metallic snap somewhere behind them. The deer started and bolted back into the woods, one limping.

They turned round to see Jerry. Pete spluttered, "What the

hell are you doing here … and what the fuck are you doing with that?" The air rifle was broken open and he was digging in his pocket of pellets to reload.

"No you don't!" said Andy, watching the injured deer regroup. "I was just filming them and you messed it up."

"Look," said Robbie thinking how to distract him, "if you want to shoot at something, why don't I set up some empty cans", and he pointed to a suitable branch in the opposite direction from the herd, "and we take it in turns to knock them down?"

"Winner gets the last beer?", said Jerry, eyeing up an un-opened can.

The intruder had shattered more than just the peace. He had violated their childhood domain. The summer rolled on and the three boys saw less of each other as they went away on their family holidays, Pete to a campsite in the New Forest, Andy to Weston-super-Mare and Robbie to stay with relatives in Scotland. Although not by design, they did not visit the woods for the rest of that summer. The incident with the deer had burst a bubble. It marked the end of their boyhood adventures. The bonds between Robbie, Pete and Andy stayed intact but had frayed a little. It was no coincidence that tensions played between them whenever Jerry was around.

Jerry had to get out of the house. His foster dad, Uncle Derek, was raging at him again about his behaviour. He walked into town and sat in the warm library, idly thumbing through the magazines and papers laid out on the table. Jerry pulled one closer that had caught his eye and, turning the pages of the local paper, spotted a picture under the sports section that featured a shooting society celebrating a recent event. It was a formal photograph taken with a lake in the background which he immediately recognised. Looking more closely, each man was dressed in tweeds and carried a shotgun in one arm and a brace of pheasants. At either end of the line were a couple of cocker spaniels on leashes. As his finger traced the faces he stopped abruptly and tapped the face third from the right. The caption underneath confirmed it. Penrose. Jerry discreetly tore out the page and stuffed it in his pocket.

4

Trouble Brewing

The next school term had begun. Jerry was like a Jekyll and Hyde. He was as crazy as ever when out of school but during school time he was like a changed person. The teachers noticed that he had become quiet and attentive. From being one of the most disruptive pupils he had become studious in class and conscientious in his studies. Miraculously, or so it seemed, Jerry had been transformed into a perfect pupil, channelling his intelligence into producing essays of a high standard with seemingly little effort, excelling in the regular written tests and contributing in class. Talk in the staff room was of the good that corporal punishment does for a child, knocking sense into them.

While some might have believed this, those who knew Jerry better caught the cold look in his eyes and knew that he was exercising restraint, watching and waiting and learning. Below the surface, Jerry was fostering a deep suppressed anger that was growing inside him. The vulnerable boy had been brought up by a series of abusive carers. One abuser still appeared in his nightmares, scorched into his earliest memories. The perfect pupil was a disturbed boy and those who spotted this were sensibly wary of him.

Jerry was excused from games on health reasons from the start of the term, by a doctor's letter that he had forged himself. This was partly to conceal the scars and burn marks that the communal showers would reveal but mainly because he thought he could put his time to better use.

From when he was a small child he had been moved at regular intervals from guardian, to care home, to foster families, often unmonitored and in very unhealthy setups, often isolated and never in one place long enough to build friendships among his age group, leaving Jerry as a loner, fending for himself. It was only time before each foster family would write him off as a difficult child with challenging behavioural issues and irreconcilably disruptive to other family members. His previous foster family had the gall to read out to him the form they were readying to sign to confirm that *"It would be best for all concerned if the boy was moved to a more supportive environment in a new location and in a new school to make a fresh start in life."*

"Fuckwits, the lot of them!" he thought.

Above all, Jerry just wanted to be accepted and he envied those in his peer group who had formed tight friendships. That was something that he had never had. He had never settled long enough to develop normal friendships and getting close was alien to him. At lunch times or at the end of the school day, Jerry would wait to catch Andy, Pete or Robbie to arrange to meet up out of school. Although not welcomed at first, he worked his way into their lives and picked them off one by one with his strange charm and daring stunts which caught their attention. He rewarded them with more.

One lunchtime Jerry produced from his blazer pocket an African toad that he had stolen from the school biology lab. It was still very much a live specimen at that time. A few days later a dead lab rat and the back legs of the toad were spotted on a cinema seat during a screening of Wind in the Willows. Later that week, the front portion landed with a splash in front of a swimmer in mid-crawl at the town's open-air swimming pool during a school competition, eliciting screams and a temporary pool closure while the offending head and torso were netted out, much to the delight of Jerry who relished the moment from the spectators' benches. The poor creature had suffered a fate even less dignified than the intended starring role in a chloroformed dissection lesson but earned Jerry fame and notoriety.

Jerry told stories about his latest antics that often seemed far-fetched. They hoped that his tales were just spawned from an overactive imagination but they often carried a grain of truth. It was difficult for the listener to discern fact from fiction. On another occasion after school, he showed Andy and Pete a wad of paper money held in a thick elastic band.

"Where did you get that?" Pete asked, wide-eyed.

"I won it," said Jerry nonchalantly. "Betting on a horse." He talked them through how he walked into a betting office in town. He saw a race coming up at Newmarket, picked a complete outsider and sat watching his horse come in on one of their televisions.

"Haven't you got to be eighteen to go into one of those places?" asked Andy.

In the next breath Jerry switched his story to having stolen the money, in equally unbelievable circumstances. His tales seemed fanciful but always carried a grain of truth. He did after all seem to be inexplicably well off for sixteen years old when there was so little money to go round. The other boys had Saturday jobs but as far as anyone knew Jerry did not work.

At school, there was talk of the fair. Flyers had appeared on vacant shop windows advertising the big fair that was coming to the town park the following weekend. Jerry invited the three of them along and to make sure he could rely on them to turn up, he said that he would treat them all to the big rides. It almost seemed as though this strange, troubled boy was willing to buy friendships that he was unable to form himself. He could afford it, so they accepted.

The fair opened on Friday. They had arranged to meet at the bandstand to share the drinks they had brought along, before walking across to the fair. Together they crossed the park towards the lights of the big wheel, soaking up the evocative sounds of music and engines, squeals from the ghost train and the smells of sweet candy floss mingled with diesel. The familiar stalls were back. There was a coconut shy, a strong man hammer challenge and families with wide-eyed children hooking yellow ducks as the bobbed along, every one a winner. Lurid coloured teddies and liquorice allsorts were handed over as prizes. As the evening light started to fade, the place came alive.

They split up. Pete and Robbie headed off in search of candy floss and toffee apples on the way to the shooting range, while Jerry and Andy went to the penny arcade. Jerry bashed against the more promising-looking coin pusher machines until they spilled ill-gotten winnings into the trays. Scooping up the coppers from the shiny coin-catchers, he and Andy did a runner before the yelling attendant had time to clamber out of his money changing kiosk.

They caught up with each other and rode the merry mixer, Jerry climbing out onto the outside rail as it spun, riding the cars like a surfer and jumping off as it slowed, rolling on the trampled grass to break his fall to yelled reproaches from the operator and a family he nearly bowled over. The four of them paired up in the dodgem cars, crashing into friends from school and each other as the music and the alcohol coursed through them. At the big wheel, Pete and Jerry jumped into a spare seat just before the ride started and swung the chair as far as the mechanical stops would allow to protestations and shrieks of the passengers beside and far below.

As the wheel came to a stop Jerry was roughly hauled off by a couple of fairground heavies, the coin-push attendant having pointed him out, and was marched off to a dark spot behind the caravans where they gave him a beating. Pete watched helplessly from the shadows with mixed feelings of terror and his betrayal of Jerry by not going to his aid. They took Jerry's pride and his purse crammed with loose change but missed the rolled up bank notes in his socks.

Afterwards, as the last rides were announced and the music stopped, Robbie, Pete and Andy regrouped and walked off, sharing tales of the evening. They found Jerry sitting on the step of the bandstand at the top of the park. His bottom lip was cut. He seemed grateful for company and shared around a bottle of vodka he was working his way through having swiped it from an open caravan behind the traction engines.

He spun his yarns, and some were so detailed they could have been true. Tales of crossing the railway line at night to ride a carriage roof on the mail train to London, ducking the bridges as they approached. Stories of shoplifting at

20

Woolworths and brushes with the police. Of shooting air pellets from his bedroom window at passers-by. In one of his more colourful stories he claimed to have broken into a young teacher's flat that morning and stolen her underwear. To a snort of disbelief, Jerry shot a cool stare before a smirk turned up the corner of his mouth. Reaching into the pocket of his trousers, he pulled out the black lacy garment to gasps of admiration, before wearing the knickers over this face like a Spitfire pilot's mask, his fingers and thumbs forming the goggles, shooting down imaginary enemy planes at one o'clock, eleven o'clock, three o'clock until the laughter subsided.

He chucked the drained bottle into the bushes and hung his head low. The fairground that had been a blaze of distant light across the far side of the park now receded as lights were switched off in all but a cluster of caravans and trailers. In a semi-sober state, Jerry dipped into his top pocket and pulled out the bent cigarette, straightening it and holding it between his lips. He patted his pockets for his lucky lighter, panicking for a moment before remembering he had left it at home.

"Here, catch!" said Andy.

The match flared and the cigarette caught.

"Thanks," Jerry said, chucking the box back which was caught in Andy's right hand.

Jerry inhaled deeply and blew out through his nose. He started to mumble about the dark side of his upbringing, as much to himself as to them, about his hate of all the people who had hurt him and how he would get revenge. He was distant and when he fell silent he seemed to the others to be in a trance. It was creepy but they waited for more words. None came. He had clammed up and shuddered violently before

21

drawing deeply on the cigarette that was now little more than a stub. That last glow before Jerry flicked it away into the dark revealed a tortured tear-streaked face. Andy thought he looked scared. Robbie and Pete saw only menace.

5

Sweet Revenge

Rain came in different forms then. There were days that were dull with a fine misty drizzle that muffled the sounds. But that day was not one of them. The rain hammered down all day it seemed, pelting the windows, bouncing over roof tiles, over spilling gutters and running in torrents along the roads, spilling down through the grilles to join the chase in the subterranean world below. A dark figure had approached the house in the dusk of the evening, concealed in the rhododendrons, crouching and sodden in a cheap anorak.

Looking out from under his hood, through the steady droplets that fell from the fur trim, he watched the family as lights turned on. He caught glimpses of them silhouetted behind the net curtains, moving from kitchen to living room. Later, much later, the upstairs rooms lit up, curtains pulled close and after a while the windows turned as dark as the house outside. All except for one room on the ground floor where a man's face was illuminated by the glow from a desk-lamp.

The figure that looked in from the garden was shrouded by the night. The rain had eased. Droplets fell from the high branches as they lost their finger holds and smacked the ground below first in an incessant patter then in a slow hum-drum way. The rain had eased and a moon peaked out from gaps in hurried clouds, casting an eerie light.

Shifting position, he observed the room through a veil of leaves. The study was next to a cavernous garage where a cream coloured Austin sheltered, its chassis still dripping slowly into a puddle below from an earlier outing which he knew all about. A strip of light shone from below a connecting door. Gathering his nerve, he crossed the silvery lawn dotted with worm casts, entered the open garage and paused to hear the clicking of a typewriter from the other side of the door. Feeling his way around the vehicle, he tried the passenger door handle. Locked. But the driver's door opened and the idiot had left a bunch of keys in the glove box. Pocketing them, he closed the car door.

The rhythmic chack-chacking through the study door stopped. The figure held his breath but the melody started again. Next he tried the car boot and opened it with the smallest key on the ring. Pulling a lighter from his pocket, he struck the flint and on third attempt the flickering flame revealed what he had been hoped to find. A smile played on the cold taught skin. He snapped the two latches on the wooden box that lay across the car boot. He would have forced the lock but the odd-shaped key fitted and turned and he reached in to touch the cold metal. After a few minutes of intense searching and after nearly giving up, he upturned a tin bucket and balancing on one foot his outstretched fingers felt a cardboard box that had been hidden at the top of the metal shelving. He locked the car, pocketed the keys and left in the shadows with the shotgun and a handful of cartridges.

The letter box snapped shut and Penrose caught sight of the paperboy hopping on his bicycle and rolling back down the drive. The newspaper lay on the mat and underneath was a brown envelope that must have been hand-delivered very early that morning. A bit odd, as normally the dog wakes up at the slightest noise, but he recalled the heavy rain as he wound his way back the previous evening with wipers on full speed. The old dog was probably having a lie-in as well. Picking them up from the mat, Penrose re-tied his dressing gown and went back to the kitchen to enjoy his first cup of tea and the freshly made toast in peace. The rest of the family were asleep and being school holidays, they would not appear for at least an hour. After a long day at the shoot the previous day, he was pleased with his progress the previous night and on word count was halfway through the research paper that he planned to submit to the Royal Geographical Society before the holidays were out.

He put on his reading glasses and glanced at the headlines, skimming over the strikes, power cuts, a photograph of the Royal Family visiting a newly opened hospital.It was a slow news day. Putting the newspaper aside, he picked up the letter.

Wiping the marmalade from the knife, he slid the envelope open. Crudely cut-out newsprint stared back at him.

"ShotGUN TeachER is dANGER To PUBlic." The rest of the note read in block capitals. *"If you want it back, meet me here at noon today. Map coordinates C4, N17. Bring this letter. Come alone. Tell no one. No police. Or going to press. Watching you. You have been warned."*

His hands were shaking when he put down the letter.

Thinking more lucidly, this could be a prank. He went to the car and found it unlocked which was not surprising after the whisky they had consumed at the previous day's shooting. He was startled to find a folded map placed on the driver's seat. With trepidation he opened the boot. The gun was gone.

* * *

It had rained again that morning. The woodland floor was soft underfoot and the air was filled with a sweet aroma of damp ferns mingled with leaves rotting into moist peaty soil.

The thick blanket of cloud that had hung in the sky for so many days had been blown away leaving wisps of pale blue late summer sky. Under the green canopies, a watery sun glinted through translucent foliage, dappling the undergrowth with a sparkling, dancing play of light. The top-most branches of the tallest trees swayed and rustled in the freshening breeze.

Penrose had parked by the hunting lodge and followed the well-trodden path weaving through the trees down towards the lake, following the lake's edge before turning into the plantation of pine trees. He had studied the map and followed the instructions to the letter. He had no intention of ending a promising career with an unfortunate news-splash that could name and shame him. He had some history after all that he would like to keep quiet about. He was head of geography with a PhD, had a steady stream of papers published and cited and off the back of this there was a real possibility of a move to a top private school with the help of his shooting contacts. He would get the gun back and then scare the living daylights out of this nutter who clearly had some grudge against him. He patted the old Enfield pistol that weighed in his coat pocket.

It was a war souvenir from his father. He would use it as a last resort if things turned nasty but he knew the woods and would have the advantage.

Checking the map and his watch, he trudged along the narrowing path into a more densely wooded spot, perhaps thirty yards away from the rendezvous.

He heard a rustling nearby. Something heavy swung from the trees and narrowly missed him, spinning and swinging like a pendulum. Catching sight of it, he twisted away in revulsion, staggered and sank to the floor on weakened knees. His heart pounded, a deafening numbing beat thudded inside his head, reverberating through his jaws, his teeth. The dog, his dog, his trusted friend, hung lifeless above him, trussed like a roasting hog, suspended across the path. A wave of panic engulfed him, cluttered with confusion, helplessness, anger. He had to run, to get away.

As his mind caught this thread of lucid thought, raw pain smashed into the side of his body. An inky blackness welled up and he lost consciousness.

After some time, Penrose's senses recovered. A chill wind bit. Trees towered above him but his vision was still blurred. He tasted blood. Slowly taking in his surroundings he was brought back to the present and he realised that he was slumped at the base of a tree, his hands and feet bound. Struggling to sit up, his left arm gave way with excruciating agony and he knew it was broken and useless. He felt a jolt of pain in his chest with every breath he took. He was going nowhere. By shuffling backwards using his feet, he gingerly propped himself up with his right elbow. A hooded figure came into focus, it was crouching to one side of him, a scarf concealing the face. There was no sign of his shotgun and alarmingly the man was playing casually with a pistol, his Enfield, that he had cleaned, oiled and loaded that very morning before he set off.

"You … bastard … what have I ever done to you?"

The man, so slight he could even have been a woman or a boy, came over and pulled a hunting knife, his bowie knife, holding a weapon in each hand. He pressed the blade to Penrose's throat above his Adam's apple, and the point traced the rough unshaven skin from ear to ear as though idly pondering the next move. Instead the steel flashed and sliced the bindings with quick precision. For a moment Penrose hoped he was to be set free, but instead was roughly pulled to his feet and was close to blacking out with the pain. Keeping a cruel hold on the broken arm, the assailant marched him in the direction of the lake, the pistol pressing into his back. When he slowed or stumbled the pressure on his arm squeezed and a searing pain shot down to his fingers, so he kept walking, terrified but resigned to his fate like a man to the gallows.

As the woods receded behind them, the ground softened under foot, their prints back-filling with water, and they started to pass reed beds, picking a weaving path over raised clumps and half submerged decaying branches. They reached a safe mound of firmer ground, like an island in the marsh, and the hooded figure stopped and jabbed the barrel in his back, pushing him onwards. Halting and looking back, Penrose saw him there, feet apart, gesturing with the revolver to keep going and raising the weapon when he hesitated. Penrose tentatively took a step forward, sinking in the squelching mud up to his knees. A moorhen bolted for cover.

When he turned again, the hooded man was holding the

pistol in both hands, pointing it at his head. There was to be no escape. Bootful after bootful, Penrose forced himself to walk on twenty yards through the stagnant black mud towards the far-off sounds of laughing ducks. His arm throbbed and he fought to stay on his feet as they slid unpredictably.

The marsh deepened and was now layered with a topping of lake water. Step by step he dragged his back foot out of the mud with a rude squelch, bracing against the pain in his ribs, lifting it high to take another step, to sink down further into the mire that now reached over thigh level. He was crying in despair and could go no further. Losing balance he sank forwards on his fractured arm and ribs, taking a mouthful of mud as his face submerged. His neck strained to keep his mouth clear of the water, but he was sinking, his head was too heavy, his body too broken. He gathered what strength was left to turn his shoulders to look pleadingly back at the hooded figure, but he was gone. As he gave up the fight, his body sank below the surface into the yielding mud.

Unseen at the edge of the woods, he watched the final moments, savouring them. The figure pulled back the fur lined hood and stuffed the scarf in his pocket to reveal the pale boy within. He ran his fingers through matted black hair and squinted up at the sun. This had been a good day. Absent-mindedly he stroked the purple scar on his neck. He felt that some of the recent hurt that had been inflicted on him had been lifted, but he had deeper injuries from his past and hoped one day to be strong enough to track down and face the one who had caused him so much pain.

Jerry retraced his route back to the woods, covering his tracks. Flies were circling the dog as he cut it down. He located the old hide nearby that he had slept in after leaving Penrose's home in the early hours that morning. It had given him somewhere to rest and to keep watch. He removed a tartan picnic blanket from the hide together with Penrose's loaded shotgun that had been secreted. With the shotgun over his shoulder, he pulled along the body of the dog on the blanket. At the lakeside, he swung the carcass into the deepest water and hurled the shotgun and pistol into the deep bog close to where Penrose had breathed his last. Back at the hide, he ran his fingers over the freshly carved markings on the trunk of one of the trees.

His final act was to destroy the hide and burn the letter. That was the easy part. He was not looking forward to heading home to face the wrath of his foster parents for staying out overnight.

6

Silver Lighter

After Jerry had tasted revenge that day in the woods, the initial euphoria gave way to an anxiety that the events would soon catch up with him. He had been careful and everything had gone to plan, but he knew that it would not be long before questions would be asked and suspicions raised.

He returned home in the afternoon. His foster parents were waiting for him frostily and sat him down across the small highly polished dining room table, a room reserved for special occasions, to face a grilling.

"Where on earth have you been? We were worried sick," started Aunt Cathy.

"Not even a phone call," Uncle Derek added. "We were on the point of calling the police."

Jerry said nothing, but he was relieved that they hadn't.

"Who were you staying with? It's not a girl is it?" his foster mother asked in alarm.

"Or drugs?" Uncle Derek added. "We can smell smoke on you, you know. Don't think we don't notice these things!"

Jerry smirked.

"He's impossible, Derek! I can't go on like this."

Uncle Derek could feel his blood pressure rising and loosened his tie. "Jeremy, answer us, damn you!" She laid a hand on her husband's forearm to calm him before he continued. "What have you got to say for yourself, boy?"

Jerry finally spoke and mumbled, "What's for tea?"

They were at the end of their tether. His foster father banged the table out of frustration, making their best china in the sideboard rattle.

"Why should we put up with you? Tell me? We don't have to, you know," the forced steadiness in his voice belying the fury in his eyes. "You lie, you cheat, you break our trust. What's in it for us? You should be grateful to us, you evil child. You don't deserve a good family home."

"Derek, we've probably said enough. Jeremy, now say sorry to your dad."

Jerry snorted. His foster mother rushed out of the room to cover her tears. "I'll do some spaghetti rings for you. We've eaten already but you can take a tray into the living room."

After the inquisition, the atmosphere might have lightened, had it not been for the jar. Aunt Cathy washed up Jerry's supper things and sat by herself at the kitchen table sipping her tea and thumbing through a holiday brochure that she had picked up in town. She consoled herself that at least she would have a holiday to look forward. She pulled out a chair to stand on and lifted down the old ginger jar that lived on top of a kitchen cupboard. They had been putting money aside every month, saving towards a special holiday to celebrate their big anniversary. She lifted the cork lid and stared into the empty vessel.

"No!" she hollered, bringing them rushing into the kitchen. "You thief!" she wailed, pointing at Jerry.

Jerry ducked just in time as the missile was thrown at him, smashing on the wall behind in an explosion of blue and white fragments.

"I can't go on like this," sobbed Aunt Cathy. "I can't live under the same roof as him any more. He's got to go, Derek," she implored. Turning to Jerry, "Get out, you monster!"

Ignoring Jerry, his foster mum said, "Derek, I don't want him anywhere near me. He's peculiar. Contact social services in the morning. Ask about rehousing him. He's a bad one and he's not staying here!" Derek was not a violent man but Jerry noticed him clenching his fists tensely as tempers flared. Jerry grabbed his coat and slammed the front door behind him.

The stars were out. He stood alone on the bandstand, flicking the spent cigarette butt over the railing. He held another between his lips and cupped his hands around the silver lighter as he struck it. At least it was a dry evening. It dawned on him that if he did not make peace with his foster parents then it was inevitable that social services would get involved and might start asking awkward questions. Before he knew it, he would be moved to a new school, a new foster family, having no say in the matter. Like every time before.

Jerry decided to sleep in the park overnight. Then in the morning when they had cooled down, he would go back home, apologise profusely and make it up to them. He would make them a cup of tea and offer to get a weekend job to start repaying their holiday fund.

Next morning, he turned the corner into his road. He noticed that the car was not on the driveway. That was odd. More alarmingly, he spotted his bags left out for him in the porch. Hurriedly he tried his key in the lock but it did not turn. The shiny cylinder was new. He rang the bell, banged the door and shouted through the letterbox, but there was no answer. His foster parents had thrown him out. How dare they? An envelope had been left on top of the bags, his name neatly written and underlined twice.

They had forced him into a decision. All his life he had been trapped in a care system that removed his ability to control his own destiny. He had no intention of getting caught in it again. He took the rucksack and refilled it with what he wanted. The rest of the clothes and possessions he heaped inside the porch. He took the unopened envelope with one hand and dipped into his jacket pocket with the other.

As he reached the end of the road, he took one last look over his shoulder and grinned with satisfaction as the porch glowed like a brightening oil lamp as flames took hold. He fingered the silver lighter again, lit a cigarette, adjusted his rucksack straps and headed off towards the main road to thumb a lift to London.

Jerry failed to show up at school on the first day or on the days after that, his empty desk standing as an uncomfortable reminder until the seating plan was shuffled. Andy, Pete and Robbie kept their concerns to themselves and quashed the rumours that were being whipped up in noisy classrooms after break times. When it was announced at a morning assembly that Penrose was missing, they were alarmed. They talked about Jerry in hushed tones as though he was recently passed. The house fire, Penrose's disappearance. Both had the hallmarks of Jerry but was he really capable of those acts? The only thing that they were sure about was that he was gone.

Maybe they should have thought about Jerry more than they did after he vanished from their lives so abruptly. But people move on and with a new term came an influx of girls to the school for the first time. Naturally their brains turned to mush. Their energies diverted to other pursuits like school discos and barn dances which seemed to be a magnet for the opposite sex. None of them ventured Over The Back again. It was relegated to a cherished memory of their childhood.

Had they done so, they would have found a charred patch of ground in the woods where their hide used to be. And on the trunk of a nearby tree, a fourth set of initials had been carved.

II

PART TWO

7

The Big City

If Jerry's life had been tough so far, as a boy living rough in London it was about to get a great deal harder. Initially he tried to sleep in the parks, learning where was safer and where was downright dangerous until heavy rain drove him to find somewhere under cover. The shadows in the city hid an underworld of destitution, mental illness and violence that no modern city in the western world would be proud to own up to. In his first few days in London, Jerry had found a man sitting on a pavement edge in Leicester Square being attended to by an ambulance crew, his throat having been cut from ear to ear. He had no intention of falling victim. In the months that had passed since then, he had witnessed with his own eyes crimes and attacks among the down and outs, crimes that remained hidden. Like a wild animal his senses had become finely tuned to living on the streets, alert to noises and dangers around him. His cunning and quick thinking had saved him so far although he had had most of his money stolen when he had let his guard down one night.

Every day, a couple of hours before dusk fell, he would roam the streets from doorway to bus shelter to railway arch to park to underpass until he found somewhere to settle for the night. His age made him vulnerable to unwanted attention and at signs of trouble he would bundle up his blanket, strap on his rucksack and move on again. He had quickly become one of the forgotten people, one of the unseen. People who for a multitude of reasons had found themselves homeless. This was a landing stage, for some a short term arrangement until they got themselves back on their feet. For others, it was their home and preferable to going back to the life from which they had escaped.

Jerry kept himself to himself and did not trust anyone else. Only his wits would keep him safe and if it was just him looking out for himself then he could not be deceived or let down. When other rough sleepers had tried to engage him in conversation, he stayed silent and wary, his sharp eyes trained on them, cat napping through the long night until dawn. But he had sometimes listened to a few of them, particularly those who wanted to tell their story as a monologue to the silent boy who sat with the blanket drawn tight around him like a protective shell, nursing his rucksack between his knees. Some spoke of escaping from something worse or were tangled in a life spiralling out of control. Others were trapped in dark times where alcohol and drugs gave temporary relief but also obliterated any hope of climbing back out. The common theme was that they had dropped through the gaping holes in the safety net that society is expected to provide to prevent their fall.

He came across a man with a green beret. A scruffy soft-mouthed dog with a lolling tongue lay at his feet.

"Can I stroke him?"asked Jerry. The man nodded. He

watched as Jerry calmly approached the dog, kneeling in front of the animal and stroking him behind the ears with both hands.

"Good boy!" whispered Jerry. He turned to the owner and asked, "What's his name?"

The man in the beret took his time to reply. "That's between me and my dog." Jerry had stopped the petting and was nuzzled and licked in the face, making him smile.

The man said, "You have a way with animals. Have you had a dog before, maybe in your family?"

Jerry remembered old Bessie from long ago. She had been his only companion and he used to tell her everything. When she was gone, he remembered being inconsolable and his guardian had hit him for crying.

"No," lied Jerry.

"What would you call him?"

"Scruff," replied Jerry.

"That's a good name," he replied.

The dog was obviously the man's soulmate, not the usual wide jawed strays some kept as guard animals. The man used to be something or so he said as he stroked the matted fur, but debt and bad decisions had destroyed everything and everyone around him. That man had too much pride to claim benefit entitlements and didn't want people from his past to know what had become of him and anyway he no longer had anything in common with them. On the streets he and Scruff could be anonymous.

Others had a story a little more like Jerry's. They had crash-landed in the misguided pursuit of a dream of a better life in the big city and had forgotten about the path to fame and fortune, distracted by the more pressing need to keep body and soul together.

There he was, one of hundreds, maybe thousands like him, living anxious existences day by day, seemingly invisible to the world around them. That world would just walk on by, averting its gaze. He clung on to his freedom and his hope and reminded himself that he had been in far worse places in his childhood where a roof over his head had been no guarantee of safety. And so, he continued to embrace this episode in his life, sleeping out in city streets, finding shelter in inclement weather or finding refuge for a night before moving on again. In clinging on to life, Jerry learned to survive independently and cherished his liberty.

In his mind he had the capacity either to sink deep into despair or to lift himself out of it and rise to dizzy heights. He harboured a dream of dining in the Top of the Tower on the thirty eighth floor of the Post Office Tower. He and his dinner companion would clink their glasses as they looked out across the city, mesmerised by the lights far below as the restaurant slowly revolved. In the meantime, it stood there above London's streets, often glimpsed between buildings as a beacon he would navigate by.

Jerry had more chances of getting some sleep during daytime but had to keep away from busy areas and cat-napped whenever he could. His dread was to be spotted by police or do-gooders as it would inevitably lead to him being incarcerated in an institution for his protection. Once when he had turned a street corner, he had come face to face with his own image on a peeling missing persons poster. As dire as his life seemed now, he had his freedom. He was sure that life would get better and in London anything would be possible. At least it might help him forget the pain of his traumatic childhood and in the big city he might even be able to carve out a future, one that would never again involve social services who bore almost as much responsibility as the one who had left his mark indelibly scorched.

* * *

As Jerry battled to keep body and soul alive, elsewhere in an elegant Queen Anne townhouse in one of London's exclusive Mayfair addresses, men in black tie and ladies in evening dresses adorned with sequins and mink filed into the dining room where the table was laid in glinting splendour under fine chandeliers. Waiting staff in pristine uniforms were lined up ready to put into action their well-rehearsed attendance at table.

The diners were seated in their named places, men at one end of the table and ladies at the other, as though battle lines had been drawn and in keeping with the house tradition. Crisp linen serviettes were unfolded in a flourish and floated down to the laps of the assembled dignitaries from top echelons of society. Two chairs were still empty, one at the head of the table and the other at the far end. There were representatives from business, politics, the law courts, the police, the church, diplomats, a senior member of the royal household and senior ranks from the civil service and armed forces. If their skill, positions and influence were directed to a collective purpose, then the male bottoms on those chairs could run a small country.

The host and her ladyship crossed the room to join either end of the table. Eyes followed them and the small talk among the guests subsided. Sir Peter winced briefly as he eased

43

himself into the carver chair that had been slid under him. He placed both hands over his horn handled walking cane as he surveyed the expectant faces, nodding at the bespectacled man with the dog collar a couple of seats away from him. The master of the house bowed his head and the reverend said grace in a thin reedy voice. Amens were murmured, glasses were charged.

Observing all from a discrete distance stood an erect owl-faced figure dressed in tails and striped grey flannels. Everything was under the watchful eye of the seasoned butler who with an almost imperceptible movement of his head, or a raise of the heavy eyebrows or a smooth gesture with one hand communicated silent directions to the attentive staff, fine tuning the service as though conducting a symphony to bring in the cellos or French horns at precisely the right time.

Black and white uniformed staff emerged from the kitchen bearing culinary superlatives on silver platters. As they tucked in, the clink of cutlery gave a tuneful melodic layer as murmurs of greetings rose to animated chatter and occasional guffaws from one section of the table.

Courses followed courses and as the last plate was finished, the butler raised an eyebrow to the row of waiters and waitresses standing dutifully in silence. At his signal plates were cleared, crumbs swept from the tablecloth with a little brush and pan and the Sheffield silver tableware was reset in front of each guest ready for the cheese course. Everything was done for them to the highest standards and nothing it seemed was too much trouble. Had they asked for their food to be cut up into tiny pieces and fed to them on silver spoons, then the butler would have seen to it.

On the far side of the flapping kitchen doors, concealed

44

from the diners behind Japanese silk screens, the worker bees set down the dirty crockery for the pot wash to deal with. Remnants of lobster soup, quail carcasses, half-eaten best cuts of meat and dauphinoise potatoes filled the kitchen bins. The meal could have fed a small army but the leftovers, some hardly touched, could still have lavishly nourished a platoon. In the safety of the kitchen, a pretty waitress pulled her friend to one side.

"Did you get your bum pinched again that time?"

"Yes, that dirty old bastard. He squeezed me as well when I reached over for the veg dishes. It's his party but if he'd done that at mine, he'd have his bollocks nailed to the wall by now and his dick on a toasting fork. Seems as though he can get away with anything here."

"Well that's the thing. I've heard that he puts on a show with us girls in front of the guests to make out he can still get it up in the bedroom. That's probably why her ladyship looks so miserable. She probably hasn't had a good shag in years. At least, not from him! Listen to this," she continued. "His strange friend, you know, the death-face vicar sitting near him? Well, don't repeat this but I'm told by them in the know that he's more partial to young boys, if you know what I mean."

"Bloody 'ell! A man of the cloth as well!"

The door had opened and the butler had drawn himself up to his full height, scowling down at them.

He spoke, in a clipped finality of tone. "You two, get back out there now and take your places sharpish! They are about to do the toast."

"I trust that you all feel well looked after at my humble abode and that the chef's creations were to your liking. I think it added much needed colour to an otherwise grey November day." There were appreciative murmurs. "On a personal note I would like to give a warm welcome to our newest member, the recently appointed chair of monopolies and mergers who brings valuable skills to our little club - Sir Francis. As the old saying goes, once a knight, always a knight. Once a knight is never enough!" This provoked a riff of laughter along the table. "Sadly his wife could not join us today. Hopefully we will meet her on another occasion."

"Well, the time has come for business of the day to be discussed. My charming wife will escort the ladies to the very comfortable drawing room where I am assured a fire has been lit and tea will be served in due course. Marcus the pianist will of course be at their disposal." There was polite laughter from the ladies and a brief clatter of applause." He beamed after them as they were led out of the room, his wife leading the graceful exodus.

Glasses were charged for the men who remained at the table. "A toast!" They all stood, glass in hand. "To the Queen!"

"To the Queen!" they replied, raising their glasses to the fine oil painting in a gilded frame that looked down on them. The butler signalled again. Port and cigars were offered, and in keeping with tradition at these gatherings, wedges of brandy-infused fruit cake were served on blue and white china. As the plates were softly placed, the prettiest waitresses received sly gropes from some of the men, less inhibited now in male company and the drink that was loosening their reserve. Except for the ashen faced vicar whose round wire-framed glasses glinted from the chandeliers as he looked up heavenwards in private consultation.

The host turned to his butler. "Privacy please, Bernard."

With a bow of the head, "Certainly, Sir". The butler took a step back, and dismissed the staff, who funnelled out in obedient procession.

Addressing the table, "Pray silence for your host and chairman, Sir Peter." He then gave another small bow, turned on his heels and retreated to his anteroom from where he could hear the buzzer if Sir Peter happened to press the call button under the table. The butler sat at his worn mahogany desk in his snug domain, glad to take the weight off his feet. He opened the top drawer and reached in to feel the cold steel of the loaded Luger P08, a memento from the War, that was sandwiched between some folded serviettes. Just in case the buzzer sounded three times.

Sir Peter remained seated. He leant back his chair, elbows on the rests, fingers rolling the unlit cigar as though deep in thought. His jowly face was without expression. There was a pregnant pause and a couple of the guests shifted in their seats uncomfortably. He looked up and scanned the expectant faces as though seeking out dissent in the ranks. These were important people, people of stature, people of power, and he had something on each of them, something that tied them into his service, dark secrets that he knew about, secrets that kept them loyal and compliant for the times when their influence may be useful to him. Apparently satisfied, he beamed at them, his ice white moustache stretching from cheek to cheek.

"Well, gentlemen, I trust you enjoyed my hospitality." There were murmurs of approval. "But as we all know, there is no such thing as a free lunch, or dinner in this case! You now have to listen to me and enjoy my wit and repartee. Anyone not prepared to will be invited to help those young girls with the washing up!" For a moment he leered at the thought of them and absent mindedly licked his lips, rolling the cigar again with his fat fingers.

His friend, the death-face vicar, caught his eye. He resumed jovially, his putty face resembling a kindly uncle but his words that followed held an ominous undertone.

"Gentleman, all of you are special people who bring special skills and I am enormously grateful for your attendance today. I believe we have a full house." Looking down the table he smiled to himself. "Even a royal flush!"

"You are all, each and every one of you, invaluable to the Firm." One of the guests started coughing violently from a piece of cake that had become stuck in his windpipe. Sir Peter's smile melted and his expression hardened as though the interruption had cut the strings from a dancing mannequin.

He continued, although all warmth had drained from his tone. "This dinner celebrates a hierarchy and mutual bond that must and will be preserved at all cost. It so happens that a troubling matter has come to my attention that I need to discuss with a few you in the forthcoming days. Bernard will be in touch through the usual channels. For some of you, your influence may be called on to correct an unfortunate issue that has recently befallen one of our own. Remember your calling and as chairman I must remind you once again of the allegiances you made when you came into this fold. Anyone who breaks ranks will be dealt with appropriately."

An awkward silence had descended in the stately dining room. A layer of rich, pungent smoke hung lazily above the table. As the members of this sinister most secret society sat motionless in contemplation or drew on a fine Cuban cigar, perhaps each was quietly recoiling at their own misdemeanours or speculating on those of the members seated near them. Maybe they contemplated the enormity of ever stepping out of line, of having their most private secrets exposed and the ruin and shame that would destroy them. While some feared the public humiliation and the fall from grace that would inevitably follow, others had a deeper understanding of the workings of this close clan. They knew what the Firm was capable of in order to survive and protect itself. Rumour was that two previous members had conspired to blow the lid on the organisation. One had simply vanished without trace. Another had been involved in a bizarre accident with dental records providing the only means of identification. Vanished or executed, same difference.

Sir Peter took in the discomfort around the table with deep satisfaction. They understood him and it reaffirmed their loyalty. A reluctant devotion but a devotion nonetheless, like that of a dog that is beaten by the same hand that feeds him. The broad smile had returned, stretching the white whiskers even further than before. "Now, Gentlemen! This 1963 vintage is something to be appreciated, all the way from the banks of the Douro. It is a flavoursome little number and reminds me of a girl I once knew. Rather fruity with rosy cheeks and a backside to match!"

"Raise your glasses and join me as we recite together the edict that binds us together." The table cheerfully erupted with the Firm's motto that they all knew by heart. *"Fortior conjunctum, fidelis usque ad mortem!"*

"Yes!" Sir Peter exclaimed, like a general rousing his troops. And banging the table in emphasis. "Stronger together, faithful until death!" The vicar's expression was sour as he joined a final toast to the brotherhood and drained his crystal water glass.

The ladies had rejoined their men, coats and shawls were collected, and the guests briefly congregated in the hallway. Sir Peter leant on his cane and he and Lady Margaret waved off the guests from the foot of the stairs before he turned and climbed his painful way to his bedroom. His gout was flaring up and he was in no mood to stay up any longer. Bernard would bring him his nightcap and have the place ship shape again by morning. The doorman in an overcoat and peaked hat, who doubled as Sir Peter's chauffeur by day, led them to the taxis that were lined up outside, pre-booked for some of the guests to deliver them home or to their hotel for the night. Some shared, others travelled solo. The vicar scuttled away on foot, his collar turned up to the cold. Two of the men who had come without partners were last to leave. Lady Margaret stood in the empty hall, reapplied her lipstick in the mirror by the hat stand and headed back to the drawing room where she was looking forward to a private audience with the dark eyed pianist.

"Brrr, this is a bit nippy! Glad we wrapped up well."

"I was going to walk it, but as you're heading my way, we may as well share a lift. We should be able to grab a taxi if we walk to the corner of the square."

"Excellent idea. These dinners are rather tiresome I find but I suppose it's his way of keeping us in line. I sometimes think that it is a bit like the masons but without the pig's blood and funny handshakes."

"Yes, I sometimes wonder whether it is worth it, all this skulduggery. But when you hear about the strings he pulled with certain members for Bertie Grace. Getting him off that manslaughter charge with the help of our friendly judge. They say Bertie flattened that woman and most of the bus shelter with his Bentley and a bottle of single malt inside him. If it had not been for the Firm's influence, making the witness and case files disappear, he'd be serving a life sentence by now."

"True enough. Oh, there's one. No, it hasn't got its light on."

"I thought the Vicar looked as though he wanted to be anywhere else but at that table. He's never the life and soul at the best of times. So, what's the old man got on him to make him stick with it?"

"Come on, you know how it works. A member's business is strictly his own business. That's not up for discussion and never will be. Anyone one of us could get a call or a tap on the shoulder and we could hardly say no. And if we did, I dread to think what would fall on us from a great height. Ah, taxi!"

8

In The Service

Bernard was in his mid-twenties when the war ended. He had cut his teeth as a British soldier in the Western Desert Campaign at the end of 1940, fighting alongside Indian, Commonwealth and Allied Forces in Operation Compass, advancing on the Italian fortified positions of the 10th army, recapturing western Egypt and capturing ports along the Libyan coast. He was then sent to Greece to support their forces in their defence against the aggressors, first the Italians and then the Germans, narrowly escaping capture. He then served in bloody campaigns in Italy and by then had built a reputation for ruthlessness and seeing a job through to completion.

He had been talent spotted in early skirmishes and his fluency in languages had not gone unnoticed. He was sent back home for a brief leave before a secondment to six weeks intensive commando course at Achnacarry Castle in the Highlands. The castle sat between two lochs, Loch Lochy and Loch Arkaig making it an ideal practice ground to replicate assaults on both land and coastal terrains. The Commando

Training Depot was used not just by the British Commandos but by all Allied Forces including US army rangers and commandos from Netherlands, Norway, Czechoslovakia, Poland, France and Belgium. The training was tough and culminated in an amphibious landing on the shores of Loch Lochy, live ammunition whistling over their heads and at their feet.

Bernard came out unscathed and was immediately posted to the 9th Commandos to take part in operations on the coast of Italy as part of the Special Service Brigade for a campaign code named Operation Shingle, where the British fought alongside the US 5th Army and Canadians. He was part of an amphibious attack force from a basin of reclaimed marshland surrounded by mountains, the task to use the element of surprise to outflank the German army.

The Battle of Anzio was a prelude to a campaign that ended with the capture of Rome. He and a selected few also went perilously deep in secret missions behind the German's Gustav Line. Bernard came into his own in the challenging terrain of the mountainous regions that straddled to the north of the ancient colonnaded city.

On one such mission, an incident had won him the nick-name of The Cleaner where his advance squad had fallen like nine-pins under enemy fire from the gun emplacement that was their target to destroy. He had lain until nightfall under cover beneath fallen comrades in one of the craters that pockmarked the terrain, testimony to the heavy Italian built Howitzer that sent shells that whistled from its 8.3-inch calibre barrel. The big gun protected the mountain pass, sited in a fortified position high above the impregnable cliff face. Their objective was to neutralise it.

As a delicate, dusty snow began to fall and swirl in the fading light, he was able to pick out pin points of lights far away in the distance as helmeted guards lit cigarettes. There was a faint glow painted in the rock face whenever mess doors opened for feeding time.

He frisked the frozen bodies relieving them of rope, mountain gear, spare thirty-two round magazines for his 9mm Sten Mark 2 and explosives, dumping his rations, digging tools and water to lighten his weight for what lay ahead.

Bernard looked up to the blackening sky above, felt the snow on his upturned face falling heavier and faster. He had a job to do and it was now or never. He glanced at the folded map one last time, took a compass bearing and checked his watch. He set off across the fresh snow, his tracks quickly smudging as flake heaped on flake. With stealth he picked his way across the snow field taking a wide sweep behind the sparse tree cover to shield his approach from the defended gun emplacement high above. He was about to take an impregnable route up the most treacherous section of cliff face to an old mule trail. In the briefing early that same morning his commanding officer had abruptly dismissed that route as foolhardy in daylight and sheer madness in the dark, preferring instead a more direct assault. That had not been his best decision that day and his decorated corpse lay where it had fallen, decoratively holed with machine gun fire around the torso like perforations in a sheet of postage stamps.

The route that Bernard now took in the fading daylight had been put down as crazy in daylight and sheer madness in the dark. It led him up an impossible overhanging crag, made scalable for him by the massive strength in his arms and bear-like hands that allowed him to heave his body weight from frozen handhold to crumbling toe hold, carefully using the climbing axe to pierce the icy crevices, hoping that any noise was muffled by the snow. Hauling himself up the final ledge, he halted in mid-climb, a smell of tobacco in his nostrils. Gruff guttural voices laughed and a discarded cigarette butt flicked past his face, sparking as it bounced off the rocky face, to be lost in the white-out deep below. He waited, adjusting aching hand and foot holds which slipped as his energy sapped from exposure.

After what seemed an eternity, he heard footsteps receding, a metal door slamming and if there was a guard right above him then he would have to take his chances. It was that or falling unceremoniously to be buried until the spring thaw with a ridiculous look on his face or ripped apart by wolves. He had never liked dogs and this thought gave him the final spur he needed.

He heaved himself up with those final ounces of energy, aware that he was in the open as he joined the narrow mule track that from the plans he had studied at the briefing led into the face of the mountain caverns. With raw cold hands he took the butterfly-coiled rope from his back, the lengths pre-tied with figure of eight bends, and with aching fingers tied the bitter end to a stout tree trunk, its branches blown away many months ago from the campaign that had taken so many allied lives and hardly dented the enemy. He crouched, eating the last lump of chocolate he had saved and taking a bite from a handful of snow, enjoying for a blissful moment the feeling of numbness as the melt water slipped down his throat.

He focussed, prepared the explosives, breathed deeply and unclipped his combat knife in readiness. He followed the track, pressing himself to the protective rocks where he could and crouching in the open until he was no more than ten yards from the guard. Bravery, madness, hatred or a combination of all three created a one-man force that quietly took out the solitary peeing guard with a slit of the throat, dropping him silently to the cold rock floor. There was another just around the corner. From the shadow of the rock face he whistled at the teenage soldier swaddled in a greatcoat many times too big who turned with a grin to greet the butt of the Sten gun. He was now clear to work. Bernard laid explosives all along the track and led the cable back to the box that was hidden near his escape tree alongside the neatly coiled rope. Charges had quickly been placed below the gun emplacement in a deep tunnel used for garbage or worse and in one of the supply tunnels that would have led in an inner chamber. Before mayhem ensued, he flattened himself against the rock wall in the bitter wind, eased open the metal door as though it had been taken by the wind and hurled the grenades through the open door of the unsuspected diners who never had time to reach for their guns.

The noise of battle had brought more soldiers from the maze of tunnels that led back into the mountain, like ants appearing from a disturbed nest. Bernard returned fire, taking them out one by one, emptying all three magazines from his Sten gun. He discarded it, grabbing weapons from the mounting pile of bodies, firing behind him as he fled back along the track to his escape tree where the rope was tied. Bullets whistled at his feet and grazed his shoulder as he threw himself forwards and pushed the charge handle all the way down. The first boom sounded. As the narrow path shook, he grabbed the climbing rope with both hands launching himself backwards into the white abyss. The mountain side caved in on itself, tipping rock, concrete, limbs and two massive gun barrels down the cliff face. There were more explosions as the ammunition stores fire balled.

Bernard had single handedly taken out a platoon and its heavy artillery. As dawn broke under blue skies, it was plain to see that the mountainscape had been changed forever.

During his war years, Bernard had proved himself to be a capable operative in combat and had learnt many of the tricks of this trade in commando training at the Scottish castle.

After he left the service with a healthy pension, he tried to settle into a routine existence but felt frustrated and idle. It was not long before Bernard was approached to join a small covert unit set up to pursue war criminals and British traitors hiding abroad. His interrogation techniques yielded information quickly. The swift executions that followed were kept away from British shores and dealt with the problems surgically. Bernard was under orders issued by a man at Whitehall. That same man took a close interest in him and after the unit was disbanded, Bernard was taken into his fold. The man was Sir Peter.

9

Pastel De Nata

F rank filled a jug at the sink and pushed the flower stems down into the water - her favourite ones - fanning them out to resemble his idea of a presentable bouquet. Placing the jug on the hallway table for her to see on her return from wherever she was, usually shopping in Knightsbridge or luncheoning with girlfriends, he scribbled a quick note.

> *"A - Have a business engagement this evening and may be home late. Don't wait up. I'll sleep in the spare room so as not to wake you. Flowers to say sorry - Fx"*

As it happened, that was perfectly true but often he would just want to get away for a couple of days, escape from the oppressive atmosphere and hope that the storm would blow over by his return and that he was not banished again like a cowering dog to spend another lonely night again in his spare bedroom under the scowling picture of his grandfather. Lucky bugger, he thought, to be killed in action with military honours. Frank's father also had a distinguished career as a member of the House of Commons. His benevolence to the Labour Party bought him a hereditary peerage. On his father's death, Frank became Sir Francis at the age of thirty-eight. This gave him an added air of respectability and opened doors for him.

His title brought a certain amount of amusement from his contemporaries. He had been involved in some highly suspect business dealings which lost him the family pile in Derbyshire, but he still retained his father's fine house in Chelsea which projected success although it was not of his making. He lived there unhappily and childless with his wife Amanda and the twice weekly visit from the Portuguese housekeeper. Frank lived off the rapidly dwindling income from the family trust where he was sole beneficiary, dabbling unsuccessfully in art, antiques and the stock market, showing a perverse and uncanny skill at buying at the top of the market before fashion and collectability fell through the floor. He sometimes wondered about his financial future once the trust income had been spent. He had scrupulously concealed the losses from his wife who most days occupied herself on the King's Road using shopping therapy to get away from him and to comfort herself by having nice things around her, compounding his woes.

Amanda hadn't spoken to him that morning, but he knew from the dark looks she had shot him that he was not in her good books. He had no idea why but that was not unusual. She had probably been hurt by something he had said or done, or not said or not done. Perhaps something misjudged that came across as belittling or unappreciative and he had no idea how any of this had come about. This was a regular feature in their relationship and he hoped that all couples went through the same daft rituals and that he was not simply a fool for accepting things that way.

When she was in one of her moods, there was nothing, absolutely nothing, he could do to avoid the trip wires that were hidden in every seemingly ordinary situation or conversation, however dull or innocuous. If she was drinking, as she was more often than not, then this would only exacerbate things. It was a question of when and where, not if. She would say nothing over the next day or so if nothing he did provoked a reaction. Knowing that there were eggshells encircling him he would tip toe around her, being exceptionally helpful, considerate, thoughtful and make cheery one-sided conversation. She would wait. The next day or the day after, as tension built between them, a meaningless trivial thing from him, a word, a gesture, a look, would trigger a fierce and violent reaction like that of a volcano that had held in its grumbling sulphuric gases, brewing and bubbling noxious fumes under the fragile surface for centuries, until a weakness in the earth's crust set off an almighty explosion. When she blew, he did not want to be anywhere nearby and certainly not in public where her erratic temper and complete unawareness of a social situation caused him acute embarrassment.

And that is how it had started. First it was working late. He explained to Amanda that he did after all have an exceptionally important job that demanded more of his time than he was able to give. But he also had needs, god he had needs, and she had made it perfectly clear that she was not going to be the one to satisfy them. Did he really say that out loud? The plate narrowly missed him and the pieces skidded across the floor.

Life took a pleasant turn for Frank when a new housekeeper was employed. Lovely Rosario was besotted with him. They had brushed past each other on the stairs on her first day. He had stepped carefully over the trailing hoover flex, his mind preoccupied, and she had swivelled on the stairs to look back up at him. Their eyes had met and they had both felt a little spark. Lady Amanda preferred to be out all day when the housekeeper was in her home and this suited Frank who found that his diary could be reorganised to allow him to work from home two days a week.

Before long he and Rose had enjoyed more than just a coffee break together. He had made it crystal clear to her from that very first time that he really could not have an affair with her. But if it wasn't an affair then what was it? He was fond of the girl who was in her late twenties. She was very sweet and always made him laugh. The double figure age gap didn't seem to matter to her and certainly made him feel young again. But Frank saw no future in it. He did not want to hurt her feelings when it all went pop as it surely would one day, or to risk Rose having an outburst in front of Amanda that would make his life even more miserable.

So, every Tuesday and Friday, she would arrive. He would by chance or design be working from home on one of those days reading committee papers at his desk while she sang popular songs from the radio or practised soulful Fado if she was feeling homesick, as she worked her way around the house. Rose would eventually come up to his study, smelling sweetly, her luxurious black hair tied up in a scarf, the silver heart locket he had given her swaying on the necklace.

"I've made you a coffee Frank, and your favourite biscuits. It's on the kitchen table."

61

He looked up and smiled., "Thank you, Rose." She lingered, rubbing her finger along the edge of the desk as though checking for dust.

"Hey, …. how's that mad aunt of yours in Lisbon?"

"Oh, my aunt, she's OK, I phoned her and she's really happy. She's borrowed," she frowned, "No, the word is adopted. She has adopted a little kitten that visits her every day. She has called it Coco and it sits on her front step while she feeds it sardines. My aunt has made a friend there, but I think I know why the cat loves her so much! Lisbon is big on sardines, Frank, I love it there and you would like the little trams and blue and white tiled houses. Maybe one day I could show you the beaches and the Torre de Belem, the little castle on the Tagus I told you about that looks like a fairy tale castle and we could eat warm pastel de nata and drink cherry liqueur and …" She would chatter away happily, perched on the side of his desk.

She seemed to have few cares in the world and when she was with him, all his troubles seemed to fall away. Her storytime at the desk was the best bit but they both knew it was a prelude. He would casually rotate his shoulder to ease some stiffness. Quick as a flash Rose would hop off the desk and stand behind his chair massaging his neck and his shoulders to ease the tension, soothing the knots in his muscles. She had a lovely touch. He would take her hands in his and wrap them around him. If she was wearing one of her short flowery dresses, then the desk was the obvious choice of approach or on a jeans day he would lead her to his bedroom suite next door. "Back to work for me, Frank!" she would eventually say, as they kissed affectionately and parted, before picking up her clothes and carrying them to her chest as she walked naked down the corridor to the bathroom. "I'll make the room look, how you say, 'spick and span' before I go. Oh, Frank, your coffee will be stone cold!"

Rose was a breath of fresh air, but the last-minute overnight trips away from work also became more frequent. Then the need to work weekends became a monthly occurrence and he managed to introduce the occasional week-long business trip to a European city without raising Amanda or Rose's suspicions to give him the space to breathe again, to be himself, to work a little and to play a lot.

With such lack of ability in many walks of life, he had been surprised to receive an invitation out of the blue to apply for the influential position of chairman of a quango scrutinising monopolies and mergers, the previous incumbent having dropped down dead on the thirteenth green, comically clutching his putter with perfect grip after sinking his ball for a birdie. Frank was told that his name had been put forward by a source that chose to remain anonymous. Privately he speculated that his title and family background probably gave the position the on-paper credibility that the Commission was looking for. Naturally, he would have concealed his dubious investment decisions had he been asked about them at the briefest of interviews but as it all seemed predetermined the subject never came up. His new role went surprisingly well, guided by a capable assistant, and he found his feet and even earned the respect of his new colleagues when he kept to the script.

A few months into his tenure, he was invited into Sir Peter's inner circle, a tight and secretive group of high-profile individuals. It felt as though he had finally really made it in life with the very best connections right on hand. His wife should have been his plus-one at Sir Peter's Mayfair residence whenever the Firm met for their formal luncheons or dinner parties. Each time she threw a migraine and made it quite clear that she was only being asked along to make him look good and had no intention of playing the dutiful wife.

One evening, Frank sat in his study listening to a record from his late father's extensive collection of piano music. The empty sleeve read 'Bach's Goldberg Variations'. The shelves had previously been lined with dusty tomes on politics, Marxism, communism, French literature and ancient Greece, almanacs and scholarly works. He had thrown them all out and redecorated to his taste. He took particular pleasure in disposing of the French works as he could never grasp the language. The shelves now supported an impressive library of books on art and antiques, bought as a load from a Sotheby's house clearance sale. The music had always helped his father to relax and concentrate and now Frank sat in the same chair and thought hard about the recent turn of events. Somehow without doing anything very much he had landed on his feet. But if he had learnt one thing the hard way, it was if something looks too good to be true, then it probably is.

Thinking back to the first of the Firm's luncheons he had attended, he had been alarmed to pick up Sir Peter's menacing undertones. He wouldn't have been at all surprised if his thug Bernard hadn't already delved into his affairs and found enough to wipe him out financially and dare he say criminally if it were ever exposed. He needed something on them in return in case they ever decided to come down hard on him. He took a sheet of ruled paper, selected two BIC biros from the collection of pens and pencils that Rose had tidied into an empty Lyons coffee tin and drew a long rectangle on the page, marking Sir Peter at the head of the table and writing down every name he could remember against the seating plan. He then annotated each member's name with two boxes - the first the skill or connection they brought to the brotherhood, and switching to red ink what he knew or suspected was their Achilles' heel. Much of it he had gleaned over a long drinking session with one or two of the more liberal members. Financial impropriety, sex with minors, caused death by dangerous driving and so on. He added a detailed commentary for each of them on a second sheet of paper.

Satisfied, Frank sealed it in an envelope marked *"In the event of my death or disappearance, to be handed unopened"*, underlining this twice, and added the name and address of his solicitor. He then flamboyantly signed and dated the envelope, before placing it in the safe hidden behind the vanity copy of a Henri Matisse that had been painted for him by a skilled forger and old business associate.

Frank was heading out that evening to meet another of the members of the Firm for a drink in a pub near Grosvenor Square. Bernstein was a senior official in the diplomatic service and enjoyed his liquor by all accounts. Frank showered and put on a casual jacket. He took a last look at the orchids, straightened the note he had left beside them and pulled the door shut behind him.

* * *

"You called, Sir?" said the butler.

"Yes, Bernard, close the door behind you," said Sir Peter. "I'm afraid that we have a predicament. One of our trusted members has had a quiet word with me. It seems that our newest recruit to the brotherhood, Sir Fucking Francis, has stepped over the line. Bernstein had a few drinks with him the other evening in a public bar and it loosened his tongue. He claims to have something on us that he could use if we ever wanted to take a swing at him, and I don't like the sound of it. The talk was of a list of some sort naming each and every one, their motivations, faults and misdemeanours. There's a lot to mine if someone digs deep enough and we wouldn't want that getting into the public eye and splashed all over Fleet Street. We have a couple of tame editors on the payroll, but the left-wing and gutter press would have a field day."

"Find out what he's got on us, get some dirt we can use on him if we must and put the fear of god into the toad. He could still be very useful to us if he snaps into line but if not, well we cross that one if it comes to it. Mind you cover your tracks well."

"Understood Sir."

"Oh, and Bernard."

"Yes Sir?"

"A dry sherry would go down a treat!"

* * *

Frank checked his dinner invitation for the charitable event and questioned himself why he had said yes to it. His assistant must have accepted it on his behalf as it didn't sound like his thing at all. He wouldn't know anyone and a tedious evening was promised but at least it got him out of the house. At the restaurant, he was shown to a circular table, with six already seated, leaving a pair of empty seats. The attending waiter took his coat and pulled back the chair for him to the right of an elderly lady dressed in black. A crisp linen serviette was delivered to his lap with an excessive flourish. The rest of the table were removing their reading spectacles having already studied the menus and chosen their wine. He caught his neighbour's fleeting glance, glimpsing an unfriendly disposition, but offered back what he hoped was a politely apologetic smile. He tried small talk but apart from covering the simplest and most trite topics, he was left feeling uncomfortable and estranged on the table.

His other nearest neighbour one empty seat away was holding court with the other side of the table, engrossed in lecturing them about cutlery, waving his soup spoon demonstratively as he challenged them that Sheffield silver was still the best cutlery in the world. None of the other guests was congenial or courteous enough to include him but given the topic of conversation, that was a relief. He looked down the menu and was alarmed to see the complicated choices in impenetrable French and the number of courses that lay ahead of him.

The restaurant was vast and waiters in black and white uniforms set down plates that had been sitting under heat lamps for too long. The portions were mean, perhaps a blessing, and wine waiters came round regularly to top up the glasses with the heavily marked up wine. As the starters were finished, he was resigned to being unable to plot an early escape. The table was too large to converse successfully and when he ventured to open a conversation with elderly lady in black, she fixed him with a stare and lashed a look of disapproval, her pinched lips moving silently in the muttering of curses or spells. The empty chair beside him was pulled back by the waiter and he took in at first the legs, then the elegant dress, the balcony cleavage and the flowing blonde hair as she joined the table, apologising for her tardiness. She was close to him in age, he guessed, and quite captivating.

The bar was packed. The surly bar maid put the brimming pint alongside the bacardi and coke and slapped down his change. Thank you, charmed I'm sure, he quipped. Not so much as a smile. The lights dimmed and conversations grew louder and shouted to carry over the music now distorted through the speakers as the DJ turned up the volume. Shadowy figures started moving more or less in time with the music on the dance floor.

Slopping the drinks as he weaved between jutting elbows and blindly shoving shoulders, he found his way back to her, still leaning over the narrow drinks ledge that separated the throng from the dance floor. Around the dance floor was a two-man deep fringe of onlookers. Girls were dancing in pairs or groups and braver blokes stepped in to show off their dance moves. A social circus had begun, displaying attempts and failures to pull, overt pairing by some, overt rejection of their primal attempts by others. If this was a jungle, as the nightclub's name implied, then most of the men around the clearing were the apes hanging from the branches and scratching their balls, too timid to set foot out there.

They raised and clinked glasses, as girls of all shapes and sizes bobbed in and out of the flickering lights as the mirror ball spun above them.

"This is more like it!" he shouted. "Who wants to be at a

stuffy dinner …"

She continued for him, "When you can have a sticky floor instead!"

They were both overdressed, but it didn't matter. They could barely hear each other above the din so passed comment to each other in facial expressions and gestures. They seemed surprisingly tuned in to each other, even though they had only met for the first time that evening. Together they cheekily rated the revellers on the floor with a phwoar for the attractive ones and shook their heads for those less blessed. She shared a wicked sense of humour.

"Come on, Frank, let's dance!" She took his hand and pulled him to the floor to join the mayhem, moving her hips fluidly to the music. He was enraptured. The bodies around them whipped and whirled and clapped and grooved until the next track came on. The floor emptied and filled again like a platform change at Kings Cross, but the pair held their ground and each other, right in the middle of the floor.

She stood on tiptoes and pulled him down to her level. "Let's go somewhere a little quieter. I can hardly hear a word you're saying!"

They returned to where they'd left their glasses. "Here," she said, closing the clasp on her black velvet handbag, "Finish your drink and let's leg it!" Her mockingly pleading blue eyes were inviting. Frank drank this in, gulped the remnants of the glass and threw his jacket over his shoulder.

The big expert hands loosened the tourniquet by one half turn to bring back the blood flow to his brain. Frank was in limbo land, suspended on the edge of consciousness. A turn and a half would kill him. "No go … no way … no no no. That dress was a devil to get off".

"The list?" He was only vaguely aware of the tightening around the artery. "Where is the list of names?"

"It's hidden, all hidden. In a special place. My special place."

"Where is the hiding place?"

"Is a secret and you never tell secrets."

"Where is it?"

"Ouch … Henri has it. He's guarding it."

"Henry? Henry who?"

Frank sniggered, "Henri's not real you know, but you'd never know."

"This is a waste of time. Let's tidy up here."

When he came to, he was sitting on the empty platform, leaning against a wall, jacketless. "How the hell did I get here?" he thought. Spotting a puddle of sick beside him, he recognised some of the contents and shifted away to disassociate himself from it. There was dinner and yes, he had ordered mussels by mistake. Was this shellfish poisoning as he didn't remember drinking much? He recalled that ghastly black widow and the empty seat. But then she had joined the table, glamorous, engaging and well-spoken but with a slight hint of a regional accent he couldn't quite place. She had an infectious dirty laugh and sent him into a spin. Yes, and they went to a nightclub. Those eyes! The dress - a devil to take off. Where did she go? Did they … or didn't they?

How the hell had he got here, wherever here was? He squinted up to look at the letters that spun and the name of the underground station slowly came into focus. "Oh no, not here. Right at the end of the bloody line, the end of civilisation!" He felt nauseous and squeezed his eyes shut. He recalled dancing, he never dances, and the girl with the blonde hair was etched in his mind. Did they go anywhere after the nightclub? His memory was hazy but out of the murk he recalled them sharing a bottle of merlot in a simple hotel bedroom. She had taken a deep sip and pressing her pursed lips to his had blown the warmed liquid carefully into his parted lips. Magnificently sexy. He had tried the same on her with less expertise, drawing half a mouthful from the shared glass and dribbled it down her chin. Why was he such an idiot!

Clinging on to the memory, he remembered stroking the smooth bare skin under her dress above her stockings and his palm brushed the clip of her suspenders. She had moved his hand away from exploring further and turning her back to him she asked him to unlace the back of her dress that was strapped on like a corset. That was one hell of dress. Standing behind her he had moved her hair off her shoulders, taking in the pale skin and the slender neck and planted kisses as he worked at the garment.

The unlacing seemed to take an age and after a final fumble, the dress fell away from her torso releasing her naked breasts that he now recalled so clearly. She had stepped out of the dress. The overhead lamp in the room was harsh and he noticed a little more bulk around her midriff than he had been expecting, but he was no spring chicken either. She unbuttoned his shirt, then his trousers, and they fell on top of the bed. Then ... he was dazzled!

"Oh god!" he shouted aloud to the empty platform, recoiling. In the bedroom there had been a flash and fizz of a camera from a male figure who had entered the room, then flash after flash as the two of them lay entwined. Someone else held him down on the bed face down and he glimpsed the girl get up

71

calmly to dress. She was wearing his jacket as she turned to blow him a kiss. He must have had something slipped into his drink as his vision blurred and he passed out. He had been set up!

* * *

Bernard reported back. "I'm afraid that the information was correct. He has made a list that reveals all the names, the clandestine activities of the Firm and a lot of personal information on our members - factual or best guess. He didn't reveal where the list is hidden, he completely blanked us. We used the serum to interview him and he won't recall anything after the needle went in."

"This is all very worrying."

"We have these photographs in case we need them later." Sir Peter slid the photos out of the envelope.

"Oh yes, well chosen. She's a sexy fox!"

The old man stroked his chin thoughtfully. "So, Sir Francis really has it but clearly has no intention of giving it up. This could bring the whole thing crashing down if it goes public. The years it has taken to build an effective team that can work above the law to get things done. All for what? We've got to find the dratted list and destroy it before this gets out of hand."

The butler clicked his heel. "Sir, I'm at your service!"

"Bernard, my loyal right-hand man! We have been through a lot together over the years and you have never let me down. But on this occasion, you are simply too close to me and we need to be careful that this doesn't bounce back on us. We'll do this at arm's length. I'm going to call in a favour."

10

Ketchup

Since coming to London, Jerry had not met anyone he trusted but as the winter cold gnawed at him relentlessly, chilling him to the core, he knew he urgently needed to find a safe place to sleep. One evening, outside a jazz club in the West End, he noticed a lad perhaps a year or two older than him, dressed in jeans with a denim jacket to match. Jerry had a good memory for faces. A couple of days ago while he sat in a doorway finishing someone's discarded bag of cold chips, he had spotted the same lad outside a busy pub at closing time. Here he was again, hovering outside the club, smoking. Every now and then, a customer going in or out of the club would wander across to the dealer in an overly casual way, asking for a light. Money would covertly be exchanged for a small, twisted wrapper. Leaving the shadows, Jerry approached him.

Denim watched the gaunt youth as he approached, and he shot a look at someone across the street out of view. Jerry stopped two paces away from him, standing there in grubby clothes and greasy matted black hair. He wore a hungry look in his sunken eyes. "Hi, I'm looking for work if you have any going. And somewhere to stay. Any ideas?"

The dealer smiled. "You look rough as shit, kid!" Keeping an eye over Jerry's shoulder for any customers, he added, "I'm a bit busy right now but the man I work for is always looking out for new talent. See the black guy near the bus stop? He's the minder. Tell him Jonny sent you and he might introduce you to our line of work. See you around, kid. Now beat it!"

The Minder was leaning heavily against the wall, motionless, and showed no obvious interest in Jerry as he headed over to him. But Jerry caught his fast-swift glances from twenty yards away, examining him up and down, taking in his hands, fixing on his jacket pockets and felt that he was being measured up from a distance. For a suit, or perhaps a coffin.

"Jonny sent me over to you. Said you might have somewhere I can stay for a bit?"

The man said nothing at first and now brought himself upright from the wall he had been leaning against, his height and bulk growing alarmingly as he looked down at Jerry who had always considered himself tall for his age.

"Well, well, Shrimp! So why would I want to help you? Do I look like a charity?" he said with menace in his voice. He then let out a booming laugh at his remark, finding it far funnier than it rightly should have been.

"OK, let's go and talk somewhere." He signalled silently to Denim, nodding his head once in the direction of an illuminated café. "When did you last have a proper meal, Shrimp?"

Jerry was taken by the Minder to a Wimpy bar next to a taxi office. He pointed with a finger to one of the fixed red plastic seats. "Sit there, I'll be back."

Jerry did as he was told, pushing his bag under the seat and sitting at the formica table in front of a tomato-shaped plastic ketchup dispenser and a half-filled ashtray. "Gino, feed this gent, he looks like he needs a square meal." The Minder headed to the toilets at the back of the shop. Jerry could only focus on his aching stomach. He had stuffed down a ham sandwich found discarded in the street early that morning but hadn't had anything since to abate his hunger. The thought of hot food was mesmerising. He had an obscured view of the kitchen staff through the open kitchen door, blue smoke hanging in the air and heard the sizzling as his food was prepared.

The Minder took a seat in front of him, his bulk like an adult on a primary school chair at parents evening. A gold chain was strung around his muscular neck. A cold draught flowed in briefly as the café door behind him opened and closed. They were joined by the lad in denim who silently passed across a roll of green and blue banknotes which the Minder took and counted with thick fingers before peeling off two notes to give back to him. The Minder pocketed the rest. Three plates of burgers arrived which Jerry didn't recall seeing the Minder order.

The ketchup and mustard containers belched up their contents and they bit into the food.

"How old are you, Shrimp? Sixteen, seventeen?" he asked, tiny bits of burger flying across the table as he spoke. "Eighteen," Jerry lied.

"Well I may be able to help you with your housing crisis," he smiled broadly to himself, finding that amusing as well. Even his teeth were oversized. One of his top middle incisors was missing and its neighbour was broken, leaving a jagged tooth that gave him a dangerous shark-like appearance when he bared his teeth. "Business is booming. An extra pair of hands would come in useful. Maybe some light delivery work to start with."

Jerry stopped chewing, his jaw set open while he thought about this. The Minder continued, "Here's my offer. You work for my boss, the big man, and he'll look after you. You can stay at the lodgings with the other worker bees. As long as you are bringing home the bacon, then the big man won't turn you into sausages!" He grinned again to himself and to Denim who sat silently looking bored but managed a weak smile. The Minder's demeanour had changed and he absent-mindedly crunched his knuckles. "The big man looks after people who take care of his business interests. If you don't show respect, then my size eleven's will boot you back on the street faster than a heartbeat and further than you can piss. Is that fair?" Jerry nodded. He felt ragged and his eyelids were weighing down.

The Minder lightened up and addressed Denim. "Teach him well!" He turned to Jerry.

"Here, these are on the house." He pushed a packet of triangular blue tablets across the table. "So that you can sample the wares! There'll be more when you make the grade and start earning your keep." Jerry frowned as he peered at the triangular blue tablets and pocketed them. When he had demolished the burger, he stood up with Denim who was to walk him straight round to the lodgings off Tottenham Court Road.

"He's given you Purple Hearts, amphetamines yeah? The boss likes to keep new salesmen, er… motivated!"

11

New Girl

D enim bent back a loose, rusted graffiti covered corrugated metal sheet that was partly screwed to a wooden frame forming part of a contractor's hoarding to keep intruders out. Red printed notices warned off trespassers but had been partly obscured by a collage of faded fly posters carrying peace and anti-war symbols, ones depicting a raised fist, a middle finger, Woodstock, Hendrix. Stuck over these was a fresher poster advertising a film about an over-sized shark.

The house behind was decaying and Jerry noticed that the windows were boarded up on all floors. So much for lodgings, this was a squat. It was obviously due to be demolished but the building looked as though it might not be able to wait. A second corrugated sheet swung back to reveal the entrance door and as they entered the squat, he was surprised to see lights on inside. It was probably feeding off an unsuspecting neighbour's electricity supply. "Here, we'll find you a place to kip on the top floor." They climbed the rubbish-strewn stairs, stepping around a couple snogging on the staircase. A sweet smell hung in the air mingling with the stale odours of damp and drains. Music drummed out of one of the rooms.

As the staircase turned, a girl's shoes came into view descending the bare wood stairs. "Ah!" said Denim. "This is Scarlet. She'll show you to the top room, Shrimp. I've got some other things to attend to." The girl was good looking, about his age with white-blonde hair. There was something wild about her even though she was dressed for a night out. She glared at Denim and barely looked at Jerry, turning on her heels to climb back up to the top floor. "Follow me!" He followed her up the flights of stairs that creaked at every step, slanting at increasingly drunken angles, forcing them to use the handrails for support. She looked back at him, "Watch your step at the top, there are floorboards missing."

A single light bulb flickered on. The room was big and had three sash windows, badly cracked all around, all boarded from the outside. There was a fireplace, cornicing and dado rails. Once upon a time it had probably been an elegant house before being condemned. The floor pitched away from them and lathe and plaster hung down from the ceiling which sagged in places and was missing in others. He counted three mattresses in the room. One was occupied by a heaped figure, unmoving.

"Here, you take that one in the corner. The other's mine and make sure you keep your hands off my stuff." She looked at Jerry properly for the first time and seemed amused. "The name's Scarlet. Welcome to your new home. Don't tell me your name, best we don't use real names here. Did he call you Shrimp downstairs?"

"Yes."

"OK then, Shrimp it is for now. There's a working toilet on

the floor below but mind how you go in there, it's slippery and take some newspaper in there with you. I've got to go out now, so I might see you tomorrow."

Scarlet hesitated and turned back at the doorway. "Did they give you any drugs to try?"

Jerry nodded.

"Well, go carefully, Shrimp. You won't sleep well if you take them now."

Jerry just looked quizzical.

She smiled. "Looks to me as though you are new to all this."

Jerry felt dog-tired. He sat on the mattress shuffling back to lean on the wall, pulling the blanket around him. He was finally under a roof of sorts and compared to what he had been through since his move to London, this was a step up and he felt safe. To wash down the tablets, he pulled from the bottom of his rucksack the near empty bottle of whisky, tipping the bottle to drain the last of the liquor. Sleep overtook him. Nothing was going to get in the way of that. But he woke in the middle of the night to green stars shining through the holes in the roof and the distant sounds of waves breaking to the rhythm of drums played on a stage by a familiar blonde girl who looked across at him and smiled the most beautiful smile.

12

Lemon Juice

He quickly learnt about the different types of drugs out there, their street prices, how they messed with the mind, and the places where they were likely to pull the most buyers. The minders usually did a recce of the locations first to scare off anyone else trading on their patch and to check for any signs of police surveillance. Drug squad officers were known to raid clubs from time to time, dealing being a more serious offence than possession. Half a dozen jazz and R&B clubs around Soho were prime trading sites.

The Marquee Club on Wardour Street was a favourite spot for them as it attracted hundreds to the live music events. Jerry had his turn hanging about by the customer entrance next to the Art Deco stone arch, selling mainly purple hearts, weed and coke for top prices. He recognised that he and the other dealers in their network were small cogs in a big business machine and was curious to know who was higher up the food chain. Nobody wanted to talk about the boss and they were encouraged not to ask any questions, although he heard from snippets of conversation that the main supply route came into the West End from the Whitechapel area of east London. There was also a shadowy figure called The Chemist who manufactured some of the new hallucinogens from a secret location in that part of town.

His youth made him useful to the traders and helped to put him above suspicion. As a foot soldier he moved invisibly from buyer to buyer, paying house calls to the regulars and dealing outside the jazz clubs. It also gave him access to drugs for his own consumption. In the early days he would receive samples of the softer drugs, as much to keep him compliant as to educate him. A twisted wrapper on top of his small share of the proceeds to keep him hungry for more.

One night he returned late to the squat after a lucrative week-long shift with a pocket full of notes for his share of the cash that the Minder had divvied up for him. As he started the long climb to his room on the top floor, he noticed sitar music spilling out into the hallway from the open door of a ground-floor room. Inside he spotted the Sloth who was normally found crashed out in a heap on the mattress in his shared room but here he was sitting crossed-legged on the floor of what was once a kitchen with a man with a wispy moustache and beads looking as though he was still living in the flower power 1960s. Layers of moth-eaten rugs and tasselled cushions added to the ambience of a drug den. The pulsing orange glow of a lava lamp illuminated a couple embraced in the corner, half naked and smoking weed.

The Sloth was heating a spoon above a camping gas burner. Seeing Jerry standing at the doorway, he looked up at him. "Come and join us, room-mate! This is where the party's happening."

Jerry joined them around the table made from an upturned

milk crate. He watched as the Sloth melted the powder under the flame and mixed it with clear liquid. Seeing his interest, the Sloth explained in slurred tones, as though teaching a child to spell, "We sometimes add citric acid - lemon juice if you like - to help it dissolve the brown. It's now ready for shooting up."

The Sloth drew the liquid into one of the syringes that lay alongside on the table. He looked at Jerry quizzically. Jerry looked from the Sloth to the hippy and back again, noticing that their eyeballs were like pin pricks and they sounded stoned already. "Here, give me your arm, room-mate and let's share the moment." He tied a tourniquet around Jerry's slender outstretched arm, the gorged fresh veins pushing quickly to the surface.

The hippy looked down admiringly through his round wire spectacles and remarked, "Lucky boy, groovy veins. Mine are like pincushions so I have to slam into my groin." He touched his inner thigh for emphasis. The Sloth drew a generous dose of the liquid into the barrel of the syringe, held it needle upwards and cleared the pocket of air. "Here," he said again, handing Jerry the syringe. "Find a vein, push it slowly along its line and you'll feel … incredible."

Jerry paused only briefly, his curiosity overcoming relicense. His hand was shaking with anticipation and hesitantly on his third approach the needle point pierced the vein and his right thumb pressed down on the plunger. The hippy was nodding enthusiastically. As the heroin entered his bloodstream, it suddenly dawned on him that this might be a point of no return, but before he could grasp the enormity of this, his mental capacity swirled within seconds into bright colours as the opiate took control.

As he languished on the rugs, the ceiling making unworldly shapes as it melded in the glow of the lamp, someone held him down firmly and he felt a second needle drive into his arm again. He heard laughing - they were laughing at him. Crawling out of the room, he tried to climb the stairs but tumbled down from the fourth step. He hugged the bannister post like a ship's mast in a storm, clenching his teeth and squeezing his eyes tight shut. Coloured lights became shards of glass and dark beasts filled his head. A face from his past loomed over him, someone was screaming - it might have been him - and then he blacked out.

A cool flannel lay over Jerry's brow and a soft hand was tenderly stroking his cheek. His eyes felt swollen and he tried to open them. Through blackened, bloodshot eyes he saw a pretty girl with tears in her eyes, looking down at him. "I thought you were a goner, Shrimp," whispered Scarlet, as much to herself as to the patient she had been nursing. "Here, drink this."

Jerry propped himself up on an elbow, took a few sips of water and dropped back, feeling bruised and battered. He was on the top floor again on his mattress in clothes that were not his and had no idea how he got there. He and Scarlet were alone together in the windowless room.

With Scarlet's help, he pieced together what had happened and was alarmed at how little he remembered. Scarlet had returned from work and thought it odd that there was no sign of him. It wasn't until the following morning that she found him, curled up in a cupboard at the foot of the stairs. He had been brutally beaten, probably drugged and was unconscious, lying in his own filth. She had carried and dragged him upstairs with the help of a housemate. She had cleaned him up and changed his soiled clothes.

"Thanks," he said, realising straight away how inadequate that was given what she had done for him. She had probably saved his life. "You're …," Jerry struggled to find a different word, but realised there wasn't another that fitted better. "An angel!"

She sat a little closer to him on the bed where he lay recovering, smiled kindly and stroked his forehead. Jerry remembered something from long ago, how his mother had done that same thing when he was upset, but he kept it to himself.

"Why did you do that for me?", he asked Scarlet. "I mean, you could have just left me."

She moved her hand over his and traced from the top of each finger across the back of his hand to his wrist and back to the next fingertip, skimming over the digits thoughtfully. "I know what it's like to be pushed around," she said. "There was some bad stuff at home that made me leave. I can see it all happening again, with the clubs I work at now. I'm scared that I am getting under pressure to do things that I don't want to do. Waitressing and dancing on stage is one thing but there are other things that go on and I don't want any part of that", she said, biting her bottom lip. "This is no place for either of us, Shrimp."

Jerry said, "The other people in this place are animals, but you. You deserve better!"

"Well, I'd better get on." Scarlet got up to leave and smiled back at him. "Oh, and I don't know how you got that name. I should know, I had to dress you!"

Jerry quickly established that his money had been stolen while he was out of his head. His mind was working again. Through his crashing headache and stomach cramps, Jerry lifted his arms and rubbed the raised and blotchy areas where the needles had punctured the skin. He felt foolish and acutely self-conscious that this girl had seen his scarred body. He had his suspicions and after Scarlet had gone downstairs he searched under the Sloth's empty mattress and feeling a lump put his hand through a tear in the fabric and pulled out his silver lighter, a switchblade and a stash of drugs.

Sloth returned later, staggering drunkenly into the dark room. Jerry was waiting for him, having first removed the light bulb. The switch was flicked up and down. "Bloody light!"

He caught the Sloth off guard, wrestling him to the floor and sat on him holding the switchblade pressed against his neck. "Open wide!" Jerry said and in the dim light in the corridor he reached for the cup. Forcing the Sloth's mouth open, Jerry poured in the gritty solution prepared from all the powders, resins and ground up tablets he had found. He held the Sloth's nose until he was sure he had swallowed the last remainder. He had seen someone do this with their poodle and the technique was just the same. "Happy dreams!"

The lethal concoction took effect within seconds. The Sloth gagged then passed out and his breathing became shallower and noiseless until it stopped. Jerry checked the pockets of the body for money and took what he found. In the dimly lit room, he quickly packed his things in his rucksack. Turning, he spotted Scarlet in the doorway, her hand over her mouth taking in the scene. Had she seen it all? He brushed past her and in his exhilaration boldly pressed a kiss to her cheek, smiling back at her before crashing down the stairs and out of the squat. He had had it with the drug scene and vowed to stay more alert and in control of himself if he was to survive to see another birthday. The fresh air outside the squat was invigorating and as he pushed back the rusted corrugated sheet to step into the street beyond, a hand fell on his shoulder.

"Don't you fucking leave without me!" A kiss landed full on his lips. She entwined her fingers in his free hand and together they fled into the night.

13

Bubbling Brook

I n a market town just an hour on the train from London, but it could have been another world from the one that Jerry had come to know, three old school friends met in town to celebrate finishing their A-level exams. This would be their last few weeks together before Robbie went off to university if he made the grades, and nobody doubted that he would, while Andy and Pete both had job interviews coming up.

They walked back together from one of the town pubs where the landlord was relaxed about serving the under-aged. Only one of them had turned eighteen but they had all been drinking in that pub for the past year, adding packets of salt and vinegar crisps or salted peanuts to their drink orders, which for some reason made buying alcohol acceptable to the unshaven bartender pulling the pints. The snacks certainly made them thirstier for more.

They had spent most of the evening either feeding the one-arm bandit, pulling its lever in the hope of lining up a winning row of cherries, or absorbed on a new arcade game of on-screen ping pong that the landlord had recently installed next to his pride and joy, the unreliable Wurlitzer jukebox that played his worn forty-five rpm vinyl records but often switched off mid-track. They took it in turns at ping pong, hitting the buttons below the screen to move the block that represented their bat left and right, each flickering square block was a ball that destroyed an advancing wall of white bricks as it bounced off it. The pints of beer they raced through did not help their score lines.

Their weaving route home took them past the town park, along dimly lit residential streets and through a shortcut known locally as muddy lane and familiar to them as the route that compulsory cross country runs would take in their early years at school, with splattered legs, red knees and chests rasping for breath in the sub-zero mid-winter afternoons. Now, so many years later under the light of a full moon, they lined up along the hedgerow.

Andy said, "Whatever do you think happened to Jerry?"

"No idea, I haven't really thought about him for years", Robbie replied.

"Oh, I have, now and again," said Pete. "It was just so strange how he disappeared. And setting fire to his old foster parents house as he did, what a nutter! Amazingly no one was hurt. It's all been rebuilt like you'd never know it happened and looks a lot smarter. I bet the new people have no idea about the strange family who lived there."

"I think he was alright," said Andy. "He was just born unlucky."

"Yeah, I know what you mean," said Pete. "Remember those parents' evenings? My mum used to dread them, particularly the chemistry master. 'How can a boy get one out of forty -

in multiple choice!' He never had anything good to say." Pete aimed higher to clatter into the clump of nettles.

Robbie reminisced, "Well my dad used to leave little notes he had written in my school desk, little jokes and riddles he must have brought with him. I would find them the next morning and it would make me chuckle."

"I always found a Kit Kat in mine," added Andy. "Jerry never had anything like that. His foster parents never even turned up."

They had relieved themselves of their bursting bladders and even before the final shakes an impressive stream of collective pee was snaking back down the path. It was something they would do whenever beer and a walk home was involved, much to the disgust or amusement of any girlfriends who tagged along. It was one of those unspoken moments of bonding between the lads, with eyes fixed straight ahead.

Where their futures would end up was out of their hands. Apart from Robbie. He was determined to make pots of money and live in a castle. This was something he regretted letting slip in their last economics class in their final school term. He had been mercilessly ribbed about it by the others ever since. But for sure, it was highly unlikely that the three friends would stay in touch.

14

The Fairer Sex

J erry had very little experience of women and his chaotic
and selfish behaviour to those in the world around him
made it difficult to form close relationships. He had
felt this acutely in his teenage years and the schools and
institutions that his various guardians and foster parents
had placed him in had on the whole been cruel experiments
that never had a happy ending and each had left its mark.
Somehow, people always found out about his unsettled
upbringing or spotted his mysterious scars that marked him
out in the school changing rooms or on the sports field. And to
young humans thrown together to sink or swim among their
peers, a child who is different in any way becomes easy picking
for bullying. As a stigmatised boy, romantic opportunities
did not naturally present themselves. His clumsy attempts
at closeness in his past had invariably led to humiliation and
after a misadventure with a simple pimpled girl called Teresa
who had completely misread his signals, and he hers, he had
vowed to stay well away from them.

The disfigured skin that ran from his neck to his torso made him acutely self-conscious whenever curious eyes settled on the roughhewn purpled flesh. He was reluctant to wear clothes that revealed below his neckline and wore turned up collars or scarfs in unseasonably warm weather. He wished he would one day find the one responsible for causing the pain in those tender childhood years, pain that still made him recoil when recalling it. The one who left those indelible visible marks and the much deeper ones that hid in the inky depths of his troubled soul.

There had been people that he had started to trust but he had a deep-rooted mistrust from his childhood over those who tried to get close to him or win favour. His suspicious outlook of the world had come about from an abuse of trust from those who should have known better. Scarlet was an exception and she was quite different to anyone he had ever known before. She could give as much as she could get and he was respectful of her propensity to lash out at those who might wrong her. In some ways, their moons were aligned.

Separately they were maladjusted kids burdened by their own difficult upbringings who would always find it difficult to fit into convention. As a pair their chemistry made them downright dangerous, with attitudes and characters that could be sullen or animated, mischievous or vengeful. They were both very bright but lacked the safety net of checks and balances that stop most people from going too far, from turning thoughts into deeds, malice into malign.

15

Lava Lamp

There was something wild and dangerous about Scarlet that he found beguiling. Perhaps Jerry saw some of himself in her. They were both ready to move on, him from the drug scene and her from the hospitality trade at a nightclub where she was being groomed for extra services. They needed a new start and when a friend had introduced them to a group of pickpockets earning their keep like characters from Dickens, they grasped the opportunity. Jerry saw this as a more legitimate trade and it was unquestionably safer for Scarlet.

They worked as a pair in distraction teams of scruffy youths, skilfully parting ladies from their purses, men from their watches. They worked together and looked out for each other, although Scarlet found it funny that he thought he could protect her. It was normally the other way around. They were wily and always kept an eye on escape routes. When they strayed into other gang's territory for the richer pickings along Oxford Street, this often led to confrontation and a couple of times when he or Scarlet were cornered, Sloth's switch-blade got them out of trouble before they lost themselves again in the crowds.

Danger and close shaves added a thrill to their daily lives and ignited something indefinable between them. A bond was forming and it was something special to them alone. But so far Jerry had never let her get close to him as the prospect of rejection terrified him but even more than that, and unbeknown to her, he didn't want to risk losing her. Little did he know that she harboured similar feelings for him but she understood that he was damaged goods and kept her own feelings as hidden as she could and bided her time. The trouble was that the longer he took to come round to her, the more she felt for him. Sometimes it seemed like agony. At night, alone in her bed, she craved to be satisfied. Pulling the blankets up over her she closed her eyes imagining how it could be, bit her bottom lip and rocked herself to sleep. She would wait until the time was right. Then came their holiday as they later called it.

For seven days they had use of a small flat above a disused furniture workshop in insalubrious Hoxton Square in Shoreditch where burglaries and car crime were commonplace. Scarlet had been asked to look after the flat for her friend Julie who had previously worked alongside Scarlet as a hostess in the same Soho night club. She had got out of the scene some while ago and was now an art student.

Scarlet turned the door key and looked back at Jerry. "Maybe you should be carrying me over the threshold?"

He pulled a face. "Don't look so weird" she laughed, "I was only joking!"

Jerry followed her up the stairs as she climbed up to the little homely flat. He was reminded of the first time he had met her on the stairs of the squat. The flat was freshly decorated with bright colours, artful posters everywhere and on the spotlessly clean checked tablecloth was a welcome note, a 1973 royal wedding tea caddy, a tin of biscuits and two mugs. One mug was a Hornsea blue and brown design of two owls and the other read 'Love Is … Treating Him Like A King'. "That's my one!" Jerry smirked.

"Well, the kettle's over there!" she retorted. "Wow!" she exclaimed, looking around her. "This is all quite grown-up."

They quickly slipped into domesticity. They did normal things like drinking tea, eating beans on toast and watching television on the settee that became Jerry's bed on that first night. On the second day they explored the area, had a fry-up lunch in a greasy spoon café and came back home with enough food and drink to last them for a couple of days. That evening, Jerry sprawled across the sofa absorbed in a book he had found on the shelves, while Scarlet soaked in her bath. He was still turning the pages when she called him from her bedroom across the hall. "Jay!" There was something soft and inviting in the way she spoke his name. He hesitated at the threshold.

A lava lamp on the bedside table glowed softly, the bulbous shapes rising and falling in the warmed liquid, throwing strange shapes and shadows. It took some moments for his eyes to get accustomed. In the gloom he could now make her out, standing by the side of the bed in a borrowed nightshirt. She crossed her arms in front of her and she pulled the hem up and over her head, tossing the garment to the floor. The pale shape of her body stood naked in front of him, the lamp casting a soft glow. He noticed the bed sheets with a corner turned down. Her clothes were folded in a neat pile on the dresser. She didn't speak and slowly approached him, her breasts drawing his gaze. She tugged the book from him, his finger was trapped still marking the page, and set it down. His heart was pounding. Jerry the victim, the delinquent, the criminal, the drug dealer, the killer. He had been scared so many times in his young life but this was the most terrifying so far.

He could feel the heat from her body, intensely close but not quite touching. She placed a hand on his cheek. Her fingers traced the waxy scars that branded him from a time in his life that made him shiver when it all came back to him. The burns below his neckline were more recent. As she slowly unbuttoned and eased off his shirt, it fell silently to the floor. He at once felt exposed and vulnerable, pulling away from her involuntarily. He had no idea how he would react to closeness or she to his scars. But Scarlet was not repelled. She did not pull away. As he stood there, rigid and square and watching her every move intently, she gazed up at him and smiled reassuringly, "Sweet Jay", and held out both hands to pull him closer.

Standing on the tips of her toes she stretched to her full height and kissed the scars on the side of his neck, and playfully nibbled the lobe of his ear. His arm was now around her back, his hand moving slowly downwards, gently bumping over the curve of her spine to settle in the small of her back. He felt his own heart drumming and she was feeling the same. Her soft full lips found his and that first proper kiss, experienced, seemingly endless and deeper than the ocean floor, was a special moment and would always stay with him.

As their breathing raced, their busy lips eventually parted, still threaded with silky saliva. With fingertips playing over the rough and smooth textures of his skin she planted warm moist kisses down his chest to his navel. She felt his excitement through his jeans and she slid her hand discerningly over the taut denim. Looking back up at him mischievously, she unbuckled his belt pulling it out of its loops, "That's for later," she teased, and guided him firmly towards the bed. At first she took charge, holding her cascading locks out of her eyes with her free hand while he tossed back his head and writhed at the delight she was bringing him. Then Scarlet relinquished all control to the boy who was becoming a man, this man she deeply desired.

* * *

As the months rolled on, the new team were making good money but they had to pool their takings. The ringleader would take his cut, the watcher had to be paid, then came the deduction for board and lodgings before they were handed their share. Sharing was not in Jerry's nature and went across the grain. For now, the living arrangements in the shared house were a lot safer than the squat they had run away from. The ringleader kept the house in some sort of order. The story was that he was looking after it for a friend who was doing time in prison.

When the two of them had enjoyed a break in Scarlet's friends flat in Hoxton Square, they had talked about going it alone as a pair one day. But to do that, they first needed to have enough money behind them to afford accommodation and food to survive, so they would bide their time. The shared house was not so bad after all and they had moved into a room of their own with two single beds that they pushed together and a door that they could lock. After an awkward start that sometimes had them in stitches, it wasn't long before their lovemaking became more natural and tender. She was not repelled by his scars and burn marks, saying it gave him character. Out of all the misery and grotesque circumstances they had shared, they were falling in love.

One lazy Sunday morning, Scarlet went out for milk, bread and whisky and returned to find Jerry crucifying bacon in a smoke-filled kitchen. It was as close to settled that either of them had felt and that day they never left their bedroom, eating, sleeping and sharing cigarettes in between.

16

Torchlight

The Dominion looked down on Tottenham Court Road. In its time the dominating landmark had hosted celebrities at their premieres spanning the years from Charlie Chaplin to Elizabeth Taylor. It was closed in the 1940's blitz and later became a musical theatre venue. Nearby the pickpockets now worked the crowds. Jerry had missed breakfast and had slipped away briefly to get a polystyrene cup of tea and a wagon wheel biscuit which he now savoured looking over the railing above the steps to the underground station where Scarlet and a couple of others were at work. He listened to the accordion played by the busker who was the group's watcher, the lookout, who in turn shared from their pickings. The accordion was an ornate white and blue Settimio that packed a punch and could be heard above the city noises, the buses and sirens. On his shoulder was clipped a fabric parrot to raise a smile and a few more coins. The watcher's job was to play his tunes and switch to *Auld Lang Syne* if trouble was spotted.

The Busker was grinding out *Tulips from Amsterdam* which

was in his usual repertoire but something that morning didn't feel right. Jerry could feel the hairs prickle on the back of his neck. He tensely clung on to the top of the rail, his sharp eyes scanning the throng of people as they battled in opposing waves up and down the underpass. He saw the Busker throw a look to someone out of his line of sight and nod a couple of times in Scarlet's direction. The music still hadn't changed. Something had gone seriously awry. He headed back down the steps, dropping the cup as he went, tea splashing as it landed. He was aware of his stomach churning and he tried to make a beeline for Scarlet but was blocked by having to shuffle behind a knot of tourists.

He felt his heart beating in double time. In what seemed like an instant two burly plain clothes cops muscled past him and he was almost pushed down the steps. Scarlet realised too late. She spotted Jerry in the crowd and shot him a look, mouthing and signing "Go, Go!" Jerry gripped the Sloth's switchblade inside his pocket but fought the urge to wade in. There was nothing he could do alone. He compliantly melted into the crowd and could only watch in horror from afar as they caught her red-handed, pushed her up against the wall with arms gripped behind her while one searched and the other cuffed. Two wallets and the contents of someone else's purse. Scarlet was dragged away, against the tide of commuters, hands cuffed behind her, to a police van that had rolled up. The Busker had turned snitch. The other gang members had already slunk away and Scarlet was going to take the rap for them all.

Jerry loitered a little way along the street outside a tobacconist and stewed, breeding dark thoughts and inhaling deeply as the accordion played a cheerful sea shanty that drifted across the street from the underpass where Scarlet had been arrested. Jerry took up a surveillance position in a café that the Busker invariably used as a pit-stop before afternoon rush-hour from where he and his parrot would return to reclaim their territory to inflict more noise on the citizens of London. Jerry recalled the long wait in the pouring rain all those years ago in what seemed like another life when he was stalking Penrose. He was thankful that he was in the dry this time but he had a long afternoon of milky tea and stale cake ahead of him. He would be careful not to be spotted and had a newspaper with concise and cryptic crosswords to occupy himself or if need be to hide behind. The newspaper came into use when the Busker came in briefly to buy a sandwich and the toilet.

After a while the afternoon commuter rush hour eased and the echoing music stopped altogether. The Busker had packed up for the day, and looking like a creature from the underworld, emerged from the underpass blinking as he ascended the steps into the late afternoon sunlight. Jerry followed twenty paces behind as the Busker headed to his usual haunts. Jerry knew his routine. He had made it his business to find out about all his associates in the gang and other people like the watchers and the bent pawn brokers whom they had relied upon.

The Busker walked a familiar route from Tottenham Court Road, turning into Denmark Street, lugging the heavy accordion case over his shoulder. He would pass the music shops and studios of tin pan alley where he would nod at familiar faces. The area of St Giles was known for its music scene as well as the less salubrious sex industry a few hundred yards away where red and blue neon signs illuminated the streets off

Soho Square attracting lonely men like moths to a streetlamp.

The music scene around Denmark Street was buzzing and drew young musicians at the cutting edge of popular music. Jerry trailed him as he walked past Regent Sounds, studios where Jimmy Hendrix, Rolling Stones and the Beatles before them had used the rooms above the basement club for practice sessions. The Busker continued on and true to form climbed the six worn steps into the churchyard, glancing up at the clock on the elaborate bell tower. There he crouched down in the late rays of sun behind the stone tomb carved with ornate scrolls, its inscriptions to an illustrious person of valour but long defaced. He shot furtive glances and clicked open the accordion case, carefully laying the instrument on one side, and fished out the coins that had been tossed into the depths and folds of the soft velvet liner of his instrument case.

He counted out his takings, lips moving silently, filling his right pocket with silver and his left with coppers. On a good day he would make sixty pounds but Tottenham Court Road was never as good as the busier tourist pitches around Oxford Street and Bond Street where there was a pecking order to secure the territory. He earned a welcome top-up from the current group of pickpockets as their lookout man. But today was not their lucky day and he had been well rewarded for his snitching by the copper. The dippers would never find out, so for him it was a win-win. He smiled to himself as he enjoyed the irony of payday from the cops and also from the robbers.

With pockets loaded with change, the Busker set off. Jerry watched him through the iron railings. Which pub was it to be today? The figure took a right out of the churchyard towards The Angel to sink a pint or two. How fitting, mused Jerry, watching the Busker push open the door to the wood-panelled bar. Frequented by musicians, bellringers from St Giles in the Fields and students, it was also the site of a tavern in the sixteenth century when it notoriously catered for condemned men on their way to execution.

As the evening fell, the Busker made his way back by underground up the Northern Line, five stops to Camden Town, following the route home to the cosy but decaying narrow boat that lay alongside the towpath under the crane of a disused warehouse that would have loaded and unloaded the barges of salt and coal and spices in a different age. He heaved himself and the accordion on board and opened the hatch, descending the two companionway steps to the dark saloon. He was looking forward to his tea of sausages and mash with mustard and ketchup.

His free hand felt for the torch that he always left lodged next to the steps but found nothing. Straightening, he was startled by a dark shape in the corner of his eye and, turning, heard a sickening crack as something heavy hit him full square in his face. Stunned, he tumbled, grabbing the edge of the saloon table to stop his fall as pain seared across his busted nose, warm liquid spewing from a dent in his forehead. The heavy torch was lifted a second time and the blow split his left ear with brutal force. Still the assailant didn't speak but now turned on the torch and shone it into his squinting bloodied eyes. He heard his own voice cry out, as though it came from someone else.

"Stop, stop!" shielding his eyes from the cruel light. "I have money."

"Correction. You had money, but I found the tin. You also had a life but today you chose to be a traitor." Jerry felt himself welling up with anger. "So for you, it's all over. The only blessing is that we'll never have to suffer that awful music again!"

Jerry shone the torch under his own chin and the angle of the beam gave his face a devilish look. He watched with some glee as recognition dawned in the pleading face looking up at him. "This one is from my girl."

With that, he brought the torch down again with a force and finality that startled even him. This creature had taken Scarlet away and had to pay the consequences. Stepping over the crumpled bloodied heap, Jerry turned the gas ring on and as he left, he flipped open his silver lighter to catch the bottom of a curtain before closing the hatch behind him. He was climbing the flight of steps back up to the road bridge when there was a muffled explosion causing ducks to fly in fright before they noisily settled back on the water, black and golden ripples illuminated by the burning craft.

* * *

Scarlet's case came up at Marylebone Magistrates Court. She was asked to stand and had to be hauled to her feet by an officer. The arresting officer read out snippets from his notebook. Her full name was read out and she winced at hearing her middle name that she preferred to forget. The accused was of no fixed abode, one previous conviction for shoplifting and a suspended sentence for a second, common assault, which she had vehemently denied. There was nothing common about it, she had maintained, "It was perfectly executed and taught the thieving bastard a lesson." From a troubled upbringing she had got in with the wrong crowd but had made no attempt to improve herself. Her defence was weakly argued with no extenuating circumstances.

For Scarlet it all happened in a blur. She was cross with herself, with being set up. Her moody demeanour, mumbled curses and shouted expletives at the district judge only compounded her misery. Her solicitor had indicated that she might be let off with a suspended sentence or worst-case scenario serve a month or two in an open prison. She did herself no favours and swore again at the judge before spitting at the policeman beside her, a gob of saliva landing on his cheek.

The judge had not had much sleep the previous night from the disturbance of a neighbour's party going on until the early hours. He frostily handed out a custodial sentence of nine months for multiple offences, eligible for review after six. There was an intake of breath in the sparsely attended courtroom. It was a harsh sentence, tainted by the defendant's behaviour in court.

"Prison will teach this delinquent young woman some manners," he murmured to himself. Those observing closely might have spotted the briefest of smiles that momentarily softened the judge's typically severe expression as judgment was passed.

A few days into her sentence, Scarlet learnt from other women that she was lucky not to be sharing a cell. Some of the others had started in a single cell, only to be joined by another occupant. The prison was heaving under the strain of overcrowding, issues with sanitation and a refurbishment project that sealed off sections of the buildings that would normally be in use.

Thank god for small mercies, she thought.

That same evening, as she returned from tea via the wash

blocks shortly before 6pm lockdown, her heart sank to find a bed frame had been moved in next to hers, leaving the narrowest space between them for the small cupboard and the toilet pan. Through the cell door appeared a terrified greasy-haired girl of similar age carrying a blanket, pillow, an enamel mug and a soft bag with her few regulation possessions and toiletries, accompanied by the wing officer.

"A room mate for you! You might find she's not very chatty, I didn't get a word out of her."

"Hello, you can call me Scarlet."

The girl smiled meekly and quickly dipped her eyes down shyly. Her forearms were scratched and bleeding from nervous scratching and she tugged her sleeves down to hide them.

"Well, I guess you'll want to settle in," said Scarlet.

She was studying Scarlet's face intensely closely which was unnerving.

Scarlet carried on talking, "Look, there's not enough room to swing a cat in here." The girl looked alarmed. "Tell you what, let's talk tomorrow. I'll get ready for bed first and get out of your way, then you can take all the time you want. They lock up in twenty minutes." The girl nodded back.

The sounds of night-time were a constant reminder to the inmates of their incarceration. Another layer of sound had been added to wreck a second night's sleep. A strange noiseless sobbing emitted from the girl next to her.

The next morning, Scarlet woke to an empty bed next to her, only to find that the girl had pulled the pillow and blanket under the bed frame where she had finally fallen asleep. Over a bland breakfast served in metal trays, a tetchy Scarlet finally let rip at the mousey girl. Scarlet's own heightened emotions at being confined and a mounting sleep debt finally got the better of her.

"Look for god's sake, say something, anything!" The girl looked terrified and still nothing, fleeing back to her safe space on the floor above. Scarlet fumed, as she finished both trays, imagining endless nights and days stretching ahead with his odd girl. Maybe she's on drugs or perhaps she's deranged, poor thing, thought Scarlet. And then the penny dropped.

Years ago, Scarlet had a friend at primary school who was deaf and dumb. At such a young age the brain is receptive to new things and she picked up a vocabulary of gestures by learning to sign with her. They spent time in secret conversations that were a mystery to the other children. She looked out for little Lucy and took exception to any spiteful teasing on her friend's behalf. She had never lost the skills entirely and enjoyed watching and eavesdropping on animated friends on the bus or the tube conversing fluidly in sign language using gesture, lip-reading and facial expressions.

Scarlet saved some toast, placed the two trays in the rack for washing, and returned to the single cell that had been converted to a diminutive flat double, coaxing the girl out from under the bed and sitting her down in front of her. As she tested her theory with slow clunky signing and took great care to form the words properly as she spoke them, she saw the girl transform from withdrawn to a thoughtful feeling person called Holly, spelled out alphabetically. In time, and they had a lot of it ahead, the two of them might be OK as room mates.

What worried her was how Holly would survive in such a place.

* * *

Jerry sank to a low point when Scarlet had been jailed. HMP Holloway had a reputation beyond its walls for self-harming and suicides. He wrote to her in that first week with a Post Office Box number for her reply. He retrieved her letter from a local post office, written in blunted pencil on cheap prison stationery. She warned him off visiting her for fear of entrapment. She said that he could be put under suspicion if he was seen to associate with her. He saw the sense in what she said but hated the situation. She kept to herself the real reason she had warned him off. She didn't want him to see her in that place and wanted him to imagine her, the two of them, in better times. He would write to her once a week and in his next and every letter he sent, he promised that he would be waiting for her on the day of her release.

Without Scarlet, Jerry felt lost and purposeless and started drinking heavily and with the drinking he became clumsy, often returning to the shared house with an unexplained bloodied face or turning up at odd hours after being away for a couple of days. He looked and began to smell unkempt and would stay in his room for days, not eating, just festering. His weight loss was noticeable and in the street people would point him out and take a wide berth around him. Attention was the last thing the pickpockets wanted and at first sympathetic to his loss of Scarlet, they started to turn on him. Before long they had no choice but to throw him out, fearing that he would make mistakes and they would be shopped as well. It was a life back on the streets again, although if he could hold himself together then he now had a new set of skills that might make survival easier than before.

17

The Mission Bell

Since Scarlet had gone, he had sunk very low indeed. One bright morning, a chance encounter caused him to pause and see himself as others do.

He had used the unsavoury park toilets for minimal daily ablutions and took a seat in the sunshine on a bench which was already occupied by a middle-aged lady engrossed in a book. He leant on his rucksack to try to grab some sleep in relative safety. The previous night had been a restless one and he had spent much of it roaming the streets. She smelled him first and let out an involuntary snort of disdain expecting to see an elderly tramp. She looked him up and down, inspecting him more closely. That sad figure dressed like a vagrant was little more than seventeen, a similar age to her own son. A distinctive purple mark ran up one side of his neck.

"Young man," she addressed him, "I don't know how you came to be in this state but it looks to me as though you have hit rock bottom. Don't give up, you can bounce back again!" she said brightly.

Jerry wanted to get up and move away from her but he felt

too weary from the long night. He stayed put and eyed her suspiciously as she spoke.

"Please believe when I tell you that there is a better life out there for you. You just have to grasp it." She pointed across the park. "There is a mission hall over there behind the church. Can you see it through the trees?"

Jerry nodded.

"If you will allow me, I will take you there now. It is run by a friend of mine. Madeleine will get you spruced up and find you some donated clothes to help you back on your feet. She will be able to find you a safe place to sleep for a couple of nights in the hostel."

She looked at him thoughtfully and dipped into her handbag. "Here, take this. It is an emergency fund but for food only, you understand?"

Jerry nodded again and took the folded ten-pound note. He looked at her quizzically, expecting to find that this was a trap of some sort. But there was something disarmingly caring about the woman, almost maternal. She seemed to see past his vagrant outer shell, his physical and emotional scars. Her eyes seemed to penetrate deeply into his soul, intuitively knowing some of what he had gone through and conveying a warmth. He felt something that he had rarely experienced out on the streets. A quiet calm.

An image of Scarlet, incarcerated in a tiny cell, had popped into his head. He turned his head away from the woman and sniffed, wiping a solitary tear away with the back of his hand. He had to turn a corner and hold things together for Scarlet. He had let her down by letting himself wallow in grief but now he had to start believing in their future.

Jerry was not used to charity and had never begged, but he

muttered an awkward thanks. He did as she asked and had a welcome hot shower and a shave. He was given a haircut and he picked fresh clothes from a donations rack. Jerry felt like a new person, respectably suited with city shoes to match. He studied his reflection for what seemed a long while, first full faced, then turning slowly to quarter profile one side, then the other. He raised his chin. His double looked down at him under half-closed eyelids, arrogantly and pompously he thought. The face in the mirror had the air of the busy people he saw every day who would walk past the down and outs at double speed.

He transferred a few things he wanted to save into a messenger bag that he found in the charity boxes. Picking up his old rucksack, Jerry walked out of the mission in his donated shiny black Oxfords, heels clicking down the stone steps. He headed for the river.

There on the bridge he gazed through the gaps in the balustrades, the brown-green waters of the Thames racing over the stone footings of the arches far below. He considered how quickly even a fit adult would drown, pulled under by the currents, bones smashing like matchsticks as they collided with the granite blocks awash at the surface. Heaving himself up to get a foothold and to the alarm of passing pedestrians, he clambered up to the coping stones that made a giant-sized handrail and walked along to the centre of the bridge where the water would be at its deepest.

Passers-by were crossing the bridge and pointing with timid, stand-back concern on their faces but none were prepared to approach this obviously deranged young man. Jerry had his audience and adopted a bird pose on the edge of the bridge wall, knees bent, crouching forwards. He pulled his arms behind him as though preparing to launch himself over the side, to fly.

A woman gasped, "Oh my god, he's going to jump!" But no one approached him.

He stood up tall on the precarious ledge in the sunshine, feeling the breeze in his clean hair, feeling the breeze in his clean hair, feet spread nonchalantly. He pointed one outstretched arm skywards and with the other hurled his arms like a fielder over the heads of some worried onlookers.

Jumping down he crossed the bridge to peer into the water on the other side. He watched as his old rucksack, his discarded clothes and bedding bobbed up once, before disappearing under the silty surface, joining the detritus making its watery way downriver on the ebbing tide.

"Out with the old, in with the new," he said to himself, smiling for the first time since Scarlet was taken.

18

Two Promises

J erry's refreshed appearance belied his itinerant existence. He missed Scarlet and every day and every night hurt with the loss. Their friendship had blossomed into something special, something he had never experienced before.

Scarlet looked forward to her weekly letters from Jerry. She sat back on her bunk in the sparse cell. Jerry talked about very ordinary things and there was nothing there that gave anything away to the casual reader. He implored her as he always did to keep her cool, to stay out of trouble and not do anything that might add to her sentence. He'd said again that he would be waiting at the gates for her on the day of her release. His promise kept her sane. The crafted letters made her sad in one line and happy in the next and completely adored as he signed it off with his initial. She imagined his voice reading the letter to her and it made her feel wanted and safe, right up to the moment that she folded it away.

Then a scream, a banging of doors, running footsteps or walkie talkies would bring her back to harsh reality and set her nerves affray. She slid his latest letter into the pages of the tattered paperback along with the others, snapping the thick rubber band over them that had fallen from the mail trolley one day. In lonely moments, of which there were many, she would re-read the letters repeatedly until she knew them by heart.

* * *

In the meantime, while Scarlet was serving her time in jail, Jerry would work crowds of tourists and commuters when he needed money. He could fund himself without too much effort by a life of petty crime, exchanging stolen watches and bracelets for cash through a couple of pawn brokers who had shops near Hatton Garden. Without other gang members to feed, he would simply eat what he killed, sharing with nobody. He took a small dingy bed-sit where no questions were asked. It had a terrifying gas heater that failed to ignite until the third attempt when it popped, shooting a flame that singed the hairs on his hand. He didn't use it again. The shower room along the landing dribbled out intermittently freezing or scorching water.

It was too miserable to do more than sleep there and he often found himself in a library, drifting through museums and art galleries and drinking tea, so much tea, while waiting for the pubs to open. There he might find a quiet corner by himself and nurse a pint or two to while away the time, practise blowing smoke rings and crunch through packets of cheese and onion crisps while composing a letter to Scarlet who was never out of his mind. When the landlord rang the bell for last orders, he would end his lonely evening buying a whisky for the road until the familiar words rang out "Time, gentlemen please!" and he would walk back via one of the takeaways on his route home.

He had his routines and found them strangely reassuring, a tonic to the adrenalin rush he got from a nifty steal or a close shave. He stayed off drugs as he had to be so careful for Scarlet's sake and could not risk messing up and being caught. Occasionally he did experiment but in a more cultural way, by going to hear new bands if they were playing locally or picking up a book that captured his imagination. Sometimes he went to see a new modern art exhibition, or to listen to the nutcases expounding their views on their soap boxes at Speakers Corner. His latest novel experience was having a Chinese takeaway meal for the first time. When he opened the bags and pots of sauces on the little table in front of the armchair, the smell was incredible. The food tasted so good to him that he was aching to tell her about the noodles, the cracker things, the sweet and sour, but it seemed too cruel when the food she had to eat in the clink was by her accounts pigswill.

On one such day, Jerry was sitting in a public library, partly to keep warm, partly to keep an eye out for easy pickings from carelessly placed bags and coats, but mainly to satisfy his restless inquisitive mind. The newspapers were upstairs illuminated by the big windows and spread out on the large table with seating all around. He scowled across at the elderly people sitting opposite for whom the library seemed to be the centre of their universe. Sadly, it had also become the centre of his. Reading one of the broadsheets at his usual speed, it seemed to be a slow news day. As his eyes flashed down the columns, he absorbed what was of interest and discarded the rest.

He stretched as the warm sunshine beamed in, dust flying and swirling, and yawned elaborately and noisily. The tutting and shushing that emitted from his fellow readers provoked an insolent, "Piss off, you old crone. Yes, I'm talking to you!"

The man next to him rose from his seat in disgust, grabbed his coat from the back of the chair and proclaimed, "Come on Mavis, we're going. I'm not going to put up with this foul-mouthed behaviour!"

"Yes, good riddance," added Jerry triumphantly.

Flustered, the elderly couple left, unaware of the theft that had taken place from under their noses. The man's wallet had been skilfully emptied and then replaced inside his gaping coat pocket.

Smirking with satisfaction, Jerry picked up the paper they had abandoned, scanning through the familiar stories. Latest on the miners' strike, more mainland bombings and a photo of the Swedish contenders for the Eurovision song contest tipped for success. Looking at the striking blonde girl, Jerry mused that they were in with a good chance. He yawned again and turned to page eight. His jaw dropped. Staring out at him from the pages normally reserved for society news and royal reports was the beast from his childhood.

There was no mistake. Those cold deep-set eyes peered mole-like from behind the same wired framed glasses. It made him shiver and a wave of nausea broke as he recollected. He must have been five or perhaps six years of age and living in a children's home when this new guardian arrived and took him away as his ward to a cold rectory in the countryside, run by a timid housekeeper. When she had left for the evening, he would be picked up by the armpits and thrown into a bare windowless room, empty but for a mop and tin bucket, a wooden chair with chewed legs and a dog basket from the old labrador that had once lived there.

Jerry could still hear inside his head the rage in the voice and the metallic sound of the door bolt being slid shut on the other side of the door. The face in the photograph was the same animal who would often hit the young Jerry. He was swiped at when he spoke with his mouthful, sometimes hard enough to knock him off the chair where he sat perched on a cushion so that he could reach the table. When he started to nibble his food before grace, he would be bawled at for being a sinful child and made to stand by his chair for the rest of the meal, his food was taken away from him. Jerry's fingers kneaded his stomach as he recalled the intense hunger pangs from his childhood that lasted until morning.

No day had been the same except that it had always ended badly for him. Shoes, Jerry recalled, the vicar had a thing about his shoes for Sunday service. His job was to shine them while he was writing his sermon the day before. The boy would work at them with the brush, a black tin of polish and spit and timidly present them to him. "Do they sparkle? Do you think these are good enough for a man of god to wear?"

He shook his head, defeated, tears rolling down his cheeks.

"Take them away, you little wretch, and do them again. I want to see my face in them, you hear?" He clipped little Jerry hard around the ears.

Sometimes his cruel guardian would play a record before tea, always the same crackly gramophone record of a lady warbling. He wasn't allowed to go to the table for his meal until he had danced through the whole song in front of him under his critical eye, forcing himself to appear happy while jigging on the threadbare rug by the hearth where the old dog used to lie. On one occasion he had stopped dancing in mid song, refusing to go on. In his fury the man punished him with relentless lashes from his belt buckle.

Jerry screwed his eyes shut to banish the memories he had tried to repress. He put his head in his hands and scrunched his hair in his fists so that it tugged at the roots. Fury gripped him as he reluctantly recalled yet more. Images cascaded into his mind with crystal clarity, like vivid colour photographs found in an album not opened for years. That ogre, his guardian, had caught him by the scruff of his neck for running indoors and had poured a kettle of freshly boiling water over him as a punishment for knocking over a porcelain vase in the chase. His tender skin had peeled like grilled bacon from chin to torso. He had screamed and cried for days, shut away in that bolted room when he should have been taken to hospital.

He snapped back to the present and leant over the newspaper again, his lips moving silently as he tracked the words on the page. That creature, awarded "For pastoral services to victims of abuse". That same pinched face had visited him in his recurring nightmares from his childhood. He now had a name and a parish not so far away. One way or another Jerry promised himself that he would find the strength to confront him. He would have his comeuppance, just as Penrose, Sloth and the Busker had got what they deserved. The face in the grainy photo was older and gaunter than the monster he remembered as a child. But behind those eyes was the same person capable of all the same evil that had been metered out to him. He shivered at the thought of coming face to face with him again.

Jerry ripped out the article and stuffed it in his pocket.

The library staff would have received the complaint from the grumbling pair and would be on their way up soon. It was time to disappear. Jerry would keep this revelation to himself until after Scarlet's release. Before then, he had some homework to do to find out all he could about this man of the cloth. For the first time that he could remember he felt afraid of what was ahead. He needed her beside him again.

* * *

Jerry had traced the vicar to a parish, south of the river. A grimy red brick Victorian church spire rose above the lime trees on the edge of a small park. It stood in a green and leafy suburb of trendy stucco-rendered town houses, starkly contrasting with a large council estate a stone's throw away across the invisible dotted line of a neighbouring borough. The housing stock there was poor and attracted more than its fair share of social problems. This patchwork of dense deprivation living alongside comfortable prosperity was familiar to Jerry and was repeated throughout the city.

He walked around the back of the building a couple of times, weaving between the gravestones and reading the inscriptions. There was service under way. On hearing organ music resonate outside the mesh-protected stained-glass window, he stopped in his tracks and took another swig of vodka. If his demon was in there as he expected, then it was not his intention to confront him, just to set eyes on him and to mark him. He drained the bottle and poignantly left it on an ornately carved gravestone to a child who had passed away a century earlier, both of her parents buried alongside. "Lucky, lucky you," he said to himself. His head spun with booze and a mix of emotions, trepidation and fear being the strongest. He plucked up courage, put his hand to the oak door and pushed.

The hymn was in full swing. There was only a sparse congregation and Jerry sat on the pew behind them, declining a hymn book that was offered to him by the warden. The murmured singing was drowned out by the discordant pipes of the organ that filled the building, except for one voice from an elderly man whose deep choral notes held their own with rich Welsh undertones transcended the otherwise dreary delivery. The final chord tremored with a long sustain and there was a miskeyed belch from the organ.

The congregation sat, and for the first time in years he set eyes on the man in the cassock who was at the pulpit ready to address. He looked older and more bowed, but it was unmistakably him. Holding the sides of the lectern as though for support, the thin reedy voice carried through the still, chill atmosphere, interspersed with coughs and a baby crying.

"Sin and sinners …", projected the voice. "Hope for the repentant who shall seek forgiveness for their trespasses."

Jerry absorbed none of the words, but their tone spun him back to his five year old self, shut in the locked room. A sickness consumed Jerry. A mixture of distress and the half bottle of vodka he had quickly drunk to pluck up courage churned inside him. He projectile spewed two pews in front of him, only to look up to see the vicar throw a look at him, that same cold look that seemed to rip into his soul and drain any joy out of him. Feeling more sickness welling up, he jumped out of the pew and raced to pull open the heavy oak door. It slammed behind him and he chucked up the remaining contents of his stomach over the stone flagged entrance porch.

He wiped his face with the back of his hand, straightened up and looked across the small park at a building constructed in similar masonry to the church. He read the words carved in the red brick above the entrance, Children's Home. Something resonated with him from long ago, Jerry had been there before.

19

Cuckoo

Jerry often spent time watching people. Women heading to the shops. Tourists absorbed in their London guides. Workers heading home from a night shift. He saw them all as his little tributaries that fed into a moving river, that surged and meandered and flowed with or against the swell. He watched them carefully, tuning himself into the bustle and the rhythm of the moving crowds. They came in ripples and in waves, some regular, others apart and it was in the turbulent waters, the chop, that he would spot the easier pickings, where they had to weave around a man on crutches or a pregnant woman or an unexpected queue for a newspaper vendor when their paths become erratic and narrowed.

The bodies he saw marching to and fro looked herd-like but all were individuals with stresses and emotions. They were just flesh and blood, some capable of betraying the inner workings of their minds to a complete stranger who spent many a long day studying them. Some were cool and wary, and to be avoided, but others were hot and flustered. He saw himself not as an opportunist but as a strategist, a big cat patiently stalking its prey for the long game, looking out for the weak, the hassled or the careless to break cover. He was at the crudest a street thief who got off on the thrill of it, but compared to his unhappy time in the squat dealing drugs, he felt that it was a more noble occupation demanding a number of highly tuned skills which all needed to work in synchronicity. Acute observation, patience, timing, daring, quick decisions, precision and dexterity, all performed by sleight of hand as a magician at the top of his game. And now that he was by himself, he had to perform at the top of his game.

He observed people closely in the weekday crowds of city workers as they funnelled their way along to work and back. Commuters walked briskly through the railway station concourses, filtering rat-like up and down the underground system or over the bridges that spanned the River Thames. In his suit donated by the mission, he looked convincingly like one of the crowd and tried to mimic their gaits, the bustle and purpose in their steps, how they walked as though anonymous and alone amongst strangers, careful to avoid eye contact. This helped him to blend with the crowd and by becoming one of them, he became invisible.

One afternoon he was sitting on a bench outside Moorgate station, adopting the pose of the city workers with a folded raincoat, legs crossed and looking to all intents and purposes absorbed in the Evening Standard that the previous occupant had abandoned. He normally took an interest in the pages but this was his work and he was keeping a sharp look out over the top of his paper for opportunities, like a bird of prey waiting for a field mouse to bolt. He had already ruined one person's day in the morning rush hour when casually, under

122

the cover of a raincoat draped over his arm, he had relieved a lady of her purse from the shoulder bag that gaped invitingly.

A young city gent who was heading for the steps caught his eye. He was a few years older than Jerry but what was striking was his similarity in face and build. He was probably heading for one of the city banks or law firms. He carried a brown leather attaché case under one arm. He had distinctive expensive looking brown brogues and a sharp-cut grey suit, despite black shoes and a striped city suit being far more common. Jerry smelt money and his hunting instinct kicked in.

Swiftly, he took up position, walking shoulder to shoulder with the other commuters, hanging back behind a bowler hatted man in full pinstripes.

He followed his target through the barrier, using a ticket that he had earlier picked up under the nose of the disinterested ticket inspector. Stepping onto an escalator that descended to the platforms, he stood a couple of steps behind him and he was again struck by the likeness. His target's hair was thick and wiry and even his ears stuck out in a similar way. The escalator approached the bottom, the steps flattened and the crowds funnelled left or right to the two platforms.

A rush of dusty air signalled that the train was approaching and he followed the man in the throng. Station announcements barked and crackled about delays and to stand clear of the doors but were drowned out by the noise of the train braking. The train was packed and people had difficulty squeezing in and out of the carriages. Jerry waited his moment, standing immediately behind the target who stepped on to the train into the last remaining space, framed by elbows and armpits of the heaving mass of bodies inside. As the doors of the old rolling stock let out a hiss, he also stepped on, swiped the attaché case from the unsuspecting target and jumped back on to the platform as the doors closed behind him.

The train pulled away and a dismayed face looked back at him and contorted, mouthing something he could easily read on his lips. So alike. Back in the fresh air, Jerry examined his haul. He unzipped the attaché case and its inner pockets expecting to find dry work papers and a cheese and pickle sandwich. He let out a whistle as he picked through the haul. A wallet stuffed with crisp banknotes, a passport, a visa application, building society book, driving licence and a bunch of keys. And a chocolate bar. All from an unfortunate lad who shared a striking resemblance to himself. Jerry's mind was racing. He had an alias. He just wondered how long it would take for his double to find out.

The Tube train lurched along the Northern City Line track and the young city gent felt sick to his stomach at what had been taken from him. All his identity documents, everything the embassy had asked for. His trip to New York now looked in jeopardy. He could get off at the first stop and call the police. No, what chance would he have to find the thief who would now be long gone? He patted his top pocket. He still had a train ticket for the week. The commissionaire could let him into his north London flat with a spare key and he had of course a ridiculously large sum of cash back at the flat. Every month his absent father posted him a neat bundle of bank notes as pocket money. Guilt money more like. He refused to touch it so it just mounted up and now filled two drawers below his sock drawer. Change of plan, he didn't need to be in the office until ten o'clock the following morning. He would head home now to get an early night and the next day he would detour to Moorgate police station on his way to work to report the loss. The thief would only be interested in the cash in his wallet and probably discarded the attaché bag. With luck someone would have picked it up and handed it in. But luck was not on his side.

The next day was a dull and mild February morning. The victim of the crime walked along the station platform and as he always did he boarded the first carriage at the front of the train bound for Moorgate so that he could jump off on platform nine right by the exit to the escalators. It was peak rush hour and the train filled up as the journey went on, passing the backs of houses and flats until the track plunged underground. He rehearsed what to say to the duty policeman and hoped by some miracle that his bag had simply been handed in. The train gathered speed and charged on towards the final stop. It was a rocky ride and he had given up his seat to an elderly woman so he held on to one of the handles that swung from the carriage ceiling, swaying with the motion.

He took the line every day since he had started his first job in his father's business and was about to start a new role he had been promoted for and that assignment would involve occasional travel to the New York office, for which he would need a visa. Being the son of an investment banker was helpful. His father made out that he worked relentlessly and travelled abroad most of the year, but he imagined it to be in a palm fringed offshore tax havens, island hopping in his private jet.

He had been given free use of one of the serviced flats in a block that the bank owned, complete with a commissionaire in the lobby and a cage lift. The property was probably lost in the balance sheets for tax reasons. He was sure it was offered to him just to get him out of the family house where his father entertained top echelons of society and lady friends when he briefly touched down in London. His mother could not cope with the long absences and after being quietly treated in a private hospital after an attempted overdose to highlight her plight, the next time she had made doubly sure of what she was taking and never woke up. He was grateful to have his independence and free accommodation. His father took no interest in him and had never once visited his flat. When he was back from one of his long absences abroad, they would meet up in an Italian he liked for pasta and tiramisu until his father would check his watch, make his excuses and leave his son alone at the table to finish his meal.

He stirred from his daydream. The train sounded different and seemed to rush onwards, taking the bends and cambers faster than normal. Tunnel lights flashed past. He waited for the usual screeching of the brakes and uncomfortable juddering as the carriage tilted left, but it just rolled on unheeded. Passengers eyed each other and his knuckles whitened as he tightened his grip on the overhead handhold for support, swaying against other bodies. They hurtled onward to the station. There was a sudden violent shudder and everything went black inside the carriages. The train was meant to stop at the platform but instead proceeded into the tunnel, smashing through a sand barrier and into a brick wall.

* * *

The news of the train crash carried fast. In the confusion that followed it had first been reported as a minor incident but had quickly grown in enormity into a major crash under the streets of London. There were multiple casualties tombed and entangled in stifling darkness under layers of metal, dirt, limbs and screams. Jerry followed the events that unfolded on his transistor radio in his bedsit. He was able to tune in to an emergency service channel to pick up a one-sided conversation. He went out to visit the area around Moorgate to experience the drama unfolding to a melancholy tune of bells and nee-naw sirens.

Blue lights carried their cargo to St Bartholomew's and other London hospitals. Much had been cordoned off for the emergency services, the fire brigade, police and ambulance services. Rescue workers worked tirelessly in cramped airless conditions to free people from the twisted wreckage. Using emergency protocol, the injured were marked with one, two or three crosses on their foreheads to indicate the severity of their injuries. Shocked emergency workers emerged blinking into the daylight, covered in sweat and soot from working in appalling conditions in a stifling atmosphere of acrid dust and soaring underground temperatures. Doctors at the coal face struggled to diagnose death, impeded by the nearby noise of pneumatic drills working to free the trapped. As news spread, crowds gathered in front of television rental shops as the rescue effort was broadcast on the BBC and ITV. Some people stood with hands clamped over their mouths, watching the horror unfold and murmuring to themselves, shaking their heads in sorrow as the toll of dead and injured rose.

Jerry set off to Moorgate to watch the scene unfolding first-hand. He stood behind the barriers that the police had put up to keep the crowds and journalists at a distance. The onlookers were respectful and muted. The reporters on the other hand had flocked from every newsroom in Fleet Street and were keen to get interviews and capture photos worthy of a front story in the next edition. A policeman with a megaphone tried to keep a semblance of control in difficult circumstances.

Jerry then walked briskly to St Barts hospital to watch the ambulances race in from the scene. He watched the first two and the efficiency of the medical teams who wheeled the stretchers into the building to an overcrowded A&E, X-Ray or to theatre. As the third ambulance appeared and dust-covered ambulance men pulled out that stretcher, a doctor climbed on to check for vital signs. The ambulance team were not hopeful and shook their heads again, as the doctor signalled that this one was sadly dead on arrival. From Jerry's vantage point, he watched the body being stretchered off the ambulance quickly to allow the vehicle to make its return trip. In the haste, the red blanket slipped off the casualty, revealing profound injuries and was replaced by the porters who would now divert to the mortuary. That bloodied dust-encrusted face was worn like a mask, but it was the same face, Jerry's face. That one shoe, the same distinctive brogue shoes his target had been wearing the previous day. There was no mistake.

Jerry left the commotion of the hospital. He had been a voyeur while others were rescuing and saving lives. The contrast made him feel insignificant, irrelevant and he sloped off feeling wretched. As he crossed the London streets all now so familiar to him, it started to sink in that fate may have just played its hand. He had just been given a second chance. If he could play his cards right, he would find a way to switch identities with the deceased and by so doing to wipe his slate clean. If he was careful and managed the situation intelligently, he could start afresh, unsullied by his past life and become someone at last.

He kept on walking and eventually came to the embankment where he lent over the rough wall, looking unseeingly into the murky flowing waters. The distant sirens were now barely audible. Deep in thought, he looked down at his hands and traced a finger back and forth over the length of his lifelines. Scarlet had done just that while they had their holiday not so long ago in Shoreditch and touching where she had made her seem closer. He smiled at the thought of her. He remembered that they had sat like a married couple curled up on the settee having eaten their beans on toast on a tray. Blue Peter was on the television in the background. She had been inspecting his palms and had said that the lifeline on the left hand shows what the gods have given you and the lifeline on the right hand is what you do with it. He had told her it was complete bollocks and she had hit him hard on the arm in jest. He could almost still feel that smarting pain and missed her so much.

There was the problem that Scarlet was incarcerated behind bars and he would have to make good use of his time until her release by making plans and setting them in motion. She would have to bide her time to get an early release but if he gave her hope then he was sure she would manage it as long as she kept a lid on her violent outbursts. He would write to her soon to tell her as much. Before long they would be together again, and he clung on to that thought. When they were together again, he would tell her about the demon he had uncovered in the library. For Jerry, he was always going to be imprisoned by his past and the evil that had been done to him as a child for as long as that creature continued to tread this earth. The two of them would have to plan meticulously but if they got it right, then one day they could both be free.

* * *

Scarlet lay on her bunk, eyes closed, imagining she was anywhere else but behind bars. Her room-mate Holly was in the hospital wing having been attacked by one of the gangs. She missed her company and the special communication that the two of them shared. The mail trolley with the squeaky wheel trundled along the bare concrete corridor. A woman with shaven head and resembling a shot-putter banged on her open cell door, barked out her surname and threw in a letter. The envelope was crisp, white Basildon Bond, not the usual second-hand brown envelope he normally used. The address was neatly written, not with biro but with an ink pen and his handwriting had changed from spider-like script to a more confident neat appearance, with "l's" and "t's" thrusting forwards on the page. Curious, she thought. Her heart leapt as she read it. Jerry sounded upbeat and chatty. He hinted at good news for them both. The last paragraph particularly perplexed her.

> *"S, I've landed on my feet for sure. Can you believe that I am living in a posh flat? Well I am! It has a doorman - a commissionaire he's called - and a cleaner. They even stock the fridge while I'm out! Can't say any more in this letter but will tell you more when I see you in person. Hold on to that and until then, please stay away from any trouble. I want you out of there and can't wait to see you. To hold you again. I'll be waiting for you. Love J xxxx".*

Scarlet distractedly picked at the stitches on her forearm that she had acquired after an incident in the canteen. She had shielded herself from the jagged can lid to save her face. It had taken two prison officers to pull the mad woman off her. A good thing too as any longer and she would have lashed out at her throat and probably killed the bitch. Had she done so, Scarlet would not have seen the light of day for years. She only had two weeks to go before she had served a full six months. She was eligible for her review and she clung on to the hope that she would be released. She closed her eyes and thought of Jerry. She knew it must be hard for him as well. She drew up her knees and hugged them tightly.

Jerry checked with the post office again and a letter was waiting for him.

> *"J, I'm up for review. If it goes well, then I could be out by the end of May. Cross your fingers for me! Love, S xxxx".*

* * *

The flat was on the fourth floor of the apartment block, which he had established from the letters and keys in the stolen attaché case. The elderly commissionaire had gazed at him curiously from the reception desk when he had first arrived and feeling like an imposter Jerry had walked straight to the lift without conversing, expecting any moment for a hand to be laid on his shoulder. As he stepped into the lift he saw the commissionaire wave and Jerry waved back at him as the doors shut. The lift opened at his floor, and Jerry felt soft, springy carpet under his feet as he walked along the corridor counting the door numbers until he arrived at 408. The key turned and his jaw hung as he looked in awe at the opulent flat.

He walked through the rooms and flopped on the comfortable settee, went to the kitchen to find a stocked fridge, pulled out a beer and carried on exploring, opening cupboards, drawers and wardrobes. Slowly he started to put together the pieces of the puzzle to reveal the life of the lookalike who had lived in the apartment up. He would have to adjust his appearance to look more like his new persona. He showered, shaved and parted his hair to look more like the boy in the photographs he found around the flat, dressing in clothes he picked out of the wardrobe. He was flabbergasted to find two drawers full of packets of cash. After jumping on the bed and bouncing for joy a couple of times, he carried armfuls of the bundles in two trips between the bedroom and the kitchen, laying them all out on the table. He started to unwrap the packets and to count the notes into neat piles but gave up after the first half a dozen. He sat back in the chair and let out a long whistle.

It would add up to an enormous sum, and he would count it another time, but it was more than he could possibly have imagined. Without doubt it was enough to buy him and Scarlet a new life together. Packing the money away and hiding it carefully in a couple of non-descript sports bags he found, he celebrated his luck by making himself a cheese omelette. He then spent a while going through the flat again and came across a housekeeping folder, which detailed the phone numbers for various services, postal services, laundry days, frequency of cleaning and an old welcome letter with a smiling picture of two commissionaires, one of whom was now on duty downstairs. So, he now knew his name which would be handy.

The phone rang and Jerry jumped. He lifted the receiver, "Hello?"

"Good morning, Mr Bishop."

Jerry took a risk, recalling the name from the housekeeping folder. "Yes Ralph?"

"I have a parcel for you downstairs which needs signing for. Would you be able to drop down at your convenience?"

He walked back into the lobby. Ralph looked up from his desk, "By Jove, that was quick!"

Jerry smiled at him, made a mental note to take longer next time. He took the new pen out of his pocket, signing with the signature he had just been practising upstairs, copied from the identification papers his double had left in the stolen attaché case.

"Thank you, good day to you, sir."

Inside the parcel was a bundle of bank notes and a brief handwritten note from his new father, explaining that he had been called away for an extended work trip and sadly would not be back in the UK until September. His PA would send on his allowance with some extra pocket money next month and he hoped it would make up for him being away again.

* * *

The corpse had taken a few weeks to identify. At first it had been mistaken, not helped by dental records mysteriously going missing. A visit to the hospital morgue by the gentleman in question had corrected this. He had indeed borne a striking resemblance to the corpse in the morgue and provided irrefutable identification to confirm the error. This visitor had further helped them to identify the deceased from a missing persons register as that of a runaway teenager from a few years ago. The coroner was satisfied and the police had solved a missing persons case. A life had been lost in the crash. Yet, another had been gained.

A memorial service was held in the spring after the tube train crash to commemorate the lives of those who had perished and to give thanks for the survivors. As horrific as it must have been, it had been carrying three hundred passengers in that peak morning rush hour and the toll of almost forty dead could have been even worse. Among the crowds who attended the service at the cathedral, there was a young city gent, perhaps a trader, dressed in cashmere overcoat, distinctive brogues and a silk scarf. In silence he laid a floral wreath beside the other tributes on the steps. Attached to his flowers was a touching message paying private respect to a young man of similar age who had perished.

Jerry had pulled it off, he had switched identity. He decided he should go out one evening and buy himself an expensive slap-up meal in town to celebrate his new beginning.

* * *

Andy had landed a job which required him to go into London from time to time. He saw the opportunity to meet up with his two old school chums, Pete and Robbie, for an evening out in town. Andy lifted the handset and dialled the number.

"Hello?" said a familiar voice. Andy pushed the coins into the phone, one rattled through into the return dish and he fed it in again. The call box smelled of urine and he held the door ajar with his foot.

"Hi Pete, it's Andy!"

There was a pause on the line.

"Andy? Bugger me, long time no hear! How the devil are you?"

"Yeah, great thanks. Look, I'm working for a lawnmower company and ..."

"Your haircuts won't have improved then!"

Andy pressed on, "Yes, well, I need to be at a trade show in London this coming Friday. I thought maybe we have our own get together afterwards in the evening? I've just called Robbie and he's up for it."

"Yup, count me in!" said Pete. "What's the plan? I can get a train ..." There was a slow beeping on the line and Andy pushed another coin in just in time.

"Sorry, last coin, we'd better be quick," said Andy.

"What was I saying?", continued Pete, "Yes, I can get a train into town straight after work."

"OK, let's meet at that Berni Inn on Oxford Street, say seven, seven-thirty. We can grab some food and then go out on the town!"

"I'm stuffed!" said Robbie, pushing his plate away. "Probably shouldn't have eaten before I came out, but thought best to line the stomach in case we end up having a heavy night."

Quick as a flash, Andy swapped it for his empty plate, squeezed a dollop of ketchup on top of the pile of abandoned chips and tucked in, cutting off the edible flesh Robbie had left on the half-eaten steak rind.

Pete returned to his chair. "Right, I've paid. Let's go. How about we find a decent pub?"

A quick pint in the first pub they came across turned into two pints, then into four. The friends reconnected as they caught up on what they were doing now and who they were seeing. Girls, and the lack of girls in their lives, were a common theme. Recent conquests were shared, one competing with the other as they claimed first base, second base and a 'nearly-third' by Robbie, only to be disqualified by Andy and Pete as it led to a smack around the chops from the young lady in question. As the beers flowed, they started to reminisce. They talked about how they used to play in the woods behind Robbie's house.

"Do you reckon," said Pete, noticing that the room was starting to spin a little "that someone a hundred years from now will find the initials that we all carved into those trees?"

"Maybe," speculated Andy, "but how high up the tree will they be by then?"

Pete tried to think about that, but instead found himself looking around the pub at the solitary customers dotted around the place and either staring into their drinks or into the far distance. They seemed to blend seamlessly into the odd-looking decor that he hadn't noticed before.

"I'm beat," said Pete. "What d'you say we move on and find somewhere a bit more lively?"

"Suits me," said Robbie, "what have we got left in the kitty, Andy?"

"Nearly eleven pounds," said Andy, who was banker for the night.

"Hang on," intercepted Robbie, rummaging in his pocket and pulling out a screwed up leaflet that he flattened on the table. "What about this place. I was handed this when I got off the train at Kings Cross. Says here there's a rock band playing and the first drinks are half price with the leaflet. Might be fun."

Pete perked up at the thought of live music. "I'm still trying to play Stairway to Heaven on the guitar," he shared with anyone who cared to listen. "I can't get beyond the 'songbird who sings' bit." Peter made the imaginary chord shapes with his left hand, strumming with the right. "It's A minor, G sharp, C, E minor 7 …"

"Shut up, Pete," said Andy casually. "Yes, it could be a laugh and it would be good to watch a band."

Andy rocked forwards on the stool and picked up the crumpled leaflet. "That's quite near here, just off Oxford Street. Let's go!"

They chattered loudly as the three friends walked the unfamiliar streets. Pete ducked down a dimly lit back alley behind a fish and chip takeaway to relieve a bursting bladder by some drums of cooking oil. A door at the back of the shop opened, illuminating him in mid-flow. Pete was yelled at and beat a hasty retreat before the angry cook could carry out what he said he would do if he caught him.

"You are such a liability, Pete," they laughed, as he rejoined his friends, grinning from ear to ear.

Back on the lit streets they walked past shop windows and lines of restaurants. Customers were seated at tables inside the windows, tucking into food from around the globe - curries, noodles, pasta, burgers, goulash, coq au vin, fish and chips.

"Hold up!" said Andy. "Look who it is! There, in the French restaurant, just standing up from the table. It's Jerry! It's him, it's definitely him."

"I'm not so sure," said Pete. "Why would he be eating in that sort of place?"

Andy ignored Pete and looked at Robbie, pleadingly.

"I'm not sure either," said Robbie, squinting. "We haven't seen him for years. He's probably just a look-a-like."

"My dad says I've got a double," said Pete. "He plays for Spurs ..."

"Shut up, Pete!"

A waiter opened the door with a flourish and Jerry stepped out onto the pavement, checked his watch, a shiny gold watch they noticed, before setting off. He was very smartly dressed in expensive looking clothes.

Andy bounced across the road while the others hung back.

"Hey, Jerry! It's me. Andy!"

Jerry stopped in his tracks and looked him up and down. "Sorry, you're mistaken."

Andy saw the rough marks on his neck just above his collar, concealed by make-up but still there. Jerry turned his collar up self-consciously and set to walk away.

Andy grabbed him by the elbow. In an instant, Jerry reached into his pocket, but stopped himself short. He turned to face him again, looking sheepish. "Leave me alone, I'm not who you think I am."

"I know it's you, stop messing about!" Andy persisted, "Look, that's Pete and Robbie across the road. Come on, join us for a quick drink, for old times' sake?"

"I don't know you!" Jerry shouted, rising to anger, "Now fuck off!" pushing Andy off the kerb into the road and causing a cyclist to swerve.

And with that, the ghost of Jerry bolted down the street, hailed a passing taxi and vanished into thin air.

* * *

On a warm day in May, the door closed behind Scarlet and there standing on the other side of the road was Jerry. Carrying a small holdall, back in the same clothes she was arrested in that day in Tottenham Court Road, she ran full pelt, dropping the bag and flew into Jerry's arms, smothering her tear-streaked face in his shoulder.

The next morning, Jerry left her sleeping in bed. She was exhausted from her incarceration, from the emotion of being free and from releasing pent up emotions again now that she was back with Jerry. She had been overwhelmed by the flat, and Jerry had to whisk her through the lobby, giving a wink to the commissionaire who was paying an uncomfortable amount of attention to his companion. Jerry would often surprise her but he had really excelled that time and she had so much news to absorb from the few months she had been in prison.

She had had a long soak in the luxurious bathroom that was so big it could have fitted in her friend Julie's entire flat. After so long apart, neither could sleep and they spent a long night of closeness and talking until dawn finally arrived and Jerry let her sleep. She had a lot to come to terms with and he had not held back. There was the bizarre change of circumstances where Jerry had assumed another's identity from events that she had yet to fully comprehend. This meant that they no longer had to rob for their living. They had the use of a fabulous flat and more cash than she could dream of, all paid for by Jerry's new estranged 'father'.

"So, what you are saying Jay, is that we are cuckoos!"

He laughed at that before his voice became serious and Jerry told her that he had found his bete noire in the newspaper cutting.

While she slept, Jerry went out to the street market and bought flowers and jam doughnuts which he laid out on a breakfast tray on the kitchen table, ready to take in when she stirred. Jerry stood at the kitchen window staring unseeingly at the street scene below. The image of their lingering tight embrace the previous evening was seared into him and for some moments seemed more real than reality. He relived how their hearts had seemed to pound against each other and that same heady rush of excitement returned to him. He could feel again the warmth of her body, the fragrance of her skin, the warm mustiness of her hair. They had held each other close through the early hours, triumphant that they had found each other, overjoyed at the all-encompassing feeling of freedom, of safety together and of being wanted. It was only them, two unlikely people who shouldn't ever have crossed each other's paths. In finding her again he felt more complete than ever before and it sent him spinning into happy oblivion.

Down the hallway came the sound of the loo flushing. He switched on the kettle, poured her a glass of juice from the fridge and they settled in for the day.

20

Gentlemen's Club

The message had been delivered. The man had been instructed to meet Sir Peter at three o'clock that afternoon. Odd timing, that was not a lunch invitation. There must be trouble.

He took a taxi, the traditional black cab Austin FX4, and was dropped off outside the West End club ten minutes early, announcing himself at the desk on arrival. He followed the marble flooring to the cloakroom where his coat was received by the uniformed attendant as though it was a regal garment and not an everyday mackintosh. It was fussily hung on a wooden hanger to join a rail of coats in return for a token. A second token was given out for his hat. He had time to visit the toilets, read the framed cartoon above the urinal, washed his hands with the bar of lavender soap and took a freshly laundered hand towel from the neat pile on the marble vanity top, before throwing it into the basket. He took a splash of cologne just because it was there, pulled a comb through his hair and straightened his tie, grimacing briefly to check that his lunch was not stuck in his teeth.

The stairs wound up, passing beneath original artwork old and modern. There was a large landing with a writing desk under the window, adjacent to which a head and shoulders portrait of a severe looking huntsman shared wall space with a Greek goddess baring all and a grandfather clock whose steady tocking and erratic mechanical murmurs gave a timeless unhurried atmosphere to the place. Two doors led off, one to the library and a second to the bar and restaurant from where a murmur of male voices and aroma of fine cigar smoke hung in the air.

The library was part of the original early nineteenth century building, an elegant room with tall sash windows to the front. Ancient bookshelves heaved under the weight of a fine collection of books many donated or bequeathed, their pages soaked in the patina of age and old tobacco that seemed to infuse every pore of the building. Old gentlemen were often found there after lunch slumped in tatty leather armchairs, crossword and whisky glass beside them, sometimes engaged in highbrow tittle tattle with a neighbouring old codger or more often simply passed out for the afternoon with a full belly. Vital signs of life were the occasional grunt as a head lolled forwards or trumping resonating from the depths of a chair.

All members had to be first and seconded through a rigorous selection process to ensure that they were suitable for the club. Even for applicants of distinction, their backgrounds were probed to check for any rough edges and if they passed that scrutiny then their social skills were put to the test over morning coffee or afternoon tea with the membership secretary. Only after that would they either be shown the door by a brief, move-along handshake, followed by a crisp two line letter on embossed club letterhead that would drop on their doormat, thanking them for their application but regretting that they were unable to offer membership. If they passed the interview then they were welcomed there and then into the fold with a warm lingering handshake and a drop of single malt or brandy to ease the pain of handing over their substantial cheque for the joining fee.

The restaurant had a different feel, striving uncomfortably to blend old and new decor, and failing in both regards. The building was a rabbit warren, a double-storey rear extension having been added in the nineteen-thirties to provide a larger room with doors out to a raised dining terrace over the private courtyard garden which was also used for functions on warm summer evenings. The club table in the main restaurant was laid for lunch on Tuesdays, stretching the full length of the room, where Pierre took great care of his front of house responsibilities and prided himself on the highest levels of discrete attention by knowing each of the regular members' preferences for drink, diets and seating. Lunch service was over but Pierre had spotted the visitor from behind the bar, greeting him courteously. "Sir Peter is expecting you." He escorted him to a private sitting room, which could be reserved for occasions where confidences needed to be discussed and etiquette observed. Sir Peter was found deep in conversation with a man who sat with his back to him. Sir Peter looked up.

"Come in, come in! Pull up a chair. You know the good reverend of course." The limbs of the reverend enfolded like a mantis as he rose from the chair, greeted the visitor with an unsettling stare through his wired-framed glasses, offered a cold limp hand, and refolded himself in the seat, tightly crossing his legs and leaning forwards earnestly.

Sir Peter continued. "Have you been offered a drink?"

"I believe it's on its way."

And with uncanny timing there was a knock at the door and the waiter set the glass down in front of the visitor on a round paper drinks mat carrying the Club's logo. It was half-filled with ice and amber liquid. There was almost imperceptible questioning eye contact with Sir Peter.

"Yes, on my account, please", Sir Peter said.

The waiter attended to the fire, adding fresh logs and poking them down. The visitor's glass seemed alive as the lead crystal mirrored the hungry flames that consumed the wedge of apple wood in the grate. The heavy panelled door clicked shut.

Sir Peter cleared his throat. "Let us get straight down to business. In fact, there are two items to discuss." He directed this at the vicar who shifted uncomfortably, recrossed his legs and crossed them again. "Let's tackle the first. No, you can put that away, best you don't write anything down."

He stroked his ice-white moustache and continued.

"We have a problem. One of our number has put together salacious information on the Firm. Frankly, I am furious. This person has compiled a list of the members containing a lot of potentially embarrassing details which he holds as security for him just in case we ever come down on him hard. That's blackmail, the little shit!"spat Sir Peter, his face turning a ruddy red.

Sir Peter reached into his pocket and withdrew a pill box, taking one of the tablets with a glass of water. He smoothed his moustache and continued. "Bernard has, how should we say, had a quiet word with the member concerned. He has reminded him what we have on him and that it would be very unwise to get on the wrong side of me. It seems that he won't disclose the whereabouts of his list and thinks he holds something that will protect him." There was no humour in his eyes.

Sir Peter continued, "If that list were to fall into the wrong hands then it could be devastating for us all and I am not prepared to let that happen."

"I see," said the man, listening carefully, drawing a long sip from the drink that he was cradling in his hands. It set the ice rattling.

"You know why I am bringing this to you. I need you to put a lid on this and it must be dealt with quickly and efficiently. We have something on him that we can use to bring him into line but there is no question of the errant member being allowed to continue to run circles around us. There will be an empty seat at our next gathering but we can recruit again."

Sir Peter observed the man closely and gave him a wry smile. "Your connections in the force and with certain unsavoury characters you use for your dirty work are invaluable. Find the list, destroy it, problem solved! Here, take this. You will find inside his name which will be known to you and his home address where he has most likely secreted the list. You, or whoever you use, can scare the pants off him but it must look like a burglary not a massacre."

"You know you can rely on me, Sir Peter."

"Good, good!" Sir Peter had lightened up. "Now switching horses …"

The vicar noticeably shifted in his seat again, head bowed. Sir Peter continued, "Our learned friend, the reverend, is to be congratulated for being recognised for his pastoral services to the victims of abuse. A very worthy accolade I am sure you will agree! Sadly his good works have put him in the firing line for unfounded and vindictive accusations. What is wrong with the world?"

The man of cloth slowly nodded his head, still bowed as though in prayer. Sir Peter continued, "If my friend will allow me to set the scene, there has again been a particularly serious assertion made against him involving, er … minors of the male variety. Complete poppycock of course but I would like you to make it disappear."

"Consider it done. I will need some details."

"Excellent, well if you will both excuse me, I will leave you talking." Sir Peter heaved himself up on his cane. "No, don't get up! I'm going to find a quiet corner to slip away for forty winks to let my lunch settle. Age is a wonderful thing but you've got to treat it with respect!"

III

PART THREE

21

The Fall

It was the dead of night. A biting wind chased through the streets and squares. Sparse leafless trees braced and bent in the gusts. Under streetlights, restless waving limbs caste unearthly shadows.

A crescent moon winked behind racing black clouds. Bins toppled. Litter flew. Cats fought. Night creatures scuttled. The city slept.

But Amanda didn't. She lay crumpled in the shadows at the foot of the building where she had fallen, her body twisted and broken. Her vision was blurred. She tried to focus, tuning into the primitive instinct to survive. Her gaze took in the dizzying rise of the facade above her and her eyes settled in horror on the balcony above her from where she had just dropped.

Screwing up her eyes, she willed her limbs to move, but nothing responded. Her chest fired up with pain at every gurgling intake of breath. She mustered a cry for help but managed just a whimper. She tried again and a hoarse scream was carried away in the wind. Above she heard the front door opening. He was coming out to find her! Shoes scuffed the top step. The pounding of her heart pulsed in her head, getting louder and louder, as shock gave way to mortal fear. Terror and pain gripped and overwhelmed her. She had been brave, but it couldn't go on forever. Her last thought before she blacked out was that he was coming to finish her off.

Beams of light swung from the road and pierced the gloom. An engine, muffled voices. The intruder froze momentarily, still carrying the poker he had swung. He bolted down the steps, ducked into a side alley and was gone.

22

Apple Core

At the station, Detective Inspector Drummond peeled the label off his apple, rubbed it down his left sleeve, admired the shine and took a big bite. He crunched through his words to the assembled team.

"Right, All. Listen up. Our esteemed Detective Chief Inspector Brisket is away at a conference entertaining our new European cousins and no doubt educating them in the joys of warm beer and jellied eels. So, until he gets back, I'm in charge and I want a quick result, not a long drawn out case like Big Micky the Flasher. Wipe off those smirks lads. Not only was it an embarrassment to the squad that it took so long to bring him to justice, but you'll embarrass Morgan again who had to apprehend him at large as it were."

Sniggers all round. Detective Constable Janice Morgan reddened.

Drummond picked up the apple and took another bite, then wiped the juice from his chin with the back of his hand. "No," he continued, "We want to get this nasty bit of work off the streets and behind bars in record time. I don't want the extra paperwork from a long-running saga. Nor the grief from our lord and master who'll chew my nuts off if we don't. Got it?"

Dropping the apple core into the nearest paper basket he licked his fingers, then wiped them down his shirt. "Right, bring me up to speed and let's get to work. Resume please Hobbs."

Hobbs was as usual the most elegantly dressed detective in the room, each shirt sleeve sporting a crisply ironed crease, a cufflink and a copper bracelet pushed to the elbow. He embraced old-school formality. The others joked in the pub to his face that he probably didn't even own a leather jacket and a kipper tie. Hobbs seemed to take it in good humour. His tie knot needed no straightening but he checked it anyway, got to his feet and opened his notebook. "The victim is female, mid-thirties," he started, a hint of an Essex accent giving away his roots. "Believed to be Amanda Castle, resident of the house. Found in the early hours this morning in Basing Crescent by a late-night taxi driver."

"The Crescent eh? Big houses, very gentile. Go on, Hobbs."

"Poor bloke thought she was dead, Guv. She was unconscious and covered in blood. A man believed to be the assailant was spotted running from the scene." Hobbs continued, "The cab driver and his passenger both got a fleeting glimpse of him and we have their witness statements. He was carrying some sort of long object. One thought it could be a crowbar, the other a fire poker. Not enough to get a useful description. Male, large build, dark clothing, gloves but then it gets hazy."

"So, we are looking for a black cat in a coal bunker. Anyone else in the house at the time of the attack?"

"We think she was in the house on her own. She is married but has no kids."

152

"Crime scene, Dougie?"

"I've done a thorough sweep, Jack." DI Doug McVitie, an overweight man in his forties with a purple veined face not dissimilar to a Toby jug, continued in his slow Scottish drawl. "The French doors at the back of the house were forced so it looks like that's how the intruder got in. He probably woke her up or she surprised him. We think she was alone in the house. Violent, yes but nothing to indicate a sexual motive as far as we can fathom. The scene looks like a burglary gone wrong."

Drummond leant back on his chair and stretched a rubber band between his thumb and fingers. "A burglary you say. Just an observation but from the witness statements we have from Hobbs, there's no mention of the assailant coming out of the house with a suitcase or a bag with 'swag' on the side that any self-respecting burglar would need to carry away the loot." He aimed the rubber band at the distant wastepaper bin, missed it and got himself back on track again. "So how did she end up in the street, Dougie?"

"I'm pretty certain the victim was attacked in the bedroom, there were signs of a struggle. She was hit multiple times with something and pushed off the balcony." He checked his notes. "Hair and blood spatters on the bedroom floor, on the outer door threshold of the bedroom and along the balcony handrail all consistent with a violent attack. Probably beaten with a heavy implement, stunned, dragged across the floor and pushed over the railings. This guy was strong, Jack."

Jack Drummond ran a pinkie fingernail between his teeth to dislodge some apple skin, then summarised. "We have the hallmarks of a burglary that went badly wrong. What I find odd is that he took the trouble to throw …", he paused to look across at Morgan's notes to check the name, "Amanda Castle off the balcony rather than stunning her and running off with the candlesticks or whatever he was after. He must have been keen to finish her off. Maybe she got a good look at him and could identify him? So, what we have so far is breaking and entering, burglary, serious assault, titling towards attempted murder. That's one heck of a charge book. What's missing from the house - jewellery, money?"

"We don't know yet if anything was taken. He's been through the house pulling out drawers and has pretty much ransacked the place," McVitie explained. "My guess is that he started downstairs where he broke in and worked his way up. The victim must have heard the intruder and may have hidden upstairs in the bedroom."

"Why didn't she ring 999?" interrupted Drummond.

"Hobbs, make a note to check that the house phones are working. Sorry, go on Dougie!"

"We are trying to track down the victim's husband, Sir Francis Castle. Forty years old, a bigwig, chairman of a government commission of some sort."

"He's going to have a shock when he finds out. Forty, eh?" mused Drummond. "That was my last birthday as well. He has a knighthood and a posh house and I have … you lot! I must have done something very heinous in a past life."

Drummond recapped. "So, we have Amanda Castle from a titled family. The press will be all over this if we don't keep them in check. Let's keep this under wraps until we know what we are dealing with. The message needs to be loud and clear 'No comment', nothing gets out and if anyone needs a statement then refer back to me. OK?"

There were collective nods around the room.

"Fingerprints, Dougie?"

"Yes and no. Lots of prints but only one match in our books. Bit odd this one, Jack. It's our old friend William Woodruff."

"The art fraudster who did time a few years back?"

"The very same. Came out of Wormwood Scrubs in seventy-two and seems to have kept his nose clean since. His prints are all over the place. But this doesn't fit his style and the descriptions given by both witnesses agreed that the man on the steps was wearing gloves."

Drummond interrupted, "Woodruff? That doesn't stack up at all. He's more the artist than the mobster. A bit of a sorry specimen as I remember. Daubing fake masterpieces and passing them off as originals was his thing. Committing GBH and attempted murder is not his modus operandi."

Albert's hand shot up and was ignored.

"I agree, Jack," Dougie said. "We checked him out of course and he has a cast iron alibi. He spent last night in a cell in a Marylebone police station cooling off for being drunk and disorderly. Back home now according to the charge officer. We've got an address for him. Lives in Bloomsbury."

"Dougie, go and pay our artist friend Woodruff a visit. He can't have been in two places at the same time, but he might be able to explain why we found his prints at a crime scene."

"OK Jack." He grabbed his jacket and headed out of the door.

"At least the poor girl is alive so we might get something out of her. What's the latest from the hospital. Dean?"

"She's still unconscious, Guv. Smashed up pretty bad by all accounts. Talisker is down at Queen Mary's. She's just come out of surgery. Doc reckons it's still touch and go. If she makes it through, we won't be able to interview her for a while but we've kept Tally down there for her protection just in case he

155

comes back to have another pop at her. Oh, and she won't be walking again if she does come through it."

Drummond paused in thought, sucking through his teeth, his brow furrowed as he looked over his reading spectacles, his eyes settling on each of them in turn. Stretching to his full height he clapped his hands together."

"Righto, you, New Lad!"

"It's Albert, Sir."

"Yes, well, New Lad! Chase up the lab for the crime scene photographs. I want them on my desk in the morning. And set up the blackboard in the incident room. Morgan, you've done door to door? Neighbours hear anything?"

"Yes sir … no sir." Blushing again, Morgan checked her notebook. "I've done door to door and either they were away that night, fast asleep or there was so much banging around in all that wind that no one heard a thing. One of them said that people in that neighbourhood tend to keep themselves to themselves. All quite aloof."

"Right Morgan, you get back to Basing Crescent and check any houses you may have missed, particularly any within line of sight of the house or alleyway he used to get away. Someone must have been having a 3am pee and may just have seen or heard something. Oh, and one more thing, Morgan."

"Sir?"

"Be a love and grab me a bag of apples from over the road. It's going to be a long day."

23

Toenails

oug McVitie rang the doorbell for a second time.
The day held little colour under a heavy monotone
sky. He braced as the wind tore down Bloomsbury
Street and licked around the corner of the grey faceless
buildings, drab and featureless and distinguished only by a
small, polished brass name plaque.

Shuffling came from behind the door, two locks turned. He
took one step back as the door eased open a crack revealing
over piled letters on the floor within. The face that looked
back at him was alarmingly pallid. Sunken eyes squinting out
from under a mop of dishevelled matted ginger hair.

"Mr Woodruff? DI McVitie." McVitie presented his identification and the dark eyes flicked down and levelled again. "I'm
here to ask you questions about a recent incident and I am
hoping that you can help us with our inquiries. May I come
in?"

The door closed again, a pause. Then a chain was slid. The
sad and sorry vision behind the threshold arrested his gaze.
He took in the bare calloused feet with yellowed toenails, the

hairless shins and the shabby silk dressing gown drawn tight but revealing unwelcome flesh where it parted.

In return, Woodruff's watery eyes looked him up and down and shot a look over his shoulder to the street behind. "Come in quickly and close that bloody door," he said in a public-school accent. "You might want to watch where you tread. My dog was trapped in the house while I was away and I haven't had a chance to tidy." Picking a route over the piled letters and through the cluttered musty hallway, McVitie took the Queen Anne carver he was offered in the only cleared space in a very squalid but elegantly furnished living room. A small shaking dog of indeterminate breed was leashed to the brass handle of a mahogany bureau.

Paintings of every genre were hung on every available wall space, some at drunken angles and many more stacked up against the filthy walls, enough to fill a gallery.

"You live alone?"

"Drink? No, well you don't mind if I do," Woodruff said, draining the remainder of a bottle of whisky. "Yes, I am all alone in this world unless you count that mutt over there. These four walls would drive me mad if I didn't get out now and again. It used to have my art studio upstairs before life took a turn for the worst, so as you can see I pretty much live in this blasted room. There's a lodger up in the garret who paints for pleasure and keeps himself to himself. I'm just glad to have someone using my old studio."

McVitie, poised with notebook and pencil, questioned William Woodruff.

"May I ask about your whereabouts last night?", said McVitie.

"What business is it of yours?" Woodruff replied. His tone

was not aggressive but there was an undisguised suspicion in his voice.

"We are investigating a serious crime that took place."

Woodruff was mystified why they had come knocking in his door, but honesty was the best policy, most of the time. "Yesterday is, I am afraid, a bit of a blur. I'll tell you what I remember before it got a little fuzzy." The little dog whined and he quieted it with a curt, "Hush, Queenie!"

Woodruff opened up to McVitie. "I met old Charlie in my local, in Lambs Conduit Street."

"What time did you go there?"

"It would have been about eight o'clock," Woodruff replied. "We had a few drinks and then I headed off on my own to the Princess for a couple more." Woodruff gave his account of his drinking session that started in his local pub, before moving to a drinkers' pub in High Holborn and finished as far as he could remember in a late-night bar in Soho. McVitie wrote down the name.

"The next thing I remember was waking up in a police cell with a bucket and a scratchy blanket."

Woodruff could not recall how he had ended the evening under lock and key. McVitie noted that his story was consistent with what the duty sergeant at Marylebone station had told him, who had given him a caution for being drunk and disorderly and had let him sleep it off in a police cell, probably to save himself the extra paperwork of charging him.

Turning to the evidence of his fingerprints from the house where the assault took place, Woodruff was less forthcoming but not obviously evasive. He had sold the occupants a collection of Victorian paintings of horses a few years back.

"The wife liked gee gees," he explained. Sir Francis had also commissioned good vanity copies of Van Gogh, a couple of Picassos, a Matisse, so he had been back and forth, helping him choose, getting them framed and hanging them.

"All unsigned and legitimate, but great works," he added. "Did one or two of them myself."

"You have explained the reason why your fingerprints were found in the house and we may need to ask you further questions at another time. What puzzles me," McVitie said, "is how you got the job in the first place to produce art counterfeits…"

"Correction, honest copies of masterpieces," Woodruff interrupted.

"To produce art counterfeits for high-ranking members of the high society," McVitie continued. "What or who is your connection to them as I don't imagine they are drinking buddies of yours given the insalubrious places you frequent?"

William Woodruff threw his head back as though looking for divine inspiration. After a moment, he laughed maniacally and McVitie tensed. "I have a little bird, you see. She pecks around the parlours of the rich and famous and passes me the odd crumb here, the odd crumb there. Little seeds she picks up. My Betty! She moves in circles you wouldn't imagine and drops a word here, a word there about the services that I can offer to well-healed art-loving connoisseurs. All legal and above board of course."

Woodruff was free-wheeling, "My little helpers produce the goods for them, like the elves and the shoemaker. All very high quality. I don't think the elves would attempt a Michelangelo but they can do passable copies of Rembrandt, Picasso, Pissarro, whatever their hearts desire so that they can hang them in their mansions and stately homes to show off to their friends. Vanity, all for vanity. And for my part, I am just the middleman. I seal the deal, check that the frames will suit the decor and hang their commissioned originals for them to enjoy, at least until they change the wallpaper or a new artist comes into fashion. Can you believe, Sir Francis wanted a Henri Matisse copy in oil, sized to stick over the front of his safe in his study. He didn't care which one, just had to be blue to match the decor. Heathens, the lot of them!"

Woodruff had met Sir Francis a couple of times at the house, an aloof businessman with little time for small talk. McVitie inferred that Woodruff was below his station and he had been smoothly passed to the housekeeper for a tour of the house and to show him the rooms where the pictures were to hang.

"An attractive girl, Portuguese," he recalled. "Rosario. Rose for short. Slender, big brown eyes and a silver stud in her nose."

Woodruff lived alone and liked to talk and in McVitie's experience it was in the off-guard ramblings where the nuggets were often discovered. "I heard from Betty who knows someone in the employment agency who has a friend who heard a rumour that Rose was romantically involved with one of her employers," he ventured.

"The house is a crime scene now, said McVitie.

"I know nothing about that. I was three sheets to the wind, I'm afraid. What happened?"

McVitie ignored his question and flicked back in his note-book. "This Betty you mentioned. Do you have her full name and a current address?"

"I don't want to get anyone into trouble."

"Mr Woodruff, we are investigating an attempted murder

161

that took place at the house where your fingerprints were found. I'd like to remind you of the trouble you will be in if you hold back information that might be useful to the investigation."

Woodruff looked alarmed. He had suffered more than he cared to remember in the brief time he had spent in prison and did not want to risk a repeat of it. He had grassed on his network to save his own skin resulting in a reduced sentence. He had given the police an inside track that had brought about the collapse of a criminal art syndicate. But snitches never get an easy ride behind bars and even now he couldn't sleep without the light on. He gave up the name.

As McVitie unlocked the unmarked Cortina parked across the street, pleased to be out of the rancid atmosphere in the house, he said under his breath, "Beatrice Du Pont, well well, he does move in interesting circles."

Looking up at the house he had left, McVitie saw a curtain twitch in an upstairs window and for an instant a man's face looking down at him. "Ah, so that must be one of Woodruff's elves," he thought. "'Paints for pleasure' my foot. Once a forger always a forger!" smiled McVitie.

McVitie rang the station from the car. "Jack, I'll brief you when I'm back but just to say, Woodruff mentioned that there's a safe in the study. It wasn't spotted before, so I'll go over there now to clock it."

McVitie sat in the car and checked that the notes he had made during his visit to Woodruff were complete. Satisfied, he unscrewed his tartan thermos flask and poured himself a coffee, sipping from the lid that doubled as a cup. He then demolished two digestive biscuits before driving in light traffic to the house in Basing Crescent, where he saw Hobbs's car parked outside.

He found Hobbs in the back garden, examining a telephone cable where it came into the back of the house.

"Look at that, it's been cut," said Hobbs.

"Well," said McVitie, "that explains why the victim didn't call for help." With the information provided by Woodruff, the two detectives quickly located a locked safe in the study, secreted behind a painting.

McVite and Hobbs returned to the police station and reported back to Jack Drummond.

"There is a locked safe in the study that the Bank of England would be proud of," said McVitie. "No sign of anyone trying to force it. We didn't spot it the first time as it's very well hidden behind an oil painting that looks made to measure. A Woodruff special!"

"A pretty substantial beast of a safe," Hobbs added, for emphasis.

"Safes in houses always intrigue me," said Drummond. "Never had one, never want one. Have another go at getting hold of the husband. It would be good to know what he keeps locked away and it might explain why the intruder ransacked the place."

Drummond then rang Brisket at the conference hotel to bring him up to speed with the ongoing investigation. They were making progress and hoped to interview the victim when she came round.

"Well done, keep me informed", said Brisket, "and if you need someone to open the safe, use old Pickett. Best safe cracker out there. Well, I'd better go. I'll ring in when I can. This conference is as dull as dishwater!"

24

Sea Legs

Frank had attended a late evening event at the Savoy and overnighted at the Strand Palace Hotel just across the road. He returned the following morning to see across the square two squad cars parked up in front of his house, one with its blue light still spinning and police tape flapping in the wind. He put down his overnight holdall that still contained everything he needed for a short-notice trip - his 'grab bag' he called it and thought for a moment. Something had kicked off and if he didn't know any better the Firm were probably behind it. He had heard of police entrapment and Sir Peter had contacts everywhere, so he had no intention of walking up the steps to his front door. Paranoia enveloped him.

He was reassured by the thought that the list was protected in the impregnable fire-proof safe in his study. He had the combination in his head and had made a point of not writing it down anywhere. And Amanda, well, they never really got on and after the row before he left no doubt she's gone off to her sisters to stay and moan about what an awful husband she had. Lucky she had never opened that brown envelope with the incriminating photos or he'd have been out on his ear. He patted his chest for his new wallet, his old one having disappeared with his jacket on that fateful night he preferred to forget. In case he had to stay away for some while, he could use what was left of the Trust money and also had access to funds of more questionable provenance from his business dealings. His broker had earned his exorbitant fees for tucking those into untraceable offshore accounts. He was already convinced that the Firm was somehow involved, and the sooner he could get off these shores the safer he would feel. He would avoid the airports which were easier to watch, so he had to make a hasty plan.

He called Rose from the nearest phone box. He then phoned his assistant at the Commission to tell him that he would be out of the UK on a family matter for a few weeks so to ask him to cancel any appointments he had made for the rest of the month. He was getting used to Sir Francis's short notice changes of plan and did not sound greatly surprised. He then hailed a taxi. Across the street a hundred yards away from the police cordon, an ignition key was turned, indicator set and a black tulip MK1 Morris Marina pulled out, trailing three or four cars behind the taxi. In the passenger seat sat a large framed man who kept a careful eye on the road ahead.

Frank waited outside the drab graffitied block of council flats, taxi engine running which thankfully kept the heaters blowing, while Rosario packed a suitcase as instructed, passport and all, before joining him. She threw her arms around him, talking animatedly. The meter ticked over as they headed towards the railway station. The ticket office only had two booths open. They were pushed for time and only just made it, clattering down the steps to the platform, clutching the tickets. The man watched the train depart, noted the time and returned to the car waiting outside.

Frank and Rose had a compartment in the carriage to themselves with a sliding door and she slept on his shoulder, then on his lap, while the train chiddelly-chunked along through the Kent countryside on its way to Dover. From there they caught the Townsend Thoresen to Zeebrugge on the green hulled Free Enterprise V with its distinctive red funnel, the three 12-cylinder diesel engines powering its 5,000 tonnes at 19 knots through the lumpy grey North Sea.

A port officer in Dover had been alerted, double checked the passenger list he had just been handed and called the London number he'd written down.

"Good afternoon, Sir. This is Dover Port Control. The two passengers are on the 14:30 sailing which is under way."

After a bouncy four-hour crossing bashing into the stiff easterly wind, much of it spent shivering on deck as Rose was beside herself to see the sea again, they arrived at the Port of Zeebrugge and by late evening were checking into a small hotel in cold, grey, boring Belgium.

"I love it here in Belgium with you, Frank."

"Well that's good, as we may be here for some while! I'm not sure what the place has to offer apart from beer and chocolate. Bruges sounds like the place to head for."

"Oh, that sounds so romantic!"

"Well it's hardly St Tropez or Casablanca and I doubt that anyone will ever make a film of it. Oh, hang on, you do speak French don't you?"

"You're teasing me again, Frank, I know they speak Flemish over here!"

Frank's face dropped.

* * *

"Bernard, I never should have relied on others. Apologises, old friend, I should have left this to you. The member whom I entrusted with the operation has just telephoned me. It was completely bungled! No list, the wife smashed up in hospital probably capable of picking the thug out of a line-up and police swarming everywhere. I am told that Sir Francis wasn't at home last night which is one blessing given the incompetence of the thugs that screwed up what should have been a simple burglary. We now have a real problem with him blowing the whistle on us."

"Ah, about that Sir. I have certain information that may be of use."

"Go on, Bernard."

"Old habits die hard, I am afraid, and I hope I have not over-stepped. I had Sir Francis shadowed last night by associates of mine from the old days. They are professional and wouldn't have been spotted."

"Ah, the old team from Whitehall days! They're good chaps, the best."

"Sir Francis was, as you say, away from home last night. He returned just before 10am, saw the police activity at his house, made a couple of phone calls from a payphone and went off by taxi. He picked up a girl on the way who loaded a sizable suitcase and they caught a train to Dover. They checked passenger logs for France - nothing - but Dover Port have just confirmed that they boarded a ferry for Zeebrugge. My guess is that he is heading for nearby Bruges to lie low."

"That list would blow the lid off the Firm - judges, military, even a minor royal for god's sake. He can't be allowed to blackmail us, that's our game. Let's nip this in the bud. It'll be like the old days when I still had my big desk in Whitehall. Sending my best agent out to hunt down the traitors! My driver will take you to the airport and my private plane is at your disposal."

25

The Waffle Hunt

They They sat at the small table, Frank sipping coffee, resigned to the possibility of many mornings like this. Rose had picked out some tourist leaflets on the way down to breakfast and was studying them, her finger touching the pictures of waffles dusted with icing sugar and anything else that amused her, in turn eating and waving a piece of raisin bread with the other hand.

"Let's go sightseeing today, Frank. Look!" She held up the picture of a horse and carriage in front of her, as though she was trying on clothes in front of a mirror and inviting comments. She tilted her head and smiled sweetly at him. In the photograph, two laughing tourists with their happy child sat behind the Belgian driver who was trussed up in full costume and a pantomime moustache to match. Even the horses were dressed up for the occasion.

He studied the picture, the boy pointing up excitedly at the Belfry of Bruges that towered above and smiled himself. Rose had a refreshingly simple outlook on life and he imagined what it might be like to have Rose as a companion, a soul mate, no cares in the world. He liked the idea.

"OK," he said, "let's make a deal. Today we do what I would like to do. I need to find a bank to change some travellers cheques…"

Rose pulled a hurt expression.

"And then get something for my back which is giving me gyp again. I wonder why?" he asked with an affectionate smile.

Rose bounced a knowing look back, laced with sympathy, and stroked his arm.

"And tomorrow", he continued, "we go on your horse and cart, if they are doing them this time of year. Everywhere seems pretty deserted out of season." He gestured at the closed and sparsely occupied cafés. "How does that sound?"

She looked pensive. "Can we have waffles today? Pleeeese!"

Her brown eyes melted him. He was a sucker for pretty girls and his resistance was never very strong at the best of times. "OK, we'll go waffle hunting later." Rose brightened and she thrust out her hand to seal the deal. Frank took it gently, turned her hand over and placed a regal kiss next to the ring that was set with a ruby stone in a nest of diamonds. It had been a birthday gift from Frank.

* * *

The private five-passenger Cessna Citation business jet touched down at Ostend airport, sixteen miles from the city of Bruges. Bernard had a telegram waiting for him. His old associates had been busy and it gave the name of a hotel in Steenstraat Quarter where he now headed. A cold drizzle was falling. He checked in to a guest house across the wet cobbled street and moved the armchair so that he had line of sight to the entrance of the small hotel where Sir Francis had booked in. He had some of his old field kit with him including his trusty field monocular.

Bernard had been recruited by Sir Peter after the war to join a newly formed small covert team of ex-commandos, a section of the British Intelligence Service answerable to Whitehall but never legitimised by the British Government. Its purpose was to track down and quietly exterminate British traitors in hiding on the continent. The goal was to prevent allegiances being forged or military secrets being sold to foreign powers in the sensitive post war and cold war eras. More than thirty operations were undertaken offshore before the squad, which never officially existed, was unofficially disbanded. Bernard had stuck loyally by Sir Peter ever since and his special skills continued to prove useful.

The city was a hitman's dream. A maze of narrow streets, vertigo inducing buildings, food to choke on, a canal to drown in, bridges to fall off, ancient steps to fall down, faulty electrics in hotel bathrooms. The ways and means were endless. This would have to look like an accident, which would be a better outcome than leaving a body with a bullet in the head that would excite the local police and attract too much attention. He was a skilled highly trained operative in his day. If it didn't feel right, then he would wait patiently until the next chance presented itself. To strike, he needed to be in the right at the right time, aided by a distraction or confusion. The execution should be swift and decisive with a clear exit route and he must be prepared to abandon the plan at any time. From what he had seen of the couple so far through his monocular, they were there to enjoy the sights of this ancient city and an opportunity would present itself.

And it did, the very next day. An elderly man in a cape carrying a tatty leather bag tailed them to Markt, the fine open square in the tourist heart of the city, and watched them board the carriage and the horse trot off on its well-trodden route through the scenic streets. He sported a Poirothian moustache finely twisted at each end. He dipped into his bag as he sat on the empty bench by the sign advertising horse-drawn tours in the near-deserted square, waiting for their return. The weather was cold again but now dry and bright and the unlikely couple huddled together under a blanket, as the driver picked up the reins. Rose revelled in the romance of the ride, squeaking with delight and pointing out indifferent landmarks. Frank was willing the ride to be over as the motion made him queasy and jarred his tender back. He tried to put on a brave face for her as they held onto each other.

The hooves clattered back over the cobbles, the sound ringing off the tall buildings. The driver pulled on the reins, easing them to a halt.

As they returned to the same corner of the square, a gentleman in a cape looked over his newspaper at the approaching horse and stood up apparently charmed by the scene, walking stiffly up to greet the animal. The driver positioned the step and took special care in helping the pretty Rosario in her unseasonably short skirt to the ground, while Frank waited his turn, standing erect up on the carriage and swinging his arms and hips to stretch and relieve his aching back. A small boisterous cluster of local youths walked by.

The gentleman in the cape mentally checked, "Position, timing, distraction, now for confusion." He had prepared. As the youths crossed in front of the horse, firecrackers exploded under the horse's legs, echoing like shots around the square, causing pigeons to fly skywards. The beast reared in its reins and bolted. Frank was hurled backwards, flung high out of the carriage and before Rosario's scream had fully expelled, he had landed, cracking his skull as he crashed down on the road in a heap. The driver ran after his livelihood, the spooked horse and carriage, that was charging on down the street out of control.

Fortuitously the elderly man was a doctor. He hastened to the body while in perfect French cursing *les enfants* for their silly pranks and knelt over it.

He commanded the hysterical Rose and one or two onlookers who had started to approach to stand well back, pulling his stethoscope from his doctor's bag. Concealed by his winter cape, he observed the pulsing blood loss that trickled away around the cobbles. He leant down as though to check for breathing and vital signs but was really frisking him for anything concealed in his jacket, finding only his passport, hotel keys and wallet.

Frank's eyes rolled open for an instant and horror crossed his face with recognition.

"Sir Peter sends his regards," the gentleman hissed in his ear in best butler-speak and skilfully snapped the skinny neck with his massive hands before he rose from the lifeless corpse, shaking his head in sorrow. He appealed with outstretched hands to an idle waiter in a long apron who was standing smoking at a doorway looking on, *"Appelez une ambulance! Il est mort,"* he exclaimed theatrically.

The waiter had gone inside and soon came back out with a dumpy cook who waddled across, hands clasped to the side of his face. He gesticulated wildly, directing others to join him, a small huddle of concerned faces gathering around the body.

"Time to go," thought Bernard. He put his arms around the distraught Rose, her tear streaked face crumpled and sobbing, and briskly escorted her back to her hotel room. There he administered a strong sedative from his bag that she gratefully took but would never wake up from. He did a thorough search of the room and took a different route back to his car, peeling off the moustache and throwing the distinctive cape into a public bin on the way, as sirens wailed from a distance.

26

Capri

Drummond had given Dean the job of tracking down the husband of the victim through his office. Dean had telephoned Sir Francis's assistant at the Commission.

"Yes, Sir Francis attended a business event in London on the night in question." He gave the detective the details of the venue in case he wished to verify it. Dean made some notes with the phone received wedged between his shoulder and ear.

"Do you know where we can contact him?" Dean asked.

The assistant explained that he was out of contact, which was not unusual for him, and couldn't provide any further information on his whereabouts.

Brisket had spoken with Drummond and by the sound of it he would not be returning to the station for a while. Brisket explained that the conference was over but he had arrived home in agony. His doctor had signed off with a grumbling appendix. If it didn't clear up after a couple of weeks' rest then the doctor had threatened him that his appendix would have to be whipped out. Brisket admitted to Drummond that he was not a good patient and would keep a low profile, although he still wanted to keep a weather eye on progress and would ring Drummond as usual for status reports.

Drummond was enjoying using Brisket's room and could be seen through the blinds with his feet up on the desk, something that Brisket would never have allowed, deep in discussion with McVitie. They had been checking through the work rota to prioritise the team's manpower to the handful of cases they were working on.

A knock at the door and a breathless Morgan entered. "Hello hello!" jested McVitie, "You look like the cat that's got the cream!"

Her face flushed beacon red and she addressed Drummond, "Sir, I think I'm on to something."

Morgan had completed the extra door-to-door visits and had finally struck lucky. Her last call was to No 78 Wellington Place. The occupant clearly remembered looking out at the street in the small hours on the night of the attack. He had been awake and up reading when he had been disturbed by someone parked outside with their engine idling. He thought it unneighbourly at that time of night and the running engine was making his sash windows rattle. He was suspicious and paid particular attention, noting down the make - a brown Ford Capri - and car registration number. At 3:15am he saw a man running out of the alleyway from Basing Crescent and jump into the car before setting off at high speed.

Drummond interrupted, "3:15am, that ties in nicely with the account by the taxi-driver. Did he get a look at the man on foot?"

"Unfortunately the angle from the upstairs window restricted the view of his face, but he got a glimpse." Morgan checked her notepad. "White male, possibly mid-thirties, athletic build, thick neck, short hair, sideburns, dark jacket possibly black leather. He was wearing gloves."

"That trumps the hazy description we had from the couple in the taxi," offered McVitie.

Jack Drummond looked thoughtful. "Any mention of a weapon?"

"I pressed him on whether he was carrying anything and he was adamant that the man was empty handed. Sir, could he have disposed of a weapon in the alleyway?"

"Possibly. Well done, Morgan. Dougie, get a uniform to check the alleyway and adjacent gardens in case he lobbed anything over the wall."

Morgan stood her ground.

"Anything else?" Drummond inquired.

"Sir, he also gave me a detailed description of the driver who got out of his car to have a ciggie."

They quickly established that the plates on the Ford Capri were false. The witness came into the station, gave a full statement, and sat down with the police artist who put together what was believed to be a good sketch of the driver.

"Jack, PC Snow has just called in." McVitie continued. "He did a thorough search of the gardens that side on to the alleyway and couldn't find anything but..."

"That's disappointing," chipped in Drummond. "He must have dumped it, he was seen carrying a weapon when he left but ..."

"Jack, he did!"

"Go on!"

178

"Snow had the nouse to lift a drain grille in the alley and found a fireside poker stuck in there. I think we can assume it was the weapon used in the assault, probably picked up after he entered the house. He's bagged it up and we'll get it checked for prints."

The results on the weapon came back the next day in a blue covered file. Drummond was disappointed that there was nothing unsmudged on the brass handle but among those on the iron shaft were fingerprints matching Amanda Castle. He read the report out loud, "Blood and hair on the heavy point were also a blood group match, confirming without a shadow of doubt that it was used in the attack. From the positions of the fingers, she must have grasped the end of the poker as she fought off her assailant in close combat."

"Brave girl," murmured Drummond, as he digested the report.

The image and descriptions of the two suspects were shared around the station and distributed by police courier to the Greater London police stations. By lunchtime they had a positive lead from Tooting police station on Mitcham Road. They identified the driver as Joshua Leonard. He had been under suspicion as the getaway on an armed raid in Stockwell, but they hadn't had the evidence to make it stick. His current whereabouts were unknown but they recalled that he liked visiting Soho's bars and clubs in London's red-light district.

Jack Drummond paced the incident room. Albert had pinned a street map to the board and had added images and notes of people of interest and witnesses. "Driver?" now had "Joshua Leonard" against it. At the top was a photo of Amanda Castle, victim with the date and time of the attack. Lines were drawn in chalk to names and notes.

Drummond said, "New Lad, add in against Woodruff's name, 'innocent prints, revealed safe, Beatrice Du Pont connection'."

Drummond looked thoughtful. "Morgan, pay a visit to Du Pont. If she has visited the house then there's just a chance she might have seen someone casing the joint. Take some pictures to see if anything jogs her memory, but mind how you go. I remember she can be quite prickly.

"I think we should pay the Lizard a call," Drummond continued. "Hobbs, his number will be in the informants card index. The Lizard dished the dirt on the Grayson twins a few years back and in return the squad saved him from doing a stretch as an accessory. He owes us some favours. He owns half a dozen sleaze pits around Soho and knows the low-lifes in the sex trade better than we do. Set up a meeting on his territory - he might be more forthcoming than if we bring him into the station."

* * *

The elegant car rolled quietly alongside the man in the raincoat and trilby, keeping pace with his brisk strides. It parked neatly ahead by the kerbside twenty yards ahead to intercept him. The rear window of the Rolls Royce Silver Shadow wound down and the occupant beckoned the walker inside who closed the door with a soft "chunk".

The gentleman with white whiskers and Prince of Wales checks was in no mood for pleasantries and fixed the visitor with a watery eye. He clicked a button. The privacy screen slid up shielding any audible conversation from the driver.

"Your people messed up. They didn't find it and in the

process managed to throw the wife out of an upstairs window. I'm at a loss for words." Sir Peter went on, "I hear she is recovering in St Mary's so there is a chance she could identify the attacker and open up a can of worms. May I make it perfectly clear that I hold you personally responsible for cleaning up this mess and bringing that dratted list to me."

The man in the mackintosh said nothing but looked alarmed.

"There's no reason to look uncomfortable. Your hands are hardly clean! You know we always look after our own as long as they play the game! And, my friend, it is your turn at the wicket."

"And ... Sir Francis?" said the man, hesitantly.

"That problem has been dealt with. We are finished here."

27

Chicken Soup

T alisker put two shiny ten pence coins into the only working drinks dispenser he had found on the second floor of the accident and emergency unit. The new coinage had only been out for a few years and was still a novelty. He still pined for the green pounds, old brown ten bob notes, shillings and the brass threepenny bits. "Decimalisation, whatever next?" he muttered to himself. "They'll be getting us to drive on the right side of the road before we know it."

He pushed the buttons for tea, white, two sugars. The coins rattled down and he waited while the beige plastic cup filled. Taking a sip, he winced at the repulsive hot liquid, tasting vaguely of tea and strongly of chicken soup. He walked back down the maze of corridors to find the stairs back down to the Daffodil wing where his empty chair was positioned on guard outside Amanda Castle's private room.

She lay in the hospital bed beneath tightly tucked-in sheets, heavily sedated. The general anaesthetic had been potent and the surgery complex. She was unaware of the drip bags, the array of tubes and wires and the bleeping of the monitors. She was oblivious to the coming and going of the post-operative nursing staff who had been in at regular intervals until she had stabilised and now visited every twenty minutes to check on her and mark up the chart that hung at the foot of the bed.

Crazy woozy dream sequences mingled with moments of near wakefulness. She dreamt of flying over the bannisters as a child. Then she fell over in the playground with bleeding knees and ran to her mother in a little chocolate box cottage where she was working at her sewing machine. When she turned to her daughter her mother had turned into a hideous witch. After some time, she surfaced slowly from her state and became aware of light moving as a shadow passed across the window blinds. Her eyelids were too heavy to lift. A smell of cologne pricked her senses but it was not one that she knew. Was that a kiss on her cheek, on her lips? A fleeting feeling of happiness overcame her, hoping for rescue from her nightmare. Then the hands encircled her throat and squeezed. The screaming and the thrashing were trapped inside her head as life drained from her.

Hospital porters pushed gurneys, nurses went about their brisk business, phones rang unanswered. To break the monotony and dizzying effect of looking at the abstract picture hanging opposite of ambiguous stairs leading up - or was it down? - Talisker had read his tabloid newspaper from cover to cover. He had resorted to completing the crossword but for one clue that eluded him.

* * *

Morgan sat at the restaurant table cupping her second tea and picking up the crumbs of the shortbread from the blue and white china plate with a dampened finger. Her contact was late. There was one other table at this early sitting, occupied by four women in their thirties. They obviously knew each other well, talking freely, fast and competitively, hardly pausing for breath as conversations bounced from one to another, filling their corner of the restaurant, first the antics of their kids, then the foibles and failings of their males, then wider views on life and living in their small worlds. Empathy, humour, bonding - all fulfilling the need to belong. Morgan was a little jealous, reflecting that she was working all hours, with little social life outside the force.

The room was starting to fill up. The tinny doorbell sounded again as the door opened and she at once recognised the elegant shape of the lady who now stepped in. Eyes turned. She was out of place here. Her heels clicked purposefully across the tiled floor. She pulled out the chair to join Morgan, draping her sable-trimmed coat over the back of the chair next to her. Sitting bolt upright, Beatrice Du Pont directed her order to the hovering waitress and spoke in clipped frostiness.

"A dry white wine."

"Thank you for coming, Beatrice. I was worried that you might have changed your mind."

Beatrice Du Pont fixed Morgan with a cool avian stare. She scowled at Morgan and almost spat out, "Your type, you police, all the same. Why should I help you when you ruined my husband's reputation?" She pulled out a packet of lilac coloured cigarettes, placed one in a holder, lit up and a thin trail of smoke snaked up.

Morgan waited.

"Dragged him through the courts when he was innocent all along. The papers had a field day. It was like feeding time at the zoo and it made a humiliating public spectacle. We lived in Cheam Village for goodness sake! He was a mild man. You lot broke him and I don't easily forgive."

"Ma'am, that had nothing to do with me, it was before my time. But I need your help. I was trying to be considerate and thought you would prefer that we met somewhere normal, but we can do this at the station instead?"

Du Pont flared her nostrils. If Morgan could read her expression then she didn't seem ready to make a quick exit. She remained seated and puckering her lips took a long sip of wine.

"I have a couple of questions please," went on Morgan. "We understand that you know someone at an employment agency who placed a housekeeper in Basing Crescent." She looked at her notes and read out the name in full.

"Ah yes, I take an interest in high society, as you may know, and the lady of the house, Lady Amanda, is an acquaintance. We also share the same bartender in an establishment in Kensington but that's as far as it goes. She seemed deeply unhappy and confided in me on that one occasion. Her rat of a husband plays away, if you get my drift. She questioned whether he might be having an affair. Well," she continued, lighting up again, and adopting a hushed confidential tone, "I know the owner of the employment agency where the housekeeper came from," she smiled triumphantly. "She reckons that pretty thing is her Frank's bit on the side!"

"Thank you, that's interesting." Morgan thought it through. So, Rose and Sir Francis were an item. Lady Amanda would have been in a terrible state if she suspected and was saying nothing to her husband. It's not surprising she hit the bottle. It doesn't mean that Rose had a motive to kill her, although her husband might have been happy to see his wife dead. But his office at the Commission gave him a cast iron alibi, he was at an event, which Albert had corroborated. The only real lead is the driver and photofit of the attacker. She looked up at Beatrice who was stubbing out in the ashtray.

"We need an ID on a couple of suspects, Beatrice, just in case you may have seen anyone hanging around outside the house on occasions when you have visited it. It's a longshot but may I show you some pictures?"

Without waiting for an answer, Morgan pulled a buff-coloured envelope from her bag and she slid out half a dozen photos including Leonard and the artist's impression of the attacked, laying them in a line on the tablecloth. "Do you recognise anyone here?"

Du Pont didn't look down at first. She was in the middle of a tropical moment and started to fan herself frantically with the menu card, her skin rouged and glistening below the neckline. Morgan was tuned in to her. Her mum suffered the same way and she poured Du Pont a glass of chilled water from the jug.

"Thank you, my dear." As her thermostat settled she studied the girl in front of her. She took in Morgan's cheap clothes, her blotchy youthful skin, the cheap jewellery and tatty shoulder bag over her chair. Unlike some of the police she had come across, this young detective seemed kind and earnest, not mocking or impudent. It was her pleading hazel brown eyes that touched her the most. They conveyed sincerity and genuine compassion, things she had not seen in a while. Du Pont had lost her husband in that sordid investigation but the same police station had lost one of their own in the final showdown when one of the real villains had pulled a gun. They were even. She drained her glass and dropped her gaze to the table.

* * *

Back in the hospital corridor, Talisker sipped the drink and closed his eyes to mull over the missing word. Seven letters, second letter "a", fourth letter "d". "Use quay to fish". Talisker frowned then smiled to himself, dipped under his chair and retrieved his newspaper from among his discarded plastic cups, sweet wrappers and crisp packets. Taking the pencil stub, he had left over his ear, he scratched the answer, Sardine.

He looked up with satisfaction as the door opened behind him and a figure in a surgeon's outfit left the room. The doctor must have gone in while he was getting a drink.

Something struck Talisker as a bit odd. The shoes were shiny black Oxford shoes, slightly muddy on the edge of the soles, not a match for the medical clothing he was wearing.

"Any change in her condition, Doctor?"

Startled, the man turned and looked him full in the face.

Tally was good at facial recognition and could confidently pick people out of a crowd across a street or in a football stadium. He recognised that face even behind the surgical mask. Talisker rose from the chair to challenge him. He saw a flash of steel and felt a hard thump below his rib cage which surged upwards, slicing through his guts. As the blade was pulled out from his belly, he crumpled forward to hit the polished floor.

28

Blue Nun

The needle dropped, the speaker crackled and the familiar chords strummed to the opening track by her favourite group. Morgan mouthed the upbeat happy lyrics that she knew by heart, but emotion welled up again and tears streaked her face, splashing on the album cover on her lap in time to the first few bars of the music. She wiped the record sleeve with the cuff of her baggy jumper, put it to one side on the sofa, drew her knees up, and cried softly into the cushion she cuddled.

She had looked up to Tally and though she had not always realised it at the time, he had always looked out for her. When the teasing from the men in the station had got too personal, he would distract them with other targets and deflect their unwanted attentions. When she was teamed up on late night surveillance operations, confined in a rank cold car into the small hours, Tally would share his flask of tea and chips. They would swap stories about what she had seen on the telly, what they had seen at the flicks, his football team's chances of winning the league or being relegated - just normal stuff. Squashed together as they were in the usual unmarked Morris Minor 1000, he had always behaved like a gentleman, unlike the other guys with their monotonous dirty jokes, lewd comments and occasional unwelcome gropes.

Her mum had warned her and tried to persuade her to get into an honourable profession like nursing or teaching. But she loved this job on the whole and wanted to succeed more than anything, to prove that she could cut it like the men. Six months ago she had filled in the forms to apply for a move to CID. She was more than qualified on paper to go for it but the forms had sat in a buff coloured envelope buried in her desk drawer, waiting until she felt ready to accept almost certain rejection. It was still a man's world, where women who made it were actresses, singers and porn stars. But there were rays of hope. She followed the news and if a woman could be elected as leader of the opposition party in place of Ted Heath then perhaps one day she might make it to Detective Inspector.

But good old Tally. He was tough on the outside but like a kindly uncle within. That wink to her that kept her spirits up when she was down, always generous with his excessive food supplies that he brought with him to maintain his fourteen stone ballast. He was the only one who stayed after work with her, making paper chains to decorate the office at Christmas. The long tales he told in those nights at watch, probably all fictitious, but they would keep her smiling and make the time pass easily as they waited for a suspect to give themselves away with a twitch of the curtains or to be caught red-handed with a holdall of stolen goods.

Janice Morgan drained the last of the sweet white German wine but it hadn't numbed the pain she felt at losing one of the good guys. She would have to look out for herself from now on. And she vowed to get justice for him.

* * *

The mood in the station was sombre and business like. This was now a double-murder investigation and they had lost one of their own. DCI Drummond had briefed Brisket by phone. He would leave Drummond to run the investigations but wanted daily updates. He saw Drummond as his number two and when his time came to retire next year, Drummond expected that he would be put forward to fill his shoes.

The hospital staff had been interviewed by Dean and Albert. They had found a locker room with muddy footprints where the clothes had been stolen and matched these to prints in the shrubbery outside the postoperative wing, men's size tens, but there the trail ended.

Morgan's interview with Du Pont had given them more background on the household. There was a part-time house-keeper and it seemed that Amanda Castle had turned a blind eye to her husband's affair. She did not pick anyone from the photos she was shown.

Drummond said, "We are now dealing with a double murder inquiry. The husband can't be traced. I want that safe opened." He thought back to an earlier call with the boss. Brisket wants us to use Pickett. In his words, 'He's the best safe-cracker in the business'. Get him down to the house, pronto!"

* * *

The study was lined with fine books meticulously organised

and neatly displayed. Ornately framed artwork hung on the walls. Under one piece, a little grey-faced man dressed in a blue work overall squatted down and opened the heavy tool bag he had carried in, unfolding a tarpaulin sheet under a painting of a woman looking down at him with wry amusement. Digging further into the bag, he set out on the sheet a row of instruments, mallets, hand saws, skeleton keys, a vice, clamps and hand drills. A second bag leant against the wall containing his welding and cutting equipment. Hopefully, he would not be needing that, but he had come prepared. Standing up, he slid a stubby pencil over his ear and looked across at the detective. "I'm ready." McVitie nodded back. Pickett resettled the glasses on the end of his nose and set to work.

The picture was discreetly hinged on the left side, and by releasing a catch on the right, it swung back to reveal the safe door, the Matisse now turned face to the wall. The safe was a high specification.

There was a commotion downstairs and authoritative voices. The job had taken two hours so far and heading out to his van after breaking tools, Pickett had resorted to fire up the acetylene torch. He had explained that there was a risk that he incinerates the contents of the safe. He had one of the policemen help him to carry up the two tanks, one blue and full of concentrated oxygen and a red tank of acetylene gas. He laid floor covers under the safe to protect against the molten slag and positioned the fire extinguisher within reach. He took off the protective valve covers, mounted the regulators and checked the hose connections.

"Right, I need everyone out of the house. Unless you want to dig metal out of your eyes when I get started. I'll call when it's safe to come in, pardon the pun!"

He pulled the welding shield over his face and pulled on the gauntlets. He opened the acetylene valve an eighth of a turn and lit the gas, adding more until the flame stopped producing smoke and feathered out. He then opened the oxygen valve to intensify the heat, adding more slowly until the blue preheat flames formed sharp cones. The oxygen was needed to intensify the heat. Acrid smoke filled the study as the acetylene torch cut through the steel, the metal glowing cherry red, until he had at last cut through the bolts.

He closed the valves to turn off the flame. He listened at the doorway. All quiet, the police had gone downstairs. He opened the safe door. Inside he found jewellery, cash, title deeds, a small oil painting, share certificates and then, yes, an envelope addressed to a solicitor in the event of his death or disappearance. That must be it. Pickett pocketed the envelope, left the safe door ajar for the detectives to sift through what was left and called down the stairs to say that his work was done and could he have a hand carrying his equipment back to his van again.

* * *

The policeman sat at a table in the corner, his folded mac and trilby placed beside him, in the tiny Seven Stars in Carey Street. It was an ancient building and old maritime pub in the days when the River Fleet was navigable. The pub had survived the Great Fire of London and was resiliently quirky, attracting members of the legal profession, local office workers, eccentrics and tourists. A steep narrow staircase challenged those who had enjoyed a long liquid lunch while discussing case law or putting the world to rights.

The tiny pub was a familiar haunt for him, located round the back of the Royal Courts of Justice near Fleet Street and conveniently just a few doors away from the old fashioned barbers shop he frequented, who invariably asked him if he would like a friction and something for the weekend. He was halfway through his pint of Double Diamond which was working wonders when a short man in an olive corduroy jacket came over to join him, pulling up a chair.

"Hello Guv, long time no see!"

"Well, did you get it?"

Typical, he thought. No small talk at all, always straight to business. He probably won't even buy me a beer. "Here," said Pickett as he pushed the envelope across to him.

He read the writing on the front of the sealed envelope. "Excellent, you've done well." He slid it inside his jacket and then pulled out his wallet.

Pickett furtively counted the notes below the table and was pleasantly surprised at the generosity.

"It's a thank you from me."

"Just like the old days, Guv!"

"Right, I'd better make myself scarce but do get yourself a pint of best before you go."

* * *

Amanda Castle's sister was picked up by Morgan and a WPC to learn that her injured sibling had been murdered in her hospital bed. She was driven to the hospital morgue to formally identify her. As the sheet was lifted to reveal her face, she had broken down by all accounts and now sat wretched in Interview Room Two waiting to assist the police with their enquiries. Morgan interviewed her with Albert, the squad's newest recruit, in attendance.

They found out from the sister that Amanda and her husband lived in the Basing Crescent house in a sexless, sham marriage, eating together, watching the nine o'clock news and then separating to their own bedrooms. It was pretty unhappy from what she saw. She did not believe that Frank would ever lay a finger on her and while he was selfish and carried his title like a millstone, he was not a murderer. Amanda had confided in her that she knew that he had been having an occasional fling with the attractive housekeeper, Rose, but she said that was only to be expected when a man was not getting his oats. Amanda had never let on to him that she knew and was quietly content with the arrangement. "We can't locate either Sir Francis or Rosario. Do you have any idea where either of them might be?"

Amanda's sister smiled, "If he has run away for a while then in all likelihood he will have taken Rose with him. Good luck to them, I say! He was never cut out to be a businessman and might be happier living a simple life where no one can find them."

Morgan nodded, thanked her for her openness and arranged for her to be dropped back home. Albert just looked perplexed.

29

Mind The Gap

Jerry was making plans. He would have to confront the vicar but he felt ill-prepared. Seeing him again preaching in church had turned his stomach and he felt vulnerable. The man had power over him.

He knew what he had to do and headed off alone for his old familiar stamping ground. According to word on the streets, there was a pub near Soho Square where people said they would sell you a pint of lager and pretty much any handgun of your choosing. He remembered the name he had to ask for.

It was a quiet lunchtime. As he opened the door to the public bar his nostrils filled with the smell of smoke, urine and slopped beer. A few tables were occupied by punkish looking lads hunched over their drinks and some older characters sat quietly, probably remembering the place in better times but unable to break the habit. Jerry bought a packet of cigarettes from the landlady and as she gave him the change he asked, "Is Rumpelstiltskin about?" It sounded ridiculous, even to him.

She looked him up and down. "Never heard of him."

"Are you sure, I'm here to make a trade?"

"Is he expecting you?"

"Yes," Jerry said, hoping it would sound convincing.

She pushed a button that rang a bell somewhere else in the building.

"OK, up you go." She opened the bar flap. "Up the stairs, first door on the right." There was an alert alsatian behind the bar. It bared its fangs at Jerry as she held him back with his chain collar.

The aroma was no better upstairs and he wondered if they had a problem with the drains. He found the open door and entered the sparsely furnished office where a man sat, his back to him gazing out of a dirty window.

In one movement, Jerry was taken off balance, there was a sharp pain in his side and a firm hand clamped around his throat. Whoever had been waiting behind the door, which had just been kicked closed, had a grip of iron. He strained to breathe.

The chair turned and he was greeted by a balding man with grey complexion in a pale-yellow shirt who studied him.

"Well, he's not the Old Bill. So, what's he doing here? If he is sitting here then he must have made an appointment. But I had no notice of anyone coming."

"I lied," hissed Jerry, his windpipe constricted.

"Ah good, an honest crook! Much better than the fibbing sort. Sit him down."

The big man frisked him and released the pressure on his neck. Jerry doubled up and coughed as he gasped for air, turning to look back at the big man towering over him who was grinning, baring broken teeth with a gap in the middle and broken incisors. They both had a double-take.

"Shrimp?"

Realisation dawned. "Minder?"

He started to laugh, bass notes resonating from his massive frame. He had more missing teeth than Jerry remembered but still had that shark-like appearance and the same gold neck chain.

The Gunsmith looked at his new bodyguard quizzically.

"I know him," said the Minder. "Worked as a mule a few streets away and he did a moonlight flit. Shame as he was a hard worker." He turned to Jerry.

"Trouble seems to catch up with you, Shrimp! But it looks as though life is treating you better. Nice clothes. Now … sit!"

Jerry sat awkwardly on the plastic chair in front of the bald man and cleared his swollen throat. "I'd like to buy a gun. A pistol. Please."

"Do you have money with you?"

Jerry nodded.

The Gunsmith squinted at him for a long moment. He pulled out a pair of off-white gloves and slipped them onto his delicate hairless hands. He pulled a curtain aside and opened the treble-locked steel cabinet that stood behind. A smell of gun oil added to the drain aroma and the whiff of Minder's cheap aftershave.

"Ah!" he exclaimed. He reached to the back and returned to the desk with a metal box which he unlocked with another key, placing the contents on the desk. With gloved hands he slid the pistol out of the bag.

He had the hint of an accent, German perhaps, that Jerry had not spotted before. "This is a war trophy so has never been used on the streets. It's clean. A Beretta M1934. Full working order and serviced by me. This one is a collector's piece. It's Italian if you didn't know and has a blowback action.

Good reliable piece."

He slipped out the empty magazine and waved it at Jerry. "Takes seven rounds." He snapped the magazine back in. "Pass me your wallet," said the Gunsmith.

The Minder put a hand on Jerry's shoulder as encouragement. The contents of Jerry's wallet were counted into two piles, one big, the other smaller.

"Right, you would like to buy?"

Jerry nodded.

The Gunsmith held up a few to the light at random to check for watermarks. He stabbed the tall pile with his finger. "This, for the Beretta. OK?"

Jerry nodded. He had brought far too much but as luck would have it, it was just the right sum. His 'adopted father' would cringe if he knew. "Oh, and the ammo? It comes with ammo, yes?"

The Gunsmith looked at him, then at the smaller pile of cash and unlocked the drawer of the desk and put a box of rounds on the desk, sweeping the remainder of Jerry's money away like a croupier.

"Thank you for your business. You'll leave through a different door. Show him out."

"Well, see you then," Jerry said to Minder as the back exit was opened for him.

"No Shrimp. You won't and you didn't," his face breaking into another big bad smile.

* * *

"Bernard, I am pleased to say that the list is now in my possession. The safe was cracked and our policeman has just delivered it to me by hand. It seems that he has finally done his job properly."

"Yes, that's good news indeed."

"Will you lay a fire for me, I'm feeling a touch chilly this evening. Oh, and when you are done, a whisky and water would be good for the old bones."

"Certainly, Sir. Will that be all?"

"For now Bernard. For now."

Bernard returned with the tray and settled the whisky and the water carafe on the table next to the armchair. The old man had drifted off to sleep in front of the warming fire, his foot up on a stool and a smile set on his face.

They had been through many skirmishes together over the years and he was hugely fond of his master. He laid a tartan rug over the old man's knees and crossed to the fire. Flames had partly scorched the unopened envelope. Bernard lifted the poker and pushed the list deeper into the heart of the fire until it was engulfed, turning the paper to crispy black leaf before it shredded into ash. The butler nodded to himself at a job well done. He set the fire guard and quietly retreated leaving Sir Peter to finish his forty winks.

IV

PART FOUR

30

Picture House

Hobbs had arranged the meeting. Taking the ticket from the booth in the cramped foyer from the listless ticket seller, he pushed open the inner door to the old Soho picture house. It took a while to adjust to the darkness. It was almost empty but his rendezvous could be with any one of a dozen or so shadows seated in the murk. Smoke rose under the beam of the projector and out of focus bodies writhed on the screen to non-descript continental music, interspersed with grunts and moans. Looking back along the rows of seats, a cigarette ember glowed a couple of times and he made out a distinctive hunched shape behind it. He eased past a drunk and took a seat on the row just behind his informant.

"Nice to see you after all this time," hissed the Lizard. "It must be something important to tempt you into my parlour."

"Can we go somewhere quieter? I need to show you some photos."

"That's the best offer I have had all day, my love! Leave it fifteen minutes as I don't want to …," his eyes were drawn to the writing on the screen and the tip of his tongue absent-mindedly traced his top lip to left and right and back again. "I don't want to miss the … climax. Those two, look aren't they adorable? My proteges! Taught them all they know. Yes, go back to the foyer and wait for me by the black door under the poster that'll make you blush. I'll join you in the cash office when I'm ready."

Hobbs found a phone box and rang into the station.

"Got him, Sir. Lizard gave a positive ID on Joshua Leonard. And better than that, Leonard regularly visits his club off Soho Square as roadie for their house musicians. They'll be playing next on Saturday evening, in three days' time. The Lizard will make sure we get into the club without a hitch but after that it's up to us."

"Good work, Hobbs. If we can get a confession from Leonard then we should be one step away from the killer. I'll work up a plan and see you back here."

* * *

Word had got out in the squad and there was a more upbeat atmosphere with the positive news from Hobbs. Stress levels were mirrored by the thickness of cigarette smoke that hung in the air.

"Morgan a word. Close the door!" said Drummond.

"Yes Sir?"

"We are putting plans in place for a sting operation at the Velvet Club. The aim is to get Leonard to talk on tape and betray the name and whereabouts of the Basing Crescent attacker." Drummond paused and shifted in his chair.

"Morgan, I know that you and Talisker were close, you looked up to him and he wanted to see you right. Tally was a close friend of mine as well and I feel I owe it to him to do the same for you. That's why I feel bad about asking you to do this but we need eyes on the ground and you're the only one, um, capable of this role."

"You mean I'm the only officer with tits and you need me to fake a hooker? Thanks Sir, and yes I want to do this and help catch that …. the killer."

"You'll have a wire and if it gets rough then we'll have Dean and Hobbs outside ready to pull you out. The Lizard owns the club. The code to get them to pull you out is 'Tiger Feet'. OK?"

Morgan took a deep breath. "Yes, Sir, I'm in."

"Good, good! I'll ring Brisket now to run through the details and get it authorised. I'll then announce it to the team so that we can run through everything." As his hand reached for the telephone, Morgan stopped at the door and turned back to him.

"Sir, do we trust the Lizard?"

"Do we have a choice?"

Drummond called everyone together in the incident room.

"Right everyone. All leave is cancelled this weekend. We're setting up a sting as we need some hard evidence on Leonard who is the key to finding the suspect. We have a lead that Leonard, the driver of the Basing Crescent attacker, is going to be at the Velvet club in Greek Street. We want him to spill the beans on tape to whoever he dropped off at Basing Crescent, let's call him Mister X for now. Mister X is believed to have carried out the break in and attempted murder at Basing

Crescent. He then returned to commit a double murder at the hospital, finishing off Amanda Castle as she lay in her bed to prevent her identifying him as her attacker and then," Drummond paused, aware that his voice had just trembled. He gripped the desk with both hands, head bowed, regained his composure and looking up at his colleagues continued sombrely. "And then carrying out the murder of our very own Talisker."

The room of expectant faces was eerily quiet, apart from an unanswered ringing phone from the unmanned office next door. There was no banter, none of the usual joking. The team had taken Talisker's murder hard.

"I don't need to emphasise," Drummond went on, "that we have a lot riding on this. Leonard is probably just a pawn in this, but he is the key. He is the link to identifying the main assailant and there may be others up the food chain if he was doing this to order."

Albert had his hand up.

"Yes, New Lad?"

"It's Albert, Sir. Why don't we just pull in Leonard for questioning. He was ID'ed by one of the neighbours, so can't we just ask them to pick him out of a line-up?"

"Good question, New Lad. Well, we don't yet have anything connecting Leonard to Mister X. Yes, he was seen standing by his car having a smoke in the early hours about the same time as the attack. Yes we have the car registration, but that's just circumstantial. It's not enough to tie him to the crime. If we pull him in now, his solicitor will just tell him to stay schtum. He'll be released without charge and he'll alert Mister X who we won't see for dust. No, we need evidence on tape and we think he'll be more talkative to a pretty girl in a bar than across the table in front of my ugly mug and a two-way mirror."

"DC Morgan here is going to scrub up and draw in the target on Saturday night. We believe that the target will be there as a roadie for the band."

"Yes, Sir."

"Dean and Hobbs, you'll be on the wire."

"Everyone, I don't want any screw ups. I have Brisket breathing down my neck. That was probably him ringing just now."

31

The Sting

The club was off Soho Square. She was dressed up like a street-girl, not her style at all. She had to borrow the clothes. A short, tasseled skirt and leather jacket from her neighbour Jackie and the go-go boots, make-up and false eyelashes from her sister. Glancing across at the parked Rover P6 that had dropped her off earlier a few streets away, she spoke under her breath: "Tango Victor Three, can you hear me over there? Dean? Hobbs?" After a short pause, the courtesy light flicked on and off, affirming. She thought of how she would much rather be sitting in a cosy car, flask of tea and digestives to relieve the boredom. "It's almost eleven. I'm going in."

The doorman stepped from the glitzy doorway, blocking her way. "Move on now, love. This is a members only club."

"Sergeant Pepper invited me," she said, smiling at him and batting her false eyelashes in the hope that it looked alluring. The bulk nodded and shifted to one side. The Lizard had done his work. She wondered what deal Hobbs had done to make such a sleaze ball cooperate with the police.

Stepping down the red carpeted stairs into the cellar bar, she was hit by the mix of dope, tobacco and cheap perfume. The club was busy which was a blessing, but she still felt conspicuous. The room was warm and the jazz rhythm from the band on the cramped stage was lethargic and drawling. Figures were seated or slumped over tables or each other in the gloom and she headed for the bar. Ordering herself a Babycham, which she assumed was the drink of choice for girls of the night, she sat at the bar from where she had a good view of the club's clientele reflected in the back mirror that ran along its length.

The band finished their set and the live music was replaced by recorded disco music. Someone cranked up the volume and a few couples started swaying to the beats. She wondered if her back-up team could actually hear anything through the microphone taped up under her blouse.

Morgan discretely studied the men to her right. On the next bar stool sat a stout man with his head on the bar, asleep or more likely inebriated from knocking them back since they opened. Standing next to him and with their backs to the stage, were three men, one a lanky man with greying stubble in denims, perhaps forty years old, a rotund man in a grandad shirt and a man dressed in black with a gold chain, teeth to match and sunshades. House girls worked the room, delivering drinks to tables and getting cosy with the clientele. She spotted one leading a suited middle-aged man through a curtain-draped doorway just beyond the bar, a dim red light glimpsed within, before the curtain swung back behind them. She noticed that Lanky Man kept glancing at the curtain and appeared edgy. He wants to but hasn't got the balls, she surmised.

She paid for her drink, took a sip to refresh her dry mouth, and placed it back on the bar. Trying to look the part, she re-applied her lipstick with the small mirror in her compact. She said as though to herself, "I don't think he's here yet," hoping the mike would pick it up over the music. "I'm heading for the toilet."

She felt eyes upon her and she thought she saw someone at a table near the stage stand up as though to follow. Walking quickly, she pushed open the grimy door. Right for gents, left for the ladies. She dashed in and locked herself in the first cubicle. Self-conscious of the wire listening in she was too scared to pee. The music thumped out through the walls.

Sitting there, the outer door opened and she could see the shadow of feet pass her cubicle. Heavy, men's trainers, squeaking on the linoleum. They stopped outside her door. Her heart missed a beat. Steps again, receding. The footsteps squeaked away and left the room. She heard the door shut but waited, straining to hear above the music. No sounds nearby, they must have left.

Realising she had effectively trapped herself, she decided to head back to the bar and cursed herself for being so stupid. Flushing the loo out of habit, she spoke into the mike, "I'm going back to the bar. No sign yet but I'll give it twenty minutes."

Unlatching the door, Morgan went to the basin, checked her makeup and splashed cold water on to her face. As she straightened up to reach for a paper towel, a hand smothered her mouth and nose, stifling in its palm any squeal of alarm as her other arm was pulled behind her and twisted in a firm grip. She caught sight of the assailant in the mirror and recognised him from the photos on the police file. Joshua Leonard!

Before she had time to react, a foot struck out, taking her legs from under her. She was pulled off balance and pushed face down onto the vanity unit. The face pressed against her cheek and barely audibly whispered into her ear, "Not a word, understand?" Her cheek bone was being pressed down into cold marble, but she nodded compliantly as best she could, petrified of what was going to happen next.

Leonard patted down her jacket and clothing and feeling the transmitter concealed in the small of her back, heaved her up against the wall before pulling the blouse apart to expose the wire taped to her skin. Carefully the wire was removed and disabled.

The door swung open again and lighter footsteps entered. "Is she clean?"

"Yes, she is now! I'll be just outside the door if you need me."

"My spies tell me that you wanted to meet my friend?" stated the woman. Her voice was hoarse, from laryngitis or tarred lungs. She had short cropped spiky hair and was stocky in build. "Well, we're mates. He looks out for me and I look out for him. So, anything you have to say, you say it to me. Got it?" Morgan nodded.

"But we're not going to do this here," the hostile woman continued. Morgan was pushed against the wall by the woman who held her with an iron-like forearm across her chest. She heard a metallic flick and a cold blade was held under her throat. The police officer, dressed as a tart, looked imploringly into the woman's face.

"You can stop the charade, Detective Constable Morgan," the woman rasped. Morgan had no choice but to inhale the rancid breath. "You'd never convince a punter in this establishment with those bright youthful eyes," she spat, "let alone a pimp.

And your two friends outside huddled in a steamed-up car, like a couple of lovers. Wherever do they find them!" The woman relaxed her hold. Morgan turned her head and glowered at her assailant who seemed bent on humiliating her.

"Right," said Spiky Haired Woman. With the knife still held against Morgan's neck, with the other hand she poked a slender finger at Morgan's temple to mimic the barrel of the gun. "You've got one minute to tell me what you want or I'll have to reluctantly give you over to the care of my mate. He has a big heart but doesn't like cops and takes his work seriously. When he's finished with you, your pretty little face will look more …", she smiled at herself, "abstract than fine art."

Morgan was in danger but she was also the only one who might glean some information that could place Joshua Leonard at the scene of the crime and she was sure now there was more to this than they knew so far. She would need to tread carefully. What troubled her was how this woman knew her name. Had the Lizard betrayed them? What would he have to gain? Or was there a mole in the operation, in the force?

There was a commotion outside the door which was opened by the same face. "Trouble!" Leonard said in a murmur to Spiky Haired Woman.

They must have twigged and sent in back-up, Morgan thought.

"OK, you're coming with us. Now!"said the woman.

Morgan was escorted out of the ladies' room and extracted via a door concealed behind a curtain that led directly through into the back of a store room, up the stairs and out the back to a side street where a black car was parked. Leonard bundled

Morgan into the back seat beside Spiky Haired Woman and he took the wheel, driving off at speed through the side streets, frequently checking his rear-view mirrors.

Reaching into the glovebox keeping one hand on the wheel, he passed a hood back to Morgan. "Here, put this on. The less you see, the more likely whoever is on to us will keep you alive."

"We've got company?" Spiky Haired Woman asked.

"Yup," Leonard replied. "Blue Ford, two cars back. I'll take a left here, hold on tight …." An oncoming motorbike had followed him into the side street and now sped past them, the full-face helmet with blackened visor craning to peer into the car windows as they flashed past.

"That's no coincidence and they are not police," observed Spiky Haired Woman, betraying a slight edge of alarm in her voice. The Cortina was now racing up behind them, a shotgun poked out of its passenger window. The road turned sharply right, burning rubber, and hooded Morgan was briefly flung across the woman who pushed her upright. As their car was back under control, Leonard floored the accelerator but pulled up fast. Ahead he saw the riderless motorcycle that was parked blocking the road. The rider was squatting, levelling a pistol and taking aim. Screeching tyres behind confirmed that they were sandwiched.

"Brace yourselves," instructed Leonard calmly, "I'm going to have to ram the bike!"

The car leapt forwards, aiming to strike the bike on its front tyre to spin it out of their way. When the shots were fired one took out a front tyre causing their car to veer into the back of a parked car, sending Leonard crashing forwards onto the dashboard. Another took out the windscreen that shattered on impact, before passing clean through the skull of Spiky Haired Woman in the back seat leaving streaks of crimson and splattered hues of grey.

Morgan pulled her hood off as the car rocked to a stop and looked around in horror. She had spotted the Cortina behind them, its doors swinging open disgorging two frightening looks thugs. She heard voices and noticed that another car had stopped behind the Cortina, the driver standing, watching from afar. In that instant she thought there was something familiar about the distant figure that she couldn't place. Morgan had to escape, but there were too many of them and all armed to the teeth. As the rear passenger door was wrenched open, she got a fleeting look at the head that peered in at her and spotted a distinctive tattoo on the muscular neck. The butt of his shotgun met her temple forcibly and she blacked out.

A gruff voice, that belonged to the man with the tattoo, spoke. "Right, this one's alive but she'll want a handful of aspirin when she comes round!" He then leant further into the car and pressed two figures to Leonard's neck to feel for a pulse. "Yeah, the driver's still alive but out cold. The other one's a goner. Yuck what a mess!"

"OK, we'll take the girl with us," said another thug from the Cortina. He seemed to be in charge and turning to the leather clad biker, "Micky, tidy up and torch it before the Old Bill turns up!"

Morgan was dragged like a lifeless mannequin out of the wrecked car, thrown over someone's shoulder and tipped without dignity into the boot of the Cortina. Her hands were tied behind her and a chloroform pad held over her face. "Sleep well!" as the boot was slammed shut and it was driven away at speed. The biker discharged his duties, driving a bullet into the back of the driver's head that rested inanimate on the steering wheel, taking out Leonard's brain stem. He mounted his motorbike across the street, kicked it into a purr and leaning back fired into the fuel tank of the car until it blew, before fleeing down the side streets to vanish without trace.

"LBC radio on 1152 AM," the radio sang. "This is Independent Radio News at three minutes past eight. Our top story this hour - two bodies were found in a burnt-out car in London's West End in the early hours of this morning.

"Two people believed to be a man and a woman died after their car caught fire and exploded following a collision in the West End. Both were pronounced dead at the scene and have yet to be formally identified.

"A police spokesman said they were called to the incident at about 11:45pm. Early indications are that a traffic accident was to blame. An investigation was ongoing with local road closures in place. Anyone witnessing the crash is asked to come forward. He added that it was tragic that there had been another loss of life on London's streets. And now time for London's weather - today will be mainly overcast with outbreaks of rain and fifteen degrees celsius or sixty degrees fahrenheit. That's all for now. Back soon with Love in London."

32

Mole Hills

Drummond was tense. He had been anticipating a call from Brisket and was wondering how on earth he was going to explain himself. He wasn't sure he knew himself as it couldn't have gone more badly wrong. He had recommended the sting operation on Leonard as a means of identifying the killer of Amanda Castle and in turn of Talisker. Brisket had confided in him that he was after a Deputy Commissioner's job and had authorised the operation hoping for a positive outcome. In the event it had turned into an unmitigated disaster. Communications had failed, the target murdered, their back-up car was physically blocked thereby preventing any pursuit and they had a burnt-out bullet-holed car with two bodies yet to be fully identified. And to cap it all, one of their team Morgan was missing and presumed kidnapped by persons unknown.

Dean had the DCI holding on the line. He would have to take it and couldn't keep dodging him. He asked him to put him through.

Brisket was livid, made worse by speaking unnaturally

calmly. His tone was cold, crisp and clipped. He came straight to the point.

"Any leads on Morgan?"

"Not yet, Sir, but we are pulling out all the stops. We know that the deceased female in the car is not Morgan and we are working on the assumption that she was taken but no leads as yet."

"I have just spoken with Dean who has filled in some gaps for me. After that sting hash up, we need to ask ourselves, Jack. Do we have a mole in the team?"

"Sir, I must admit that the same question has occurred to me. It's almost as though every move we make is anticipated."

"Quite." The line went quiet briefly. "Who do you have working on the case?"

Drummond ran through them. "McVitie, he's solid. He's pretty much been my right-hand man as you know and I trust him. One hundred percent. The others in this case apart from myself are Dean, Hobbs and Morgan. We have been using support from the boys in blue, PC Snow in particular."

"Hmm, Hobbs eh? Any new faces in the team?"

"Ah, I forget, yes there is Albert."

Brisket leapt on it. "Albert, what do we know about him?"

"Well, to be honest not a great deal. He has only been with us for a couple months but he's settling in well. Bright lad did an engineering course at Polytechnic of Central London before switching to police training at Hendon. He has a lively mind but I like to keep him in check. He has been put in charge of looking after the incident board so has as good an overview of this case as anyone else."

"Interesting. Interview him, Jack. Dig deep! There might be something in this."

"I'm assuming, Sir, that you are not thinking that I am the mole? I can assure you that I am not but I would want to be treated like the rest of the team. I don't want any special favours."

"Jack, you are not a suspect. If you were then the whole pack of cards would come tumbling down. Report back to me, just me, when you have something. We've got to keep this between us for now. And focus on this Albert. You may have something there. I'd also like you to look into Hobbs. Pull his file, he could also be a person of interest."

"Yes, Sir."

"And Jack, I've left you to your own devices but this has turned into a mammoth mess. It reflects badly on me. I'm getting a lot of negativity from those above."

* * *

Jack Drummond put the phone down, feeling hollowed out by the experience, his boss casting suspicion on the very team most of whom now sat on the other side of his window. He pulled the blind down. He phoned Dean's internal line and heard it ring twice outside.

"Yes, Guv?"

"I don't want to be disturbed, no calls, even if Liz's corgis are on fire. Got it?"

The personnel files were in the bottom drawer of the locked cabinet and he had them sitting on his desk to refer to. He pulled out a blank sheet of paper and wrote down the two names to consider each in turn.

'Albert'. He thought through the worst scenario. The boy had full sight of the incident board from when Amanda Castle

218

fell. His job was to know what was going on in the whole team and keep maps, locations and procedure updated. So, Albert, the incident room boy and an intelligent one at that. He always knew what was going on, the latest developments and could have passed on everything, including the proposed sting operation. He had the opportunity to rearrange the facts on the board to throw the team off the scent. He could have been passing on information to those who might benefit.

Drummond thought, but Albert has a cast iron alibi. He was with me when Tally was killed in hospital. And his shoe size is … size eight and a half. Tally's killer wore tens from the prints in the hospital. And another thing, considered Drummond with growing optimism. Albert was here with me while the sting was underway. Motive? None. And he is fresh faced. I see innocence and a keenness to succeed in the force there. He was too young to have underworld connections. So, mole suspect one - ruled out. He put a line through his name.

'Hobbs'. He referred to his file. Bugger, size ten shoes are a match. Drummond thought through recent events. He was away from the station when Tally was killed visiting Toenails, but ample opportunity to drop by the hospital before going back to the station. Hobbs came back from seeing the Lizard and it was he who suggested setting up the sting which failed. He was boxed in the car with Dean listening to Morgan's wire, perhaps to allay all suspicion? Opportunity - yes. But what motive could he possibly have?

Drummond pondered over his personal life. Hobbs lives alone, as far as I know. He seems to want to emulate his senior, maybe he thinks it will help to smooth a promotion." He chewed the pencil. "Thinking about it, he dresses like Brisket, similar overcoat and hat. That's a bit weird, granted.

Hobbs might even fancy Brisket a bit for all I know, he bats for the other side after all and has never made any secret of it. Always combing his hair when he's not wearing that hat. But Hobbs a killer? He put a question mark next to the name and replaced the personnel files.

He called in Albert, and then Hobbs, for a general chat and to ask a few pertinent questions. Albert allayed his concerns but he still had an odd feeling about Hobbs who seemed nervous at being probed.

Drummond then shouted for McVitie. Dean replied that he had gone for a leak and wouldn't be long.

"Shut the door, Dougie. This is highly highly confidential. I can't emphasise that enough. We may have a mole in the ranks or so our esteemed DCI believes. He gave out two names and asked me to look into them. Well, I am happy that it is not New Lad. Butter wouldn't melt in his mouth and he'll make a fine copper. The other one is Hobbs. I think he is sound but I just don't know him very well. Any money concerns or anything that might make him a blackmail target?"

"Jack, thanks for bringing me on in this. It's a bit awkward talking about our mates like this but when we've lost one of our own and have another missing, I accept that you've got to turn over every stone. But Hobbs, no, I don't have any reason to think he would do the dirty on us. He can be a funny fish until you get to know him, but I've spent time in his company on long watches and the like. He's a good egg."

"Thanks, Dougie. Keep an ear to the ground. In the meantime, we have a damsel in distress. She's trained and can look after herself but it's been forty-eight hours now. Where are you, Morgan?"

33

Bootful

J anice Morgan awoke from semi consciousness to a searing pain in her head. She was lying in a pitch-black room on a cold hard floor, unable to stretch her legs or free her hands from the bindings that cut into her skin. With difficulty propping herself up with knees and elbows, she was able to sit upright against the wall, which felt smooth through her thin clothes, like a tiled surface. As her mind cleared, she realised how cold she was.

In the darkness, her other senses peaked. Wherever she was it smelled bad. It was dank with a putrid rotten smell, like meat that had gone bad. She recalled the smell of forgotten overripe pheasants found in her grandad's shed and resisted the urge to wretch. There was a drip, drip somewhere nearby. She strained to listen and picked out a faint murmur of voices from above her. There was a creaking of floorboards as someone moved around. Heavy footsteps, they seemed to encircle the space she was in, causing timber joints to creak and sigh in unison. A bolt slid and then another. There must be a door and stairs which were out of her view. As the door opened, it let in a strip of flickering light that picked out part of a staircase and its handrail, and hooks that hung from the ceiling. "That's artificial light," she thought, "it must be night-time."

She wondered how long she had been down there. There was the scrape of a ring on a metal handrail as someone descended the stairs. A dark shape stopped. A torch clicked on and shone at her, dazzling her. "She's awake," a gruff voice called up. And then directing it towards her, "Are you thirsty?"

Morgan squinted into the blinding light and nodded. Her tongue felt swollen and she tasted dried blood. He stepped down the remaining stairs and keeping the torch aimed at her, he pulled a can from his pocket and cracked it open. She heard liquid fizz out and splash the floor. He set it down within her reach and aimed the torch at the can of Tizer that stood in an orange puddle.

"Drink this." Her hands were bound together but with difficulty she managed to lift it and get some of it in her mouth. It was sweet and sugary and at that moment it was just what she needed.

"Hey, don't go!" she said, shielding her eyes. "How long are you going to hold me here? I really need the toilet."

Ignoring her, keeping his torch trained on her, he pulled a strip of material from his back pocket that had been torn from a tea towel and tied the improvised blindfold around Morgan's eyes. He climbed back up the steps and Morgan was again plunged back into darkness.

Time went by and she had slept. She woke up shivering in her skimpy clothes to different sounds. There were background noises of engines and a clattering, like someone pushing a trolley over a bumpy surface. Factory sounds. They seemed to be coming from the other side of the wall. The direction of the sound was disorientating and difficult to discern. She even questioned whether she was in a basement after all. There was a commotion. Men's voices could be heard above her, rising and falling as the floor creaked. She strained her ears. Most of the conversation was muffled but some she was able to pick out.

"What did you bring her here for?" asked a male voice, more educated than the Tizer man.

"Not doing this ..."

"This wasn't the plan..." It fell silent again.

Then the bolts slid. The man that came down the stairs was different. He had lighter steps and there was no scraping sound on the handrail as he descended. He stopped a few steps from the bottom and clicked on the torch, shining it at Morgan, who sat hunched and blindfolded.

The blindfold had been poorly tied and she had managed to ease it up a little, just enough to see below it but not so much she hoped that anyone would notice. She strained her eyes to pick out any features. Below the beam of torch light, the open door illuminated his lower third, knees down and she caught sight of the bottom of a mackintosh, pale grey trousers, spotty socks and black shoes. She dimly recalled glimpsing the man in a mac standing next to his car, behind the Cortina. It struck her uncomfortably that it was also the same combination that Hobbs often wore. The man held the beam on her as he turned and went back up the stairs without speaking. But he did give one thing away, which lodged in Morgan's mind. A ring scraped the handrail as he climbed.

Morgan woke much later to a cloth being pressed into her face. That was the last she remembered of the stinking basement as the chloroform filled her lungs.

* * *

Derek walked back to his car. He had an ear worm and was still whistling the Barbra Streisand number that they kept playing on the radio. He wished he had parked nearer Tesco as his arms were falling off under the weight of the bulging striped plastic bags filled with the shopping. He was chuffed with himself as he had managed to buy the lot using just the Green Shield stamps they had been collecting. He only hoped he would get there before the plastic handle of the heavier one ripped off. He could feel it stretching under the weight.

At last, he spied his reliable old Austin parked in the side street. He reached down to lift in the dodgy bag first, taking the weight underneath to avoid a calamity, and pushed the release button with his free hand to open the boot. He staggered backwards, dropping the bag, its contents skidding away in an eggy mess.

A red angry face streaked with mascara looked back at him through matted black hair from the floor of the car boot and urgent muffled sounds came from behind the gag. The body thrashed as best as a body can when tightly bound in yellow washing line.

* * *

Morgan had been checked over at hospital, her head wound cleaned and stitched, and ignoring medical advice was back in her flat showering carefully to avoid getting the dressing wet. After a quick cup of tea to wash down the painkillers, she emerged after twenty minutes in fresh clothes, climbing back in next to Albert who was to run her back to the station where Drummond was waiting to de-brief.

"Thanks for the lift, I'm not sure I'm safe to drive today." She held her hands out, fingers outstretched, and they still trembled.

"You sit and I'll do the fetching for once," said Drummond. "Tea and digestive? Apple? Cherries?"

"Just a tea, please Sir. White and I think I need some sugar in it."

Fifteen minutes later the door opened again, Drummond carrying the tea and joined by McVitie carrying a plate of biscuits. They'd found some custard creams.

"I'm sorry to use the interview room," apologised Drummond, "it's just handy to be able to record your witness statement where we won't be disturbed and I doubt you want to go through the ordeal more than you have to. You are not, absolutely not, under any compulsion to do this now but whatever you say may help us piece together what happened and more importantly help us get to whoever is behind this. If you are ready, shall we get started?"

"Yes Sir," she said. She thought back to Tally and knew that everything had been connected somehow. She took a sip of the sweetened tea and a nibble of biscuit. McVitie took a new cassette tape out of its case, slid it into the machine and pressed down two buttons simultaneously to start the tape recording. He nodded to Drummond who spoke the date, the time and gave the names of those in the room.

Morgan took a deep breath and began. "They held me in a basement, at least I think it was. They kept me in the dark and shone a torch in my face whenever they came downstairs, so I never got a good look at them. There were at least three different voices, could have been more."

McVitie asked, "Any idea where you were taken?"

"No, I was knocked out after the car crash," she said as she gently touched the top of the dressing on her temple and winced. "I don't know where they took me. Albert said they torched the car?"

"Yes, the driver and a female passenger in the back seat were found," said McVitie. "The vehicle was burnt out. Forensics found the car riddled with bullet holes and dug a few out but haven't found a match yet. They probably shot out the fuel tank before they escaped. Both occupants had been shot, one shot fired from a distance in front of the car and the driver …"

"That would be Leonard," Morgan confirmed.

"Ah, that makes sense," said McVitie who continued. "From the injuries the driver was shot at very close range in the back of the head, execution style."

The door opened again and Albert put his head round, carrying a brown paper bag which Drummond took off him.

Morgan recalled more details, "There was a motorcyclist. I didn't see him as they'd put a hood over my head, but I heard him pass. The engine sounded like a two stroke, possibly a Suzuki. Not a big bike, and not a little fizzy either, something in between. A two-fifty maybe. My cousin is into bikes and has a GT250."

Drummond speculated, "So maybe he sped off in front and he was the gunman. Well, one of the gunmen. This was an ambush and premeditated at that. A van parked right across Hobbs and Dean, boxing them in so they couldn't follow."

"I noticed that the cavalry never showed up," she said glumly.

Drummond reached for the cherries and offered them round. "Do you have any idea who the woman was?"

"No but she was a nasty bit of work, Sir." Morgan gave a description of Spiky Haired Woman and continued, "She held a knife to me in the toilets after Leonard had removed the wire I was wearing."

"That explains the loss of contact in the club," said Drummond.

McVitie said, "I've just remembered something. Now where is it?"

Morgan and Drummond watched as he sifted through a file that he had brought in with him and pulled out a photo.

"Here it is!" continued McVitie in his rich Scots accent, "I dug back in Leonard's file when his name came up and he has a half-sister. Her own record isn't that clean. She was charged with grievous bodily harm a few years back but never served time. That's when this photo was taken."

Morgan studied the photo. She remembered the brute of a woman with the spiky hair and visualised the broad face in the photo with the different hair style. She was in no doubt. "Yes, that's her. It's a match!"

Drummond whistled. "Maybe after Leonard's time behind bars she took it on herself to look out for her half-brother."

Morgan continued, "Yes, it did seem as though she was protecting him. She called Leonard 'my friend' so I had no idea they were half brother and sister. It makes sense now."

"I was doing a lot of thinking while I was being held. Who was pulling their strings?" she asked.

The room fell silent. Morgan's brow knotted, deep in thought. There was something else chewing at her. She tapped the photo as she spoke.

"She knew my name! She actually addressed me as DC Morgan. How did she know that?"

McVitie shot a knowing look at Drummond.

Drummond changed tack. "Going back to your captivity, Janice. Do you remember anything that might tell us where you were being held? Little details could be useful. How long did it take to get there, anything you spotted along the way that may narrow down a location?"

"As I said, I was knocked out, so I don't remember anything until I woke up in the basement. A dark room, no windows, no pavement light. I do remember there were hooks hanging from the ceiling and the room was tiled. It stank to high heaven, sort of putrid smell. The floor above was quite bouncy as I could hear people walking around."

"Go on," encouraged Drummond.

"Two people came downstairs, both male. I was tied up and only got a sideways glimpse of the stairway which had a metal handrail on the left side going down, or right going up. First a heavy-footed man. Gruff voice. It made a metallic sound when he came down, so I guess married, ring on left hand, but no ring sound going up. He gave me a can of drink. A second person came down later, a more educated voice from what I could hear upstairs. Lighter footed. He wore a ring on his right hand as it only made a metallic sound on the handrail as he went up. He didn't speak to me and again shone the torch in my eyes, but I caught a glimpse of him 'knees down'. Black shoes, mac and pale grey trousers. Oh, and spotty socks."

"How did you get out?"

"Someone put a cloth over my face and it knocked me stone cold. The next thing I remember was waking up to see an old man opening his boot who was probably more scared to see me!" Morgan winced again and pulled out the painkillers, downing another two with a slurp of cold tea.

"Are you OK to go on?" There was a growing pile of cherry stones in front of Drummond. "Let's go back to the shooting. Some horrible stuff happened there but some of the detail might be important."

"The car that was chasing Leonard's stopped about fifty yards behind. I saw two thugs get out with sawn off shotguns, one smashed me in the face of course. The one that stuck his head in the car had short hair, a thick neck. He had a tattoo on his neck," she said, touching her own neck to show them where. "It wasn't words or a picture like an eagle or a skull." Morgan shut her eyes tight as she tried to recall. "Got it! It was a motif, like two diamonds, one on top of the other."

"Here, can you draw it?" offered Drummond.

"She took the biro and sketched them. She drew the diamond shapes, but they didn't look right. She scribbled out her first attempts and then tried standing three crosses on top of each other, touching, giving the two diamond shapes in between. There, that's it!"

"There's something familiar about that," said Drummond stroking his chin, which had a two-day stubble from the long hours he had been working. He shook his head. He was dog tired and his mind was not as sharp as it usually was. "Let's we go back to the shooting. Some horrible stuff happened there but some of the detail might be important."

Morgan felt nauseous as she recalled the woman next to her who had been splattered over the inside of the car. She pushed the custard creams away and composed herself again.

"There was a shooter, dead ahead. It must have been the

motorcyclist as Leonard said something about having to ram the bike. And something else is coming back to me," continued Morgan. "After I pulled the hood off I saw someone else get out of a car which was stopped behind the Cortina. It was some way off and I didn't get a good look in all the commotion as the back window was splattered with blood. But it was a man and he was wearing a mac and carrying a hat. You know the sort that Hobbs wears? A bit like that."

McVitie shot a second look at Drummond, their faces set stern. There was a tap on the door. "Yes?"

"The police psychiatrist is waiting. Here to speak with DC Morgan?" Drummond clicked off the tape recorder.

"What?" retorted Morgan.

"Yes, I asked Dr Felix to drop by," said Drummond. "You've been immensely helpful considering what you have been through, but it was a traumatic experience. If you want to stay working in the team rather than take leave, and I really need you here, then he needs to sign you off as fit for work."

He looked down at the large pile of cherry stones staining the table and addressing Morgan said, "Take him to Brisket's empty office. You'll be more comfortable in there."

* * *

Drummond sat in his own office, staring at the symbol that Morgan had drawn on the page. There was something familiar about it, possibly from an old case file but which one? He was about to lift the receiver to call Brisket who had a longer memory than he had, but something stopped him. He spotted McVitie through his window blinds and shouted through his closed office door.

"Dougie!"

"Yes, Jack?"

"That tattoo that Morgan drew, spotted on the neck of one of the thugs in the Leonard shooting. I've definitely seen it before but can't place it. Does it mean anything to you?" McVitie studied it and he raised his eyebrows in recognition.

"Give me a moment, Jack, I need to dive into the archive."

Drummond looked through the phone messages that had come in while they had been in the interview room with Morgan. There had been two from Brisket asking for an update. He was halfway through turning the dial when McVitie bounced back in, slapping the file down on the desk. He replaced the phone receiver.

"Here, this is the one. I worked on this as one of my first cases when I moved to CID in sixty-four as a junior. A bank robbery on Fenchurch Street which left a security guard mortally wounded. This guy was part of the gang and look at the photo!"

The black and white prison photo clearly showed the tattoo down the left side of his neck. "He went down for a ten year stretch but had early release. GBH, manslaughter, extortion, robbery, the list goes on."

"Quick, show it to Morgan before she sees the shrink to see if we have a match."

McVitie returned. "Yes, it's him."

"Dougie, I've flicked through your file and look who else was in the gang!"

Drummond turned over the photos of the other gang members that he had lined up on his desk, as though they were playing a game of cards. Drummond gasped. "That's Pickett, the boss's favourite safe cracker!"

Drummond put his palm over his eyes. "I have a horrible feeling that I might know the answer to this but tell me, who was the investigating officer in sixty-four?"

McVitie confirmed his worst fears.

* * *

The police psychiatrist was on the bench in the waiting room, knees crossed, tapping his feet incessantly with nervous energy. He was shown into Brisket's office and Morgan joined him.

Dr Felix sat in Brisket's chair and spoke in an Irish drawl. "Anyone held in confinement against their will is going to have some difficult episodes until they come to terms with it. It may take months. How severe will depend on their personality and whether they are prone to emotional imbalance, bipolar being at extreme ends of the scale, or if they are more on the level with less pronounced peaks and troughs the recovery may be swifter. They may experience anxiety, depression, and paranoia ranging from mild to severe. In severe cases they may believe that they see their attacker in a crowd or imprinted in familiar faces, even family members. Nightmares can be commonplace as their subconscious self re-lives the episode. In my experience, the person who bottles up their emotions is more likely to display long-term symptoms so counselling and time off work are highly recommended."

He pulled out a printed form, carefully secured it to his writing board with an over-sized bulldog clip and settled it on his knee, pen poised.

"I will be submitting my recommendations to your station DCI. Do you have any questions for me?"

Morgan had heard little of what he had said and had been gazing over his shoulder, studying the sporting photos on the wall. Golf club line-ups and a photo of a social in the Kings Arms dated 1968 celebrating bringing the Bullion Four to justice. She frowned, something struck her. "Shit!"

"I'm sorry?"

She grabbed the photo from the wall. "I know that you are only trying to help but I need to see DI Drummond. Right now, and no, it can't wait!"

"Sir," said Morgan, bursting into the room. "I don't think you are going to believe this."

In the framed photo of the busy pub in celebration was DCI Brisket, then a detective inspector, in centre stage with a few others toasting a case success raising a glass of fizz in each hand. On a coat rack in the background hung a mac and a trilby hat. Almost out of the picture was a man in a corduroy jacket looking on, sporting shaggy sideburns before they had turned grey. It was Pickett the locksmith. But what really struck her was the man of the moment. Brisket was wearing a signet ring on his right hand, the same hand as one of her captors.

34

Falling Out

Scarlet had not seen her mother since she was fifteen years old, when she had run away from her home as the only child of a single parent. She never knew her father. Her mother struggled with alcohol dependence and had a string of boyfriends ranging from decent upstanding men to the abusive and violent. Sadly she had never hung on to the good ones and it was one of the worst boyfriends that led to Scarlet escaping to London for a new start. She left a lot of bad memories behind, but the guilt gnawed at her for abandoning her mother. Now that she and Jerry were together and feeling settled, she had a growing urge to go back to her old home to visit her mum, maybe to track down some old school friends, to stay there for a bit and fill in the gaps of what had gone on at home since she ran away, or at least a censored version of it.

Jerry felt uncomfortable and tried to put her off. "If you go back there, you might find that she doesn't want to see you, or she's moved or living with some vicious bastard …"

"Jerry, for once this is about me, not about you."

He was hurt. "But I've got to face him soon and I could really do with you by my side. Besides, you might like it at your mum's so much that you decide to stay and never come back! And she might have moved by now, it was years ago when you left, so it could be a wasted journey."

"I found her in the phone book. She's still living at the same address."

"When did you find that out, you didn't say?"

"A couple of days ago, but that's not important. Jay, I'm going to see her, like it or not. I'll get the train up there tomorrow. I don't know how long I'll be away, and I'd like you to come with me."

Jerry felt rejected. She had gone behind his back. More worrying, he could feel his blood rising and he knew how this could develop if he didn't control his emotions. She was the last person he wanted to frighten away, to hurt. She had gone behind his back. He knew he wouldn't deal with it well and had to get out for a bit. He grabbed his jacket and a couple of joints he'd left in the tobacco tin. She watched him leave. The door slammed as Jerry went off to clear his head.

When he returned an hour later, he was clutching a small brown paper bag.

"I'm sorry, I just can't go with you to your mum's. Not this time. I've got the chance to meet Him in a couple of days if he reads the letter I posted through his door. I can't miss this opportunity to be free of him."

There was disappointment in the eyes that followed him as he paced.

Jerry hesitated before he continued, unsure of himself and suddenly tongue-tied with embarrassment from what had sounded so good when he had rehearsed it on the walk back from the street market.

"Come on Jay, spit it out!" There was a hard edge to her voice, as though talking sternly to a child.

"I've, er, bought you something. It's something I thought about when I got you the flowers the other day. You may think it's nothing but to me it means a lot. Hear me out!" he continued, looking very serious. "Sometimes, I think we need to be reassured, that you feel the same for me as I do for you. I know you say sometimes that I'm not good at talking about deep things, like emotions and, well," Jerry struggled to expel the next word, "...er ... love. So, I thought that something more ...visual ...might help us both."

"What? Sorry, go on!" She was trying not to smirk. He's bought me a ring and he's working up to a proposal, she mused. It was not quite how she had imagined it. It was clumsy and awkward but still rather sweet.

Jerry went on, "I know that we have strong feelings for one another."

"Yes, I'm with you so far."

"Love can be big or small, but it's never nothing, it can never be extinguished. If it's small, then the other one should do something about it. If it's big then we need to tell each other how great it feels. What we feel for each other is here," he pointed to his chest, and then moved his finger closer to where it should be.

"So, there or thereabouts, two inches to the right and up a bit?"

"Yes, it's in a little box stored in the heart and it's here for all time, locked away. We can have love for others, like your mum or friends or a pet, but they may only have a little bit stored away. Maybe in a matchbox on a top shelf, but that's

OK as it's still in there."

"Jay, what were you smoking out there?" Scarlet looked at this odd boy who seemed to be getting stranger by the minute.

He was in his stride and wasn't going to be put off by her. Jerry emptied the paper bag onto the kitchen table and the contents rolled to a halt. The cheapskate, she thought. He had collected from the market dried peas, hazelnuts, almonds, brazil nuts and walnuts. Just two of each. He laid them out in two neat rows in ascending size order, each opposite its pair. "You see, sometimes we love each other this much," and he touched the small hazelnut, "and sometimes this much," and he held up the largest nut. "If you go away, I don't want to think of your love for me ... shrinking."

"You daft twat!"

"No, I want you to take them," he pressed on. "You take yours and I'll take mine. If we are ever apart again, then we can use them as ... as a secret code for how much we feel for each other."

"Alright, Jay, whatever you say!"

"You go to stay with your mum. I'm fine with that. I haven't got anyone, so I don't know what that feels like, but it sounds like something you've got to do. Oh, and here, take this as well, my lucky lighter. But I want to see it, and you, back again!"

They embraced and kissed. "It's a shame we've got to give up this flat," Scarlet said, looking around. "It's been good here."

"Yes, but my 'adopted father' turns up at the end of the week so I need to bag everything up by then and disappear. He moved back to the table. "OK, I feel ... this for you," he said, picking up the largest nut. "Now, your turn. Touch the nut that expresses how you feel about me."

A cheeky grin spread over her face. "I prefer these to your

lovenuts any day." She cupped his balls instead. "Come on, lovebird, let's go to the bedroom and you can wish me bon voyage properly!"

35

Bad Cop

Drummond had dug deep, but into Brisket this time and the evidence against him was mounting. They still needed physical evidence against him to build a convincing case that would hold up in court. Brisket had attempted to throw them off the scent but Drummond was as tenacious as a bloodhound and his nose was twitching.

Their DCI had worryingly close connections with members of a dangerous and highly organised group and the more they looked into him the further the tentacles reached beyond the recent murders.

Drummond had called a contact in Internal Investigations and discovered that they had an open file that showed anomalies where substantial proceeds from crimes had simply gone missing. Delving deeper at Drummond's request, they found that his name came up as one of the investigating officers in half of a dozen cases over the years, all building society robberies or drug swoops. The connection had not been made before and with such a rising star in the senior ranks of CID. They had simply missed it.

A watch was put on Brisket's house, but it was reported back that he had not been home for the past few days. "So much for a grumbling appendix," said Hobbs. "It doesn't seem to be slowing him down."

Pickett was picked up and brought in for questioning. From that point, things moved quickly. He had a story to tell but wanted to avoid prison at his age. Hobbs played the good cop, McVitie the bad, and a deal was struck with Drummond's blessing who was watching through the mirror with Morgan alongside him. Pickett spilled the beans on the location of one of the gang's hide-outs where it was highly likely that Morgan had been held captive.

The squad raided the disused abattoir in Smithfield the next morning. Upstairs they found empty ammunition cartons hidden in a cupboard and recent ashes from a paper fire in a waste bin. The kettle was still warm. Someone had the good sense to bust open a locked door and they found a staircase leading down to a long-abandoned butchery where Morgan had been held, the old meat hooks still hanging from the beams. A former door to the yard and pens had been bricked up long ago. Dusting for fingerprints they found a match to Brisket on the handrail and two sets of prints on a can of Tizer, Morgan's and those of another member of the gang.

As soon as Drummond found out that they had irrefutable evidence on the DCI that would hold up in court, he marched into the incident room and triumphantly wrote "Brisket - The Mole" on the blackboard. The chase had begun and they just needed some luck.

Pickett had been detained all day while the Smithfield operation was underway. They were convinced that he had more to tell them. Hobbs had got chatting to him and discovered his achilles heel. He had a sweet tooth and came back with two large blocks of Cadburys. Across the table he watched Drummond and McVitie munching.

"What we'd like to know", said McVitie, "is where you think we can find our DCI. Not next week, not tomorrow, but today!"

Drummond broke another strip of chocolate, cracked it to pieces which he again shared with McVitie. They watched Pickett squirming and salivating. "Oh, and this second bar. It's all yours if you tell us."

Pickett licked his lips, "In for a penny, in for a pound as they say! And our deal still stands? No witness statements, I get protection?"

Drummond nodded and added, "But it's got to be worth it."

"One piece now?"

Drummond complied and broke off a single chunk from the foil wrapper, placing it on the table within easy reach but leaving a finger on top until the drooling Picket spoke.

"There's something going down," he said, addressing the chocolate, "Really big."

Drummond lifted his finger and the locksmith greedily put the chocolate chunk into his mouth and briefly savoured the moment with eyes screwed shut. It was as though someone had flicked a switch and information starting cascaded from the old weasel.

"I've heard on my grapevine that a couple of containers have been off-loaded at Tilbury. Soft toys stuffed with drugs, the hard stuff. They've already been cleared through customs. The supply route is fragmented but Brisket's people are involved in protecting the UK end of the supply chain to make sure it gets to the streets. There's a warehouse in east London where the consignment will be broken down into package-sized quantities and distributed in mail vans. Simple, genius!"

"Where's the warehouse?"

Pickett shrugged his shoulders, palms upturned.

There was a knock at the door. Drummond stepped outside to see Morgan, the plaster on her forehead was weeping. "Are you surviving?"

"Thanks, never better," said Morgan. "Sir, you need to see this. Forensics have pieced together some of the larger debris of ash from the slaughterhouse." She handed him a photocopy showing a mosaic of the larger segments of ash found, some with partial text just legible on them, others with parts of building plans. Morgan pointed to the paper with her forefinger, "This piece of the plan shows 'Bay Eight with what looks like a cross marked on it'. Here's another that just says 'ICTO'. Albert worked it out. It's Royal Victoria Dock!" She gave him a folded plan of the docks. "We've just matched it on the plans for the site, but it's not clear which building. There is a hell of a lot of warehouses there!"

"Well done, Morgan!" Drummond returned to the meeting room. He showed McVitie what they had found out.

Drummond laid the documents in front of Pickett. "We believe there is something going down at Royal Victoria Dock. It's a big place, lots of empty warehouses. Can you help us identify this?" He pointed out the piece on the plan.

"I've done a bit of locksmith work at the docks in years gone by. Let me think now, there is the old oranges warehouse, the meat trade shed, bananas. No, the shape's all wrong. That looks like the old tobacco warehouse!"

Pickett was driven home in an unmarked car clutching his bar of chocolate.

Drummond groaned and rubbed his belly that was bulging more than usual over his trousers. "I think I'm getting a stomach ulcer from all of this."

"Or overdosing on cherries," said McVitie. "Jack, I think it's time to brief the team. Shall I gather them together?"

"Yes," Drummond affirmed, glancing at his watch. "Incident room at quarter past.Oh and Dougie, …"

He never finished. An animated Dean had just burst into the room.

36

Slopped Coffee

I n the railway station café, Jerry was feeling miserable.
For the umpteenth time, he watched sulkily as Scarlet
pulled out the crumpled timetable and rechecked the
station clock.

"You don't need to go, you know," said Jerry petulantly,
tearing the corner off another sachet of sugar and pushing
his finger through it to draw swirls on the café table. "I really
need you here."

She had been trying to ignore him and was becoming
increasingly irritated with herself for letting him take her
to the station. Why hadn't they just had a farewell hug at the
flat?

"Look Jay, this is hard on us both, I know that, but it won't
be for long. A fortnight maybe, three weeks tops! I still wish
you were coming as well but I just need to make this trip, for
me. To … find out who I am. You can understand that, can't
you?"

"Jerry, can you stop doing that!" she snapped. "You're
spilling it over me." Scarlet had packed her old clothes and

244

Doc Martens in a travel case. She had put on make-up and was wearing one of her new outfits, now adorned with sugar crystals. Jerry had told her that she looked classy and he already confessed to her to feeling a pang of jealousy that she was dressing not for him but for her mum. And for whoever else she was going to meet back at her estranged home. She liked that he felt that way.

Her emotions were already heightened by the anxiety of not knowing what she would find when she arrived in the place she had called home all those years ago. She so hoped for the mother she never had, the sort of mother who would be standing in her apron when she arrived home, a smell of a cake baking in the oven to share. A mum who would welcome her estranged daughter back, untying the apron, dusting the flour off her hands and give her a massive hug before becoming part of her life again. They would ring each other and see each other for birthdays and Christmas. And Jerry would be there with her. At least, a well-behaved version of Jerry, not the jerk sitting across the table to her playing with the sugar packets. Or she would find the same nervous woman, a pale shadow of herself. A life destroyed by a succession of boyfriends attracted to vulnerability and control. That mum didn't bake cakes for daughters. She only found comfort in a bottle.

Scarlet thought a while. "You're making your own journey in a way."

"What?" he said, an incredulous look on his face.

"Yes, you are going to face the man who made your life an utter misery. It's not going to be easy for you I know but maybe it is for the best that you also do this thing alone. Put your past behind you, whatever it takes. I know you can do it, whether I'm there or not."

Jerry said, morosely, "After seeing him in his church the other week, I don't know if I want to go through with it by myself. He's got this, I don't know, power over me. I can't explain it."

"Jay, now look at me. Look at me. In the eyes! That's better." He looked deep into those eyes and knew that when she left it would rip him apart again. He was liable to lose control, to go off the rails.

"Sure, I'll be fine."

She took his hands in hers, ignoring the gritty sugar this time. "Jay, listen to me, you can do this thing. If you can forgive the vicar and move on, then do it. If you need to make him pay, then do what you have to. But either way, you must end it." She smiled. "Look at what's happened to us! We've been through a whole heap of shit together but things have got better, we've got lucky on the whole. Best of all, we still have each other! So be careful, my Jay. I'll be back."

"If you leave", said Jerry, "I might not be here when you get back." It was a hurtful thing to say to her.

She bit her lip as she didn't want him to see her cry. She wrenched her chair back violently, scraping it on the polished floor, and stomped out to sit outside on the bench on her own on the bracingly windy platform. The train was still twenty minutes away. She saw rain starting to spot the platform edge just beyond the cover of the canopy that was sheltering her and she watched it, furiously. He stubbornly stayed put at the café table seated opposite the empty chair where her cup of tea still stood, steaming and hardly touched, except, he noticed, for a perfect lipstick mark on the rim. A puddle of tea was caught in the saucer in her haste to get away.

He could see her through the café window but rather than go to her, he drummed his fingers loudly making ripples in her tea. An elderly lady on a nearby table coughed as a rebuke. He stopped, fixed her with a cold stare and told her to piss off and mind her own business. She made a noisy palaver of getting her bags and coat together, muttered something about the young these days, no manners, and pulled herself up in a huff, tutting and grumbling. Jerry got up to pay and slapped the coins on the counter. The café girl behind the till eyed him cautiously and spotted the scars on his neck.

Keeping her eyes firmly fixed on him, Café Girl slid the coins from the countertop into her palm, ringing up the sale and dropped in the money quickly into the sorting trays before closing the till drawer. She continued to watch him through the window as he went out to the platform to stand in front of his girlfriend. His girlfriend turned her head away from him in rejection. He sat next to her and tentatively put an arm around her. His girlfriend now faced him and spoke slowly. If only she could lip read, thought Café Girl. He pulled his arm away and his posture was defensive, elbows in, head down gazing at his shoes, like a man defeated. His girlfriend studied him closely in profile. She took his hand in hers. He turned to her and they paused looking into each other's eyes for what seemed an eternity. They embraced, tightly and passionately. The train arrived, doors swung open. They looked earnest and appeared to say frantic things of importance.

Doors were being slammed shut and the station guard blew a whistle to warn of imminent departure. The two lovers parted, reluctantly it seemed, holding on to each other until the final moment when she dipped into her handbag and placed something in his hand, closing his fingers around it, cupping his hand in hers. She mounted the train. As it pulled away, he stood there fixed to the same spot on the desolate platform watching it glide away. His eyes dropped, he opened his hand and started to shake, tears streaming down his face. Scarlet caught a glimpse of his broken face through the dirty carriage window, took her seat and checked the inside of her bag. "Oh shit, poor love," she murmured. "I gave him the bloody dried pea!"

Café Girl shook her head, smiling knowingly as though she had seen it all before. She wiped the formica countertop and picked up a tray to clear the tables.

37

Shadows

The vicar had received the note from Jerry, posted through his letterbox, explaining that years ago he had been in his care. His charge had asked to meet him, to help him come to terms with what had happened, to put this to rest and allow him to move on in life. Jerry had asked to meet him in the old meeting hall by the wharf the next afternoon.

This was not how Jerry had imagined the showdown. He considered simply wiping him off the face of the earth. A cold-blooded execution. But he wanted to move on in life and needed to face him, to hear what he had to say. He had wanted to plan this with Scarlet, but she and Jerry had fallen out and like it or not he was going to have to face his tormentor alone.

He had removed from the flat anything that might raise suspicion if his adopted father visited, being meticulous in his final circuit of the rooms to take away notes on the fridge, letters he and Scarlet had written to each other while she was in prison that she had saved in shoe box on a high shelf. For authenticity, he left one packet of cash in the bedside drawer. Most of the hoard of cash had been exchanged for gold sovereigns to make it easier to hide and transport. It was enough to buy a modest house one day and he still had access to his double's building society accounts which hadn't been touched, not to mention the flat if his adopted father didn't mess things up.

The lift door slid open and he walked out into the lobby for what might be the last time. He casually told the old commissionaire that he would be away for a while visiting a friend but to keep his post on one side for him. As he stepped into the busy street, feeling the weight of the pistol in his jacket, he didn't notice that he was being observed from the café across the road by a figure who had just stood up to leave. Jerry crossed at the traffic lights and turned the corner to the Tube station. Unbeknown to him, his shadow did the same.

38

In The Dock

Dean burst into Drummond's office. "Guv, we've spoken to the security company. Their guard did a routine check yesterday on the warehouses at the docks. He spotted activity at one of the units which is normally shut up. He spotted a Cortina matching the description in the Leonard shooting, a motorbike and a Jag parked alongside. He took the registration numbers and called it in. We've checked them out. The Ford and the bike have false plates but the Jag, well, it's DCI Brisket's private vehicle."

"Got him!" said Drummond.

Drummond addressed the team. They hadn't seen him as animated as this since the Christmas party in seventy-three. That was the last time any booze had crossed his lips.

"We have anywhere between three and six suspects, including your DCI Brisket who has a long charge sheet waiting to be read out to him. The plan is to round them up so that we can get them on centre stage at the Old Bailey. Now I know feelings are running high because of what happened to Tally and Morgan here, but keep cool, be professional.

"Every available officer is to head for Royal Victoria Docks. McVitie will oversee operations here so keep in radio contact. We've got to expect that they'll be armed, so vests must be worn, no exceptions." Eyeing Hobbs he added, "They are not a fashion choice!" He looked around the room in a headmasterly way over the top of his reading spectacles

"Now, on to hardware. I know some of you are attached to your Walther PP's but I don't want to see any today. They might have worked for double 07 but I don't want any jamming up today. Hobbs will sign out the hardware but just Webleys and Smith & Wessons!

"Questions? … No? Good luck everyone."

Drummond turned to New Lad. "Albert," he said, using his name for the first time, "Good work on putting the pieces together. You are not firearm trained yet so you can drive me and Morgan. We're going blue light all the way. Let's see, we'll take the Rover!"

Albert's eyes lit up as though it was Christmas morning.

Fifteen minutes later, three cars from the squad raced in convoy across the city, crashing the red lights.

They slowed as they turned into the approach to the docks and a uniform pointed out one of the vast disused warehouses halfway down the dockside. They sped past the long expanse of water, wavelets running in the breeze, passing a couple of the last cargo ships to use the docks. The docks were closing down and were to be dismantled as the industry moved to container shipping downriver at Tilbury. The dockside cranes towered above them, like the invaders from War of the Worlds. In their heyday there was plenty of work to go round and the dockworkers kept the pubs full and tills ringing, but not any longer. A rust-streaked vessel was under refit on the far side of the dock, sparks flying off welding equipment working on its foredeck. Barges were rafted together and a fuelling barge was moored in the far distance.

The radio crackled on the operations frequency. It was McVitie doing radio checks. They parked under cover of an outhouse at the back of the warehouse, furthest from the dock and took up positions.

"It's too quiet," said Drummond. "They must know we are here if they have anyone on lookout. The approach is so exposed." He radioed in, "Charlie Oscar Two, over."

"This is Charlie Oscar Two," came back Dougie's Scottish drawl.

"Dougie, Jack here. Get Old Street to scramble firearms support. I've a horrible feeling that we might be fighting the bad guys with pea shooters. We need some serious backup down here, over."

"Roger that, out."

"Sir, armed suspect up on the main roof," said Dean. "My guess is that they are …"

They flattened as a rocket launcher on the roof fired a volley at them. It missed but hit the car, which exploded, bucking in the air before bouncing back on its shattered axle, blackened and windowless. The burning wreck now blocked their retreat.

"We're sitting ducks," said Drummond. "I don't want heroics but we've got to get ourselves out of the line of fire. On my word, in groups of three run for the warehouse under that canopied door. We can then find a way in."

The walkie-talkie bleeped. "Jack, the firearm unit is fifteen minutes away, over."

"Roger that, out." The officers were huddled. "Support is on its way. Most of you trained with D11 in Gravesend, they're good guys and have some sharp shooters. Albert and Morgan, you're with me. On three."

They found a broken fire door where the threshold had rotted out. "OK, split up into three groups. Dean's team left bay, Hobbs centre and I'll take the right."

They worked their way through the aisles of empty racking that rose above them, noticing old spider traps fixed to stanchions from when the product was stored on a big scale. The pungent aroma of tobacco had permeated the fabric of the old warehouse and filled their noses as they worked their way to the front of the building. The warehouse was split into bays and they were about to enter Bay 8. Two loading doors were open to the dockside service yard, the vast expanse of water shimmering beyond. There was activity ahead and they crept forwards. Forklifts were busy ferrying heavy pallets from a shipping container that had been craned off the lorry and moving them inside the warehouse. Parked inside were half a dozen vans recently painted in Royal Mail livery. Pickett had got that right as well. Shouted voices came from ahead.

They took cover behind a stack of timber pallets. "Bandits ahead," whispered Drummond to Morgan and Alex.

"Sir," said Morgan pointing, "Just outside the right-hand loading bay. It's Brisket!"

A hail of bullets from a gantry high above sent splinters flying over their heads as they sheltered behind stacks of old wooden pallets. Drummond gave the order, "Engage!" Morgan aimed her Webley revolver at one of the gunmen. The first shot ricocheted off metal. A second squeeze of the trigger found her target and he slumped down onto the open grid walkway. Hobbs took out another who had been indiscriminately spraying rounds from his automatic weapon, dropping with a thump as he fell off his perch. The officers bashed their way through to the open loading doors, returning fire where they had to defend themselves. Dean caught a bullet that grazed his shoulder, but otherwise they were unscathed.

Drummond ducked down for cover and unclipped his radio. McVitie was on the line immediately, hearing gun fire on the line. "I'm listening, Jack?"

"Dougie, we'll need ambulances standing by, but they must not, repeat not, approach the scene until ordered. There is a major firearms incident underway and we're under siege. We have one officer down and multiple casualties."

"Copy that. Already made the call, Jack. Ambulances are waiting at the main gate."

"Sir, ahead!" said Morgan urgently, as she crouched down reloading her revolver. The forklift truck drivers had picked up weapons and were taking aim. From behind the lorry parked in the dockside service road, came a dozen or so heavily armed men, some carrying sawn-off shotguns, others automatic rifles, marking every officer in their sights. The police squad were no match.

"Cease fire!" yelled Drummond. The sounds of gunfire ceased. They had been snared.

A voice they all knew carried authoritatively from behind the mob. "Give up, Jack! Tell your officers to throw their weapons down," said Brisket. "You are not going to win this battle."

The figure in a mackintosh, carrying a hat in one hand, weaved nonchalantly around the heavy-set shoulders of the thugs who were twitching for the order to shoot them down.

The protective huddle shuffled to let him pass to the front, where Brisket brushed his trilby, set it on his head and tilted it to a jaunty angle.

"Do as he says!" said Drummond to his officers.

There was a clatter as the officers laid their arms on the floor. Quick as a flash, unarmed Albert grabbed a discarded pistol.

"No!" shouted Drummond. It was too late. There was a loud crack and Albert's gun flew out of his hand, the end of his thumb falling alongside it.

"Line up against the wall!" barked Brisket.

"Do as he says!" said Drummond, adding "That's an order!" The CID officers did as they were told.

A gunman with a tattoo on his neck and a shotgun at his waist kicked the discarded guns out of reach. In a gruff voice said, "That's it, backs to the wall, hands on heads!" He then re-joined the others.

"It was him, Sir" Morgan whispered to Drummond. "He was the one that rifle-butted me in Leonard's car!"

Drummond didn't hold back and spoke directly to Brisket, "You disgust me, you toad. You, a common criminal of all people. To think I looked up to you!"

Brisket laughed. "You think I did this to protect a criminal syndicate, a dirty gang of thieves. You don't know how far off the mark you are. No, I am part of something much much bigger than that. And you know, whatever you try to throw at me, it'll never stick!" he smiled. "I know people in high places." With that, Brisket reached inside his coat and pulled a gun from the holster. He raised it to Drummond's temple.

What Brisket didn't factor in was Morgan. She was almost bursting with a fury and hatred for Brisket that she was struggling to control. This beast, Tally's murderer who thought he was above the law and still flaunted himself as a figure of authority. He didn't deserve the badge that she felt so humbled to wear.

She launched herself at Brisket, taking him off guard. Driving her shoulder forwards, she shoved him back, forcing him to stumble. She felt a searing pain as a bullet tore through her thigh. Gritting her teeth, she ignored it, running at him again and driving him back like a rugby prop. With one last desperate shove she threw herself at Brisket, taking them both over the dock edge and into the water. Then hell let loose.

A firearms response officer from the response team had just positioned himself at gantry level on one of the towering cranes armed with a 7.62mm Lee Enfield sniper rifle. He had a birds eye view and proceeded to pick off the gang one by one. There was confusion and five of the criminals were easy headshots from the elevated firing line. Another marksman had climbed the second crane and took out four more of the armed gang before a Makarov submachine gun discharged its thirty-round magazine at him. The burst hit the marksman full in the stomach. He flew off the crane and was dead before he splashed into the water.

At the same time there was a rear-guard action from other support officers who had entered the warehouse from the back, following the route that Drummond's team had taken earlier and adding firepower from within the warehouse.

Two powerful workboats had been commandeered from the welders working on the cargo ship further along the dock. The first discharged officers who clambered up the quayside ladders and using the element of surprise took out two of Brisket's army who were taking cover armed behind the forklift trucks. Another gangster was spotted scaling one of the towering cranes where the first police marksman was still at work. A well-aimed round found its target and a curdling scream rang out until he dropped heavily onto the steel rails. The boat circled the injured Morgan who was coughing up the sweet oily water. She was driven at speed, foam flying in the wake, to the waiting ambulances at the dock entrance.

The second motorboat went to rescue Brisket who was trying to swim out towards the middle of the dock but was clearly struggling. As a craft boat came alongside, he hung on to the end of the boat hook, gasping and considering his options. He was roughly heaved in and as he dropped unceremoniously into the boat, a gunshot rang out. Brisket's face splattered with blood, but it wasn't his. The driver and officer who had picked him up had been taken out with a single shot from the man with the tattoo. He had lain flat on the warehouse roof, out of sight preparing his moment. Brisket looked up at the roof and put a hand over his eyes to shield the sun. Tattoo man now stood erect and saluted his boss like the captain on a sinking ship, before hurtling backwards with the force of a bullet unleashed by the police marksman on the crane.

The writing was on the wall for Brisket, but he wasn't going to go quietly. He pushed the lifeless corpse off the driver's seat, grabbed the wheel and revved the powerful engine to its maximum, pointing the craft at the fuel pontoon moored ahead. It was well protected with rope and rubber fenders and on impact the fibreglass bow just ripped off and the vessel started to sink. Brisket hauled himself out, clambering onto the floating platform. He stood up, drenched and shivering, squinting back at the distant warehouse. He could just make out the figure of Jack Drummond, standing at the edge of the dock gazing across. Brisket pulled his pistol from the holster again and fired two rounds into the fuel storage tanks below his feet.

The pontoon blew up with a loud crump sending up a plume of black smoke and a raging fire. A white crested wave hurtled down the dock to the very far end where it slapped at the dockside and kicked back. As the moored boats and the cargo ship stopped rocking, bits of Brisket sank into the deep along with a signet ring.

39

Salt and Vinegar

J erry had arrived five minutes early at the entrance to the old meeting hall. He remembered the place when it had been a soup kitchen for the rough sleepers. Rain used to come through the roof even then. There was now a board nailed to the fence identifying it as a construction site for a refurbishment project, but this had stalled when the charity had run out of money.

He had not planned to go alone but now that he was there, he felt ready to face the vicar. In the afternoon sunlight, with the familiar scents in the breeze blowing off the river and the perfume from the overgrown lilac, the place seemed serene and unthreatening, its door ajar. He was there to talk to him and to seek reconciliation, not revenge. On impulse, he slid the Beretta under a corrugated sheet that lay outside in the small car park. He still had the switchblade if he needed it. His tail watched him as he moved to the door.

Jerry took a deep breath and stepped inside to find the vicar standing at the end of the hall silhouetted against the vast window, the rays of the afternoon sun giving him a holy demeanour.

"I wasn't sure that you would turn up," Jerry started confidently as he slowly approached him. "You must have recognised me after all those years. I've been waiting for this moment for so long."

The vicar said nothing and stood his ground, wearing a contemptuous expression behind the wire framed spectacles. Unseen, a figure had crept in and was hidden from them both behind a pile of scaffold planks, the pistol held tightly in both hands.

Scarlet never went as far as her mum's and decided Jerry that needed her more. And she needed him. By the time that the train had pulled into the station of her home town, she had already decided to catch the first one back. He had asked her for help and she had put herself first. But if Jerry had come a cropper and she had not been there for him, then she would never have forgiven herself. They hadn't parted on good terms and he had clearly made up his mind to go it alone. So, she had followed him. That time in the squat, he had called her an angel. It now seemed a lifetime away, but there she was. Still his guardian angel.

She had watched Jerry conceal something under a corrugated sheet and enter the old meeting hall. She noticed a car waiting a little way along the street, quietly purring, a driver waiting at the wheel. Vicars didn't drive Silver Shadows, she thought. She had pulled the gun out from Jerry's hiding place and tip-toed into the building, nestling herself down behind a large pile of scaffold equipment. Male voices echoed deeper into the hall, Jerry and one other. Scarlet peered from behind her cover and lifted the pistol into position. She strained to listen. Her forefinger lay along the trigger guard and she tentatively brushed the trigger with her fingertip, readying herself if she had to take a shot.

Scarlet froze as she felt the jab of a barrel in the back of her neck. With a painful twist of her arm, she yelped as the Beretta was expertly removed from her grasp. Wings flapped in the rafters high above, disturbed by the noise.

Jerry turned as he heard the cry from the back of the hall. "Scarlet? What the hell are you doing here?"

Bernard kept his Luger pressed against the back of Scarlet's head, her arm bent behind her, and walked her out to join Jerry.

"Get your hands off her!" shouted Jerry.

An elderly voice stepped out from the shadows, his cane tapping on the dusty quarry tiles. "Quite a little party," said Sir Peter.

Jerry looked wildly around him. The vicar had betrayed his instructions by not turning up alone. Jerry lunged for him.

"You come a step closer boy, and your pretty little girlfriend gets it!" roared Sir Peter.

Jerry stopped rigid, slowly raising open palms to show that he was unarmed. He turned to Scarlet. "What are you doing here?" he repeated more calmly.

"Trying to look after you, you idiot! Did you really think he would turn up on his own? And Jay, at the railway station. I meant to give you a walnut, not a pea!"

A walnut! Jerry's spirits lifted and as their eyes met he smiled. The vicar saw his back turned and picking up a sturdy length of wood that had been lying at his feet, swung it with all his might into the side of Jerry's head. In a split second of Scarlet yelling "Look out, Jay!" he felt pain crashing into his skull. His world went black as he dropped to the floor.

"That was effective!" said Sir Peter. He pointed his cane at Scarlet, "Bernard, perhaps you could oblige?"

Bernard hit her with the pistol, using just enough force to stun her but not to kill. He had been taught the technique in combat training in his commando base in Scotland before his posting to the Italian front and had used it to good effect many times since. Bernard dragged the girl's body across the filthy floor to join the unconscious Jerry.

Jerry came to as a bucket of water was thrown over him. He had been tied with a rope around his waist to one of the supporting columns. Next to him sat Scarlet, tightly bound but alert and brooding dark thoughts. Blood was congealing on the side of her head from the whip of the pistol.

The vicar stood next to his victim, arms folded and shaking his head in sorrow. Jerry looked directly into his eyes, unable to control his fury.

"You bastard," Jerry spat at the vicar. "You remember me, I know you do. I was that child in your care that you beat, that you abused. You can't deny it!"

Sir Peter had been sitting down while Bernard had trussed up the two youths. The old man now stood with the help of his cane, to observe them more closely.

The vicar replied in a thin, insipid voice. "What nonsense! I have no recollection of ever seeing you before."

Scarlet shouted at Jerry and, imploring to Sir Peter, said "Jay, show them! Show them what he did to you." And with his tied hands, Jerry tried to rip at his collar to expose his skin, but to no avail.

Sir Peter sighed, "Bernard, assist please!" And Bernard took from his pocket the Sloth's switchblade that he had frisked from the unconscious Jerry, cutting his shirt down to the waist.

"You see now, do you remember what you did to me?" Jerry spat at the vicar. "You, who use the Church as a cloak of respectability. Behind it all you are preying on children for your own gratification, on vulnerable boys like myself, leaving us with lives tortured by what you did to us." The vicar shook his head in denial but he was evidently uncomfortable at how the focus had shifted to him. Jerry continued.

"The scars are in my mind, in my nightmares, let alone the burns you can all see to my flesh that are a testament to what you did. They remind me of it every day of my life. Every single day!" He fought back tears and steadied his voice. "And despite all this," he recalled from the newspaper clipping, "you've been given a commendation for your work in pastoral care. It sickens me!"

The vicar grabbed Jerry by the hair. "Pray I never have to hear such vile and untruthful allegations again." Turning to Sir Peter, "Peter, let's finish this. Let's send these devilish scums down to where they belong and we can put this all behind us."

Bernard levelled his Luger at Jerry's temple, the first in his sights, awaiting Sir Peter's command to execute the two kills. But Sir Peter raised a hand.

"No Bernard, allow me on this occasion. Sometimes I need to get my own hands dirty."

Bernard offered him the Luger, but Sir Peter shook his head. Tapping a few paces towards the miserable figures, wincing from the gout in his inflamed toe joint as he took each step, Sir Peter stopped in front of Jerry and pulled a gleaming sword from inside his cane. Scarlet, held securely by Bernard, screamed, "No!" and screwed her eyes shut.

Sir Peter focused his gaze on Jerry and lifted the sword. Jerry met his stare, refusing to look away. Sir Peter winked and before Jerry had a chance to process what was happening, Sir Peter spun round and drove the sword into the vicar, running it up to its hilt. The vicar, with alarm and betrayal written in his face, stood briefly immobile, then swayed back and forth. He took one step back, withdrew the sword stick and the vicar toppled forwards, arms outspread in a crucifix.

The former spymaster admired his handiwork. "I've still got it in me," he chuckled.

"Are we finished here?" Sir Peter asked Jerry.

"Yes, we are. I have no bones to pick with you."

"Well I have, you piece of shit," Scarlet said, addressing Bernard and pulling at her bindings.

"Set them free and gently does it," said Sir Peter. "Ladies first and all that!"

She spat at Bernard as he bent down. The butler looked wounded but didn't flinch. Bernard's bear-like hands untied Scarlet. He lifted her up in one swoop, waited for her Doc Martens to stop flailing at him and stood her on her feet. He smiled down at her as she set her best venomous stare. "No hard feelings?" Bernard took Sloth's switchblade that he had confiscated from Jerry's pocket and threw the folded knife to her.

As Scarlet set about untying Jerry, Bernard removed the magazine from the Beretta, dismantled the gun with ease and put it back together again in seconds. He tested the firing action, replaced the magazine and laid the Beretta at a safe distance away. "I haven't seen one of those for years. Not a scratch on it, quite a collector's piece!"

Bernard followed Sir Peter out of the building and hailed

the driver.

As the elegant car carried them back in comfort, Sir Peter confided in Bernard. "That was very poor judgment on my part. Did I tell you that he married us in a little church in the most perfect ceremony and we became friends of a sort? He is the one who gave me the inspiration for a clandestine group who could conquer inequality and get things done to set this country on the right track. Little did I know he had his own agenda. I'm an old fool, Bernard."

Bernard stayed silent.

"I've been thinking," Sir Peter went on. "Maybe it is time to plan for succession and in a year or two pass the chairmanship to a younger member of the Firm. Now there's someone I have in mind who I think could fit the role admirably."

* * *

Jack Drummond read through his operational report again under the light of his desk lamp. He signed it off, before neatening the papers and driving a staple through the top left corner. He added it to the buff coloured file in the wire tray that was filled with the reports from his other officers. The cleaner's floor polisher was whirring outside in the corridor. He felt his stiff shoulder, sat back in his chair, yawned like a walrus and stretched his arms out, taking care not to overdo it after the exertions at the docks. "What a day!" he said to himself. He couldn't recall a more challenging one. He checked the clock. "Right, time to go."

As he closed the door of the office that he had commandeered, he prised off the name plaque 'DCI Brisket' that stared back at him, snapped it in two and tossed it with a clatter into the nearest bin. "That's better than you deserve!" He paused, then deviated on his way to the coat rack, briefly touching the tops of the chairs of each of his colleagues. First he went over to the empty desk where his fallen colleague had sat, bowed his head as he supported himself on the back of the chair, squeezed his eyes shut and simply said, "Tally!" A tear ran down his cheek which he wiped away.

He touched the next empty seat. "Dougie, what would I do without you!"

He strolled to the next desk, "Dean, you took one for us but thank god you're alive."

"Albert. Poor kid, this has probably put you off the force forever."

"Hobbs, I nearly did you an injustice and it was our DCI all along. Forgive me, my friend."

"Morgan …"

"Sir!"

Janice Morgan was standing in the doorway supporting herself on a crutch, quietly watching him and not wishing to intrude.

"I came back to get you, Sir. They patched me up and let me out of the hospital as I didn't want to miss this. The whole team's over at the Red Lion waiting for you, even Albert who has a lovely bandage where his thumb used to be," she said smiling. "Oh, and Sir, they plan to get you very drunk, so go carefully!"

"DC Morgan," said Drummond, looking embarrassed. "Best we keep this to ourselves, I don't want anyone thinking I'm soft in the head!"

Morgan hobbled in and grabbed his coat from the peg which

she handed to him. "I didn't hear a thing, Sir!" she lied.

He patted his jacket, checking for his wallet. "Righto, let's go. Drinks are on me!"

* * *

"So, you came back," said Jerry, tutting as he carefully moved the blood-crusted hair from the wound above Scarlet's eyebrow. "He spoiled your beauty but you'll live."

"Yes, Jay," she said and then kissed him tenderly, before pulling his torn shirt back over him. "It seems like I can't stay away."

She turned, looking down at the corpse that had bled a dark crimson pool from where the highly polished sword had pierced straight through him.

"Jay, does this bring you closure? Can you put your demons to rest now?"

"Almost. Will you help me?"

She nodded solemnly. She patted her pocket and took out his silver lighter that he had given her before they left the flat. A wicked smile had crossed her face. "Let's roast the pig!"

They waited just inside the old meeting hall as the smoke wove its way up to the rafters and fanned out, raining little smuts of ash inside the hall. The light through the large west window had started to fade and they stood transfixed, mesmerised. They watched the flames burn through the old newspapers they had scrunched. It worked slowly along the lengths of rope that they had coiled on top, catching the edges of the cardboard boxes and wooden crates they had heaped up. Smouldering embers fell to singe the black coat, the sombre suit, the dog collar that lay below, until there was spitting from the fats in the pyre as the flames mercilessly consumed the body.

"OK, now it's done," Jerry said with relief. He was smiling and so was she. "I'm free, I'm really free of him now! It feels like a weight has tumbled off my shoulders!" The fire was spreading inside and was lapping at the old timber columns. They pulled the heavy door shut and inhaled the cool air outside as they walked away. The noises of the city returned.

"I don't know about you," said Scarlet, taking his arm, "but I'm starving."

"Let's get some chips?" suggested Jerry.

"Oh yes, I could murder a bag of chips. I warn you, I like lots of vinegar."

"I don't like vinegar at all. Just salt, OK?"

"Haven't you learnt anything, Jay? As that toff said, 'Ladies first and all that!' There's a chippy round the next corner, I'm sure of it."

Starlings were flocking, communing densely on overwhelmed trees before lifting noisily against the pink dusk sky and spiralling as a mass into the air. The chatter of the birds mingled orchestrally with the sounds of the sirens, the hum of evening traffic and the squeaking of braking taxis. The tidal rhythm of the River Thames provided the bass notes to the music of the city.

As the light faded, a young couple, one tall and the other short, walked along the river promenade sharing a bag of hot, greasy chips that were liberally doused with vinegar. Beside them, the dark river ran. It hid at its whim many things in its murky depths, and with a splash from the pistol it hid yet another.

The waters carried away the sins of a city as the rushing tides filled and emptied, flushing from the west out to the Thames Estuary in the east. Sometimes at ebb the hidden crimes resurfaced, beached on the mud banks at low tide.

As they strolled hand in hand, out there in the inky darkness the waters had given up the decaying body of a man. The three buttons of his green corduroy jacket were still tightly fastened. He now rested with an assortment of bottles and driftwood on the strandline of a mud bank. Where his eyes should have been were two gaping sockets, hollowed out by the seabirds above the water and by the eels from the depths below, creating a look of permanent surprise. The hands that had been so skilled in their mastery of his trade were missing below the wrists.

Half a mile upstream, the man had been pulled out of the back of a van, his feet tightly bound, held down as they hacked at his hands. The thrashing body had been rolled to the edge and dropped over the embankment. The locksmith let out his final scream as he tumbled into the dark waters with a splash, paying dearly for his betrayal. The tide would turn and he would be dragged back down to the depths to disappear under the racing currents until the next tide and the ones after that would carry him on his journey out to the sea.

As the unlikely couple walked on through London's streets with fingers entwined, they felt taller than giants and happy that they were together again. For alone they were troubled souls. But together nothing would stand in their way.

About the Author

TIM PARR grew up in West Sussex. He spent his early career in London and now lives and works in land-locked Oxfordshire. He has three grown-up sons and two senior cats. In his parallel universe he lives by the sea on a west facing bay, fixing up an old sailing boat while his imaginary spaniel snoozes by his side. Below The Strandline is his first novel.

If you have enjoyed this book, please leave a review on the retailer's site or at Goodreads to help spread the word!

You can connect with me on:
🌐 https://www.goodreads.com/tim_parr

Subscribe to my newsletter:
✉ https://timparr.uk/contact

Printed in Great Britain
by Amazon